CRUELEST MONTH

AARON STANDER

WRITERS & EDITORS

INTERLOCHEN, MICHIGAN

•

ISBN: 978-1478358145

Printed and bound in the United States of America

FOR BEACHWALKER

WHO HELPS THIS ALL HAPPEN

1
~

Ma French bumped along the snow-covered two-track in her dilapidated GMC Jimmy, her golden retriever Roxy peering attentively out of the windshield. She slowed to a crawl and turned into a two-track that had been flattened by snowmobiles. Rolling forward a few dozen yards, Ma switched off the engine and pushed open the door, using her arm and shoulder to overcome the resistance of the worn hinges. She stood and waited as Roxy walked across the seat and dropped to the ground next to her, then turned back to retrieve a steel-tipped walking stick. Together, they followed a narrow, winding path of hard packed snow for several miles through the dense brush until they reached the shore of a small lake.

Ma stood for a long moment and took in the panorama. Her gaze moving from left to right, she viewed the perimeter of the ice-covered plain. Three sides of the lake were bordered in marshland. The dusky skeletons of long dead pine trees angled helter-skelter at the verge of the marshes. Beyond, scrub forests of oak and maple in saturnine nakedness stood on the rolling terrain. A dark overcast added to the grimness of the tableau.

Ma looked over the expanse of ice toward the old resort. She could just make out the dark forms of a few of the buildings near the shore. Winter was starting to loosen its grip. Ma knew with the coming of warm weather the inland lakes would start to open. She wanted to make this trip to the landlocked resort before anyone was around, and while it was still easy to get there.

A few inches of water separated the shore from the layer of snow-crusted ice that covered the lake. Ma took her walking stick and tested the ice, probing carefully, then stepping gingerly across the band of water to the ice. With Roxy at her side, she followed the shoreline, hoping that if she did break through, the water wouldn't come above her rubber farm boots—boots her husband had worn for years before he became too sick to work.

Ma half circled the lake, coming ashore in the area where the dock extended far out into the water during the summer. She followed snowmobile tracks up past the main house—its interior obscured by wooden shutters—several hundred yards to the ridgeline. A derelict windmill stood at the top. The tower was covered with a thick layer of rust and most of the blades were missing, the remaining ones twisted and distorted. Just below it was the massive storage tank, steel bands on wood, now collapsing inward.

Ma crossed the ridge and looked out at Lake Michigan. Most of the shelf ice had disappeared in recent weeks, leaving the shoreline open to the waves. She moved toward the rolling surf, stopping on a bank high above the water. With trembling hands she pulled a plastic bag from her jacket pocket. These were the last of them, the last of Pa's ashes. She had spread the others near his favorite deer hunting blind, and in the yard where they had buried many generations of dogs during the almost half century of their marriage.

The first two places were special to Pa. *Perhaps,* she thought, *this is more important to me. This is where it all began that first summer when we met.*

She slowly poured the ashes from the bag, letting the wind carry them away. Roxy stood at her side, silent and watchful. Ma folded the bag carefully and put it in her pocket. Then she turned and retraced her steps back up to the ridgeline, this time heading into the small family cemetery. Ma gazed across the undisturbed blanket that covered the area. She could remember a time, years ago, when a wrought iron fence surrounded the plot. Now only bits and pieces leaned drunkenly.

Ma carefully brushed the drifted snow from the base of the largest headstone.

Rose-Marie Hollingsford 1870—1962

She remembered when they brought Mrs. Hollingsford's body back from Chicago for burial. It was late spring, and she and the other folks that worked on the estate had already completed most of the necessary work to open the place for the season. She was thinking about how kind Mrs. Hollingsford had been to her during the four summers she had worked there, only sixteen that first summer.

Roxy's sudden barking pulled her from her memories. The retriever was pawing at something. Ma dropped to her knees to see clearly the object of Roxy's attention. She pulled a jar from the sand. The glass had a greenish tint with the brand name *Ball* in raised letters on one of the four sides. Wiping the sand from the glass, she squinted at the contents—it looked like a roll of newspaper bound by several dull-red rubber bands. She pulled off her mittens, clasped the bottle firmly with her left hand and applied pressure to the lid. It slowly gave way. Pulling off the rubber bands, Ma peeled away the newspaper and unrolled a large wad of new $100 bills. She stood suddenly and looked around, up and down the shore and back toward the woods. Then for several minutes she stared at the money, flipped through the bundle. Scanning the area a second time, she shoved the bundle into the pocket on the right side of her jeans. Ma put the newspaper back in the jar, screwed on the lid and dropped it, pushing a layer of sand over the glass. Then she picked up the rubber bands and put them into her jacket pocket.

Dragging a reluctant Roxy, Ma quickly retraced her route past the main house, outbuildings, cabins and boathouse. She crossed the ice, and began the long trek back to her car, pausing occasionally on her retreat to listen carefully while surveying the terrain. Anxious and in a heightened state of awareness, she found nothing suspicious or alarming.

2

Ray Elkins, sheriff of Cedar County, was in the early stages of reentry, a.k.a. the downside of taking a vacation. From the moment he walked through the back door to the department, everyone he met had to comment on his rich tan, a rarity in northern Michigan in late March. At the first few encounters, he felt obliged to explain that it was just a "skier's tan." It ended at his collar. He quickly learned that it was easier to say "thanks," rather than try to explain.

Ray spent the early hours at his desk responding to letters and e-mails. His long-time secretary, Jan, had arranged the paperwork in order of importance so he could efficiently attend to the most pressing issues. Jan, also a skilled gatekeeper, gave him several hours of cover to begin the process of catching up. He was starting to think about lunch when Sue Lawrence, a key member of his small department, knocked at his closed door and uncharacteristically waited until he pulled it open before entering.

Although the Cedar County Sheriff's Department had a command structure similar to other police agencies of its size, at least on paper, Elkins' management style was more collegial than top-down. His approach was shaped by years he spent in university teaching and administration, and was further influenced by his desire to give every member of his small staff a role in improving the effectiveness of the department. Ray encouraged people to grow their professional skills, providing money and time for additional training.

Sue Lawrence had joined the department right out of college and quickly became the person he assigned to major criminal investigations. Sue was bright, insightful and took advantage of the in-service training available from state and federal agencies, especially the FBI.

Over the years Ray and Sue had also developed a strong friendship that had almost spilled over into a personal relationship. Ray worked hard at maintaining a professional distance, wary of the risks and negative consequences of crossing the line.

"Great tan," commented Ray, remembering that Sue had spent a week in Florida with her parents before his own vacation.

"It's starting to fade," she responded.

"Anything happen last week I should know about?" he asked.

"Nada. How about the week I was gone?" she asked.

"Same."

"It's about time things slowed down. Remember when deep snow and frigid temps used to keep the bad guys indoors or out of state for weeks at a time?"

"It's just one more negative consequence of global warming," Ray shot back. "How was your vacation?"

"A week with the parents, not too exciting. I hit the beach every day, read a stack of books. We went out to eat a lot. That's what they seem to do in Florida. I think my mom has stopped cooking. How about you?"

"We skied every day. Salt Lake has great snow. And in the evening we did the opera, the symphony, chamber music. I got back Saturday, slept most of yesterday."

"What does your friend do?"

"He says he's an investment banker—I've never quite figured out what that is. It appears that he's sort of retired or has taken a sabbatical. He obviously doesn't like to talk about it, so I left it alone. His main focus now seems to be skiing, music, volunteer work, and a long-term girlfriend."

"In that order?" asked Sue.

Ray thought about the question before responding. "That was probably true last week. My presence might have skewed the data."

"The opera," Sue started, "the one we went to, I really enjoyed that. The next time your love life falls apart and you have an extra ticket, I'd be happy to go again. Only this time it would be nice not to work a homicide scene before the show. The onstage carnage was enough for one day."

Ray's focus was drawn to his secretary standing in the doorway. "Yes?"

"Sorry to bother you," Jan said, "but I have a Mrs. French waiting in the outer office. She insists that she has to see you. She says that it is very important."

"It's okay, bring her in."

Less than a minute later Jan escorted Ma French into the office. Ray steered her to his conference table. He sat at the end of the table, while Sue sat across from her.

"Sorry to hear about Pa," said Ray. "I saw the obit in the paper and hoped to get to the funeral but...."

"I understand, Ray," she said. "I read the papers, too. Horrible things were going on. And I appreciate the card and your nice note. It meant a lot. That card is something that I will hold on to."

"Jan said you needed to see me."

Ma unbuttoned her coat—an ancient, heavy, red and black wool hunting jacket—and extracted a small brown paper bag. She set it on the table in front of Ray.

"What's this?" he asked.

"Money, lots of it. Ten thousand dollars by my count. All in hundreds."

"Do you want to tell us about it?"

Ma French made no attempt to summarize her story. She started with the economics of dying, and how she and Pa had talked it over with the undertaker in the fall when it was clear he wasn't going to last much longer. They found that a cremation was far cheaper than burial, and Pa liked the idea. Then she told Ray and Sue how Pa had asked her to spread the ashes nearby in a deer blind, in the burial place of the family dogs, and on a bluff overlooking Lake Michigan near Camp E, their nickname for the Hollingsford Estate. She explained that they'd met there the summer before she graduated from high school.

Ray was tempted to prod her a bit to summarize, but he took a deep breath and allowed her to continue. Mamie, her given name, but not one used by the locals for decades, told them about her trip over to Lost Lake to spread Pa's ashes, how she'd parked and walked across the ice-covered lake to the grounds of the old estate. Then how she had followed the snowmobile track through the woods to shore. Finally, Ma told them about stopping at the burial plot and her dog Roxy unearthing the jar with the money near Rose-Marie Hollingsford's grave.

"Did you see anyone else that day, from the time you left your car until you returned to it?" Ray asked.

"No one," she said. "Not that time or the next day."

"You made two trips?" asked Sue.

Mamie flushed. "Well, when I first opened the jar and saw the money, I didn't count it or anything. I just put it in my pocket and looked around to make sure no one saw me. When I got home, I laid it out on the kitchen table and counted it. I couldn't believe how much was there. Right from the beginning, I knew it wasn't right—all that money and me just taking it. So I thought I should put it back. I went over there again the next day after I got off from work."

"What days and times are we talking about?" asked Ray.

"Wednesday and Thursday. Last week. Both times I was over there it was probably 'bout four-thirty, quarter to five. But the second time it was different. When I was there the first time, there was no footprints, but Thursday there was prints everywhere. I could see someone had been raking around, looks like they used their hands. You know, open fingers. I got scared. Headed out fast. Got back to the car and out of there."

"Did you see anyone?"

"No."

"How about the footprints? Did it look like someone might have followed your trail from Wednesday?"

"I thought about that. I didn't see none. I think they came on a sled. There's still enough snow along the shore, but it's going fast."

"How about when you were on that access road?"

"No. I didn't see anyone either time. What are you going to do with the money?"

Ray sat for a long moment before he answered. "I would like you to count the money again in front of us. I'll then give you a receipt. Sue will check for fingerprints. She will record the serial numbers and send them on to the FBI. They'll see if there's a match to any bills in their database that are connected to criminal activity. In the meantime, it will be held in the vault of the county treasurer."

"And if no one claims it, and it's not part of law breaking?" probed Ma.

"Let me check with the prosecutor's office. I think after a certain period of time, pending no other claims, the money has to be returned to the finder."

"That would be something," she said. "I desperately need a new roof and lots of other stuff."

"Don't talk to anyone about this," Ray warned. "Did Bobby see you with the money, or did you tell him about it?"

"No."

"Don't go back to the Hollingsford Estate."

"I won't, Ray."

"Tell me again about your connection with the Hollingsford Estate. You worked there as a teenager?"

"Yes, it was my first paying job. One of my cousins worked there, and she got me in. We stayed right there on the property all summer. It was my first time away from home."

"What did you do?" asked Ray.

"Domestic work mostly, helped in the kitchen and laundry. There was a lot to do. They had china and crystal and silver. Everything had to be polished and dried spot-free. As you know, I grew up on a farm not far from there, but I didn't know people lived like that. They had late dinners every night. Everything was by candlelight. It was beautiful."

"And you said you met Pa there?"

"Yes. He was older than me, been in the Army for a few years. He was the handyman, and he also helped the chef some. Pa had cooked in the service. We fell wildly in love, the way kids do, got married a year later when I graduated high school. Pa stayed on as the assistant caretaker for a few years."

"Why didn't that land become part of the National Shoreline?" asked Ray. "It's just about at the southern border."

"I heard a lot of talk, something about how the family lawyers were able to keep the property. The Hollingsfords had lots of political connections. Last I heard the place belonged to Faye Hollingsford, she's gotta be way up in her 90s by now. I think she was one of the granddaughters of the people who built it."

"This Faye, has she or other members of the family used the place in recent years?"

Ma thought about it. "No. I don't think anyone from the family has been there in 25 or 30 years. I don't know why they hold on to the property. Maybe sentimental reasons or something."

"But there's been a caretaker?" said Ray.

"Yes, Perry Ashton. He's been there for years; took over when his father died. Perry opens the place in the spring, shuts everything down in the fall, just like someone from the family is going to show up. Every month he gets a check from a law office in New York. He used to live in the house on the highway next to the road that runs into the estate. That was the winter place for the caretaker."

"But he doesn't...."

"No, not no more. I think he's supposed to, but he doesn't. No one checks. These days he spends the winter in town with his girlfriend. They live out at the estate in the good weather."

"The girlfriend, do you know her name?"

"Let me think, first name is Carol and last name is…something… maybe Truno."

"So no one watches over the place during the winter?" Ray asked as he penned Perry Ashton and Carol Truno at the top of a yellow legal pad.

"True. There was never a problem in the old days. It's just too hard to get through all that swampland, and almost no one knew it was there. But you know those damn snowmobiles can go everywhere. If you put up fences, they tear them down. There's been some vandalism over the years. Perry told me he took all the valuables out of there years ago. He's got them stored some place in town."

"Other than the vandalism, has there ever been any other trouble?"

"What do you mean?"

"Drugs or anything that might have involved the police?"

"I don't think so. The place has always been sort of its own little island, if you know what I mean. Whatever happened there was family stuff and nothing bad." Ma paused, holding Ray's gaze. "There was one thing, years ago. It happened in the spring, caused a bit of a stir."

"What?" pressed Ray.

"A body, a boy in his early teens, washed up on the beach."

"When was that?" asked Sue

Ma's reply was slow in coming. "Maybe 20 years or a bit more. Perry found him. As I remember, he was a kid from down around Sandville. Paper said Sheriff Orville thought the kid was probably skinny-dipping down around South Bay, got caught in a rip current or something and drowned. His body got carried up here by the wind and waves. I never thought that added up. Like if he went skinny-dipping, why didn't they find his clothes on a beach somewhere. There was a lot of talk at the time.

And who would be swimming in the big lake then? It was early spring; the water was still awful cold. Too cold even for kids."

"So what happened?" asked Ray.

"I don't think anything happened. Orville and his deputies did their investigation and said it musta been an accidental drowning. Kid was from a poor family. Other than his folks, probably no one really cared."

"Anything else about that case? Do you remember the victim's name?"

"Ray, that was a long time ago. If I ever knew it, I long ago forgot. Life moves on."

Ray looked across at Sue. He knew that they were sharing the same thoughts. Over the past several years, they had uncovered numerous examples of incompetence on the part of Ray's predecessor, Orville Hentzler, and the collection of cronies and relatives he employed as deputies during the more than 40 years he held the office. Most of the records and reports from Hentzler's long tenure in office had been lost in a suspicious fire that took place shortly before he left office.

"How is Bobby doing?" asked Ray, moving the conversation back to Ma.

"He's struggling with his dad's death. They've always been buddies. I've started taking him to an adult daycare when I go to work. I think it's been good for him to meet other people. My job is my big worry right now."

"How's that?"

"The new business manager at Leiston School, he's looking to cut costs. There's talk that they're going to hire an outside contractor to handle things like food service, laundry, custodial, and grounds. Rumor is that some of us will still be able to keep our jobs, but we'll get paid less and probably lose our health insurance. I don't know how we'll make it." Ma looked at her watch. "I dropped Bobby off at the barber shop. I know Leo will look after him till I get there, but I shouldn't make him wait too long."

"We'll only keep you a few more minutes. Let's count the money and Sue will get it logged in and give you a receipt. And remember what I told you."

"You know I will, Ray," she responded, pulling herself out of her chair.

Five minutes later Sue returned to Ray's office. "What do you think this is all about?" she asked.

"Your guess is as good as mine. The automatic response is that it must be some kind of drug deal, but that doesn't quite make sense, does it?"

"No, I don't think any of our dealer friends would need to wander off to some remote place in the woods to make an exchange. That's too much like work. They are more into passing packages from one Escalade to another. And I can't imagine bad guys leaving a stash of cash with the expectation that their distributor would leave the goods under a pine tree. What do we do now?"

"Keep an eye on things and see what develops. This drowning Ma mentioned, I'd like to know more about it. How busy are you?"

"Lots of little things need to be finished up. But less jammed than I usually am."

"Will you see what you can dig up?"

"Sure," she responded. "First I have to find a name, then look through the non-existent police reports from that time and…."

"There will be a death certificate, and maybe there's a state police report." Ray paused for a long moment. "Mrs. Schaffer, Helen Schaffer."

"Who's that?"

"She's been the main secretary at Consolidated Schools for decades. See her, you'll get a name and probably some family history. She's a really bright woman with an incredible memory.

"And I forgot to ask, how did Simone do when you were away?" Ray asked. Sue had acquired a Cairn terrier during the course of a recent murder investigation.

"The couple I boarded her with was really wonderful. They kept her with them in the house. They said she seemed to be fine, but she was off her food. I'm trying to remember, did she eat okay when she stayed with you?"

"She was great. Clean plate club."

"Ray, you didn't…"

"Not a chance. Nothing but dog food."

3

~

The next morning, Tuesday, Sue started her exploration at the County Clerk's office of the death of the teenager who'd washed up on the shoreline at the Hollingsford Estate. The youngest elected official in Cedar County, Julie Sutton, a woman of boundless energy and enthusiasm, greeted her.

"Hey, Susan, great tan. How was Florida?"

"It was good. I need a favor."

"A favor or a miracle?" Sutton shot back.

"How do I...?"

"You need some information?"

"Yes."

"A favor request would be something we've got on the computer, something that's happened in recent decades. A miracle request is a birth or death record from 120 years ago. In fact, I just completed one. Been working on it off and on for weeks. This lady in New York, one of those ancestry.com addicts—most of them need a Twelve-Step Program—contacted me about a distant relative, a great-great grandmother twice removed, with three or four possible spellings of the last name, who may have been born in this county around 1880 and may have died around 1920. With a lot of digging I solved the case," Sutton said, beaming. "Someday I will have this all computerized, and a search like this will be just a few key strokes." She paused for a moment and smiled wistfully. "And it won't be near as much fun. Now, what can I do for you?"

Sue took a deep breath. "I'm searching for the name of a boy, 15 or 16. He died about 20 years ago, probably in May or June. I think that it will be an accidental death, a drowning. He may have lived around Sandville."

"That should be easy," said Sutton. "Give me a few."

Sue had barely started checking her e-mail on her iPhone when Sutton reappeared. "I think this is what you're looking for," she said, placing a death certificate on the counter at an angle where they could both read it.

Sue quickly scanned the document. "Terry Hallen," she said.

"Yes," said Sutton. "We usually only have a few drownings a year, and sometimes none. This is the only one from that time that fits."

"Why all the blanks?" asked Sue. "This form is only partially filled out."

Sutton chuckled. "It's from the bad old days when one of my bungling predecessors didn't mind the store." She pulled the form to her side of the countertop and looked at it closely. Then she pointed to a signature. "Here's part of the problem—your department. Look at the signature for the person who completed the 'cause of death' section, Dirk Lowther. There was a real piece of work."

"You didn't like my departed colleague?"

"What a scum ball. A total sleaze and a poster boy for Grecian Formula. Don't get me started."

"I think I have," said Sue.

"You know, I first worked here when I was in high school, the co-op program. If Dirk came in when no one else was around, he would hit on me. Real aggressive, obscene, like he believed every high school girl wanted to drop her pants for him. Hell, he was lots older than my father. After I repeatedly insulted him, he finally left me alone."

Sue pulled the death certificate back to her side of the counter. "So a physician signed here, but it doesn't look like there was an autopsy."

"That's correct. It was pro forma. My understanding is that back in the day, a body would be turned over to the undertaker, and he would look at it after getting a doctor's signature on the form. If there weren't any gaping knife wounds or bullet holes, there was seldom an autopsy. Things were pretty casual."

"Can I take this with me?"

"Yes, it's a copy." Sutton stood back and crossed her arms. "Why the interest in something that happened years ago?"

"It just came up in another investigation, and I was a bit curious. You never know what you're going to find. Thanks."

Driving toward the south end of the county, Sue felt a pang of regret that she had been less than honest with Ray. Yes, she had spent part of a week visiting her parents in Florida, but she'd also enjoyed a long weekend in Chicago with Harry Hawkins, a man she'd met earlier in the fall during a criminal investigation.

Initially she'd found Hawkins, a lawyer, pompous and distant, but as she got to know him better, she'd started to see a very different person. Over the past several months he'd kept in contact via phone and e-mail, and he'd invited her several times to spend a weekend with him in Chicago. She had finally surrendered to his persistence.

Hawkins met Sue at O'Hare and took her to dinner and a movie before escorting her to his apartment in a Mies van der Rohe building on Lakeshore Drive. The next morning they jogged along the beach before breakfast. Then they spent the afternoon at the Art Institute, followed by an intimate dinner in a small French bistro. That evening he arranged for front row, mezzanine seats at the Lyric Opera for an especially steamy version of Carmen.

When Sue awakened on Sunday, Hawkins had just returned from picking up fresh croissants filled with a buttery dark chocolate. They ate, drank coffee, and read the *Times* in the sun-flooded living room. All too quickly the weekend reverie was shattered by the dash back to O'Hare.

Sue felt a warm glow and glanced at herself in the rearview mirror. Harry Hawkins knew how to treat a woman. *But is there anything really there?* she asked herself, then started at the sound of her voice. She frowned. It was lovely spending time with a smart, interesting man. And for months she'd been struggling with the feeling that she needed to take her life in another direction. But while becoming involved in a good relationship might be part of moving her life forward, Sue wasn't waiting for some Prince Charming to play "Misty" for her. She was also looking at graduate programs in art and public administration and considering law school.

Sue parked in the *Visitors Lot* near the entrance to the administrative offices of the school district, a small red brick building across the parking lot from the new middle and high school complex. Once inside the building, she identified herself to the receptionist, a perky high school girl with short black hair and a pleasant manner. Sue was guided to a work area where the receptionist announced her presence to a woman who had her back to them. She was bent over a large computer screen and hammering away on a keyboard.

"Helen, someone is here to see you."

The keying continued for a long moment before the woman swiveled her chair in their direction.

"Oh," she said, rather unsettled by the appearance of a stranger.

"Mrs. Schaffer, I'm Sue Lawrence." Sue passed a business card across the desk.

Helen Schaffer held the card by the corner, lifting her head to use the bottom lens of her trifocals. She looked at Sue for a long moment, studying her face. "You weren't ever a student here, were you?"

"No, I was not."

"I didn't think so, but my memory isn't what it used to be." She opened a drawer and placed the card inside. "How can I help you?"

"I'm looking for information on a former student, Terry Hallen. Do you have any of his records, or do you remember anything about him? He would have been enrolled here about 20 years ago."

"Terry Hallen," Schaffer mused. "I haven't thought about him for a long time, but he's not someone I will ever forget. Just a beautiful kid: big blue eyes, a shock of brown hair. He supposedly drowned. I could never quite believe it. Didn't seem right."

"How so?" asked Sue.

Schaffer didn't respond immediately. "Well, maybe that's the way I feel when any of our kids die or get killed. It's not right. It's not natural. And Terry was special. His people were so poor. We were always looking for clothes for him and his sister—they didn't have anything. But they were smart, sweet kids. They were the kind of kids that get beyond their circumstances and do something with their lives. And then he was suddenly gone. It made no sense."

"How did it happen? Our records of Terry's death are very incomplete."

"One story was that he was fishing off the pier near the lighthouse and got washed off by a rogue wave. As I remember it, he was missing a few days before they found his body miles up the lake."

"You mentioned a sister," said Sue.

"Yes, she was a sweetie, too. Let me think—Caitlyn."

"Did she graduate?"

"No. As I recollect, it was the end of the school year when Terry died. I don't think his sister even finished her exams that year. I do remember calling the home. Her mother told me that Caitlyn and her younger sisters, twins they were, elementary, fourth or fifth grade, had gone off to stay with a relative. The next fall I called again before the fourth Friday count. The phone had been disconnected. That happens, you know. People disappear. Sometimes we get requests for records from their new school district. Not always."

"Could you check that?"

"Yes. It will take me a few minutes; we have the old records stored in an annex."

"I'd appreciate it. Is there anything else can you tell me about Terry or his sister?"

Schaffer stood up and began to move toward the door. "They were from Sandville. Not much of a town then, almost nothing left today. That's the poorest part of our attendance area, right on the county line. Lots of problems, most connected to poverty. And kids aren't always kind; I mean other kids. If there's someone slightly lower on the ladder, they think it's okay to dump on them."

"Are you talking about bullying?"

"That's the term we use today. I'm sure the students from Sandville got more than their share of abuse. They were at the bottom of the heap."

"Do you think Terry or his sister were bullied?"

"I don't know specifically, but I wouldn't be surprised. We're more sensitive to that kind of thing these days. But so much goes on that's beyond adult supervision. You know, on the bus or at the bus stop, in bathrooms and hallways. It's like we're on different planets, the adults and kids, and unfortunately we're never able to control some of the bad stuff that happens in their world."

"Do you remember anything more about Terry's death?"

"There were a couple of articles in the paper. And there were some rumors. People always talk. I can't tell you if there was anything to them. I'm sorry, that's all I can remember."

"Rumors, what kind of rumors?"

"Like I said, I can't remember details, but some people thought it didn't quite add up. They said maybe he was killed. Why would anyone kill him? Anyway, they didn't have anything more than feelings. There was no evidence. "

"One more question," Sue said as Schaffer put her hand on the door. "What else can you tell me about Sandville?"

"Not much. Some," she said, shrugging. "I guess it was a flourishing village back in the lumber days. A hundred years ago, there was a railroad and two or three mills, a store, post office, a saloon, and a couple of churches. When the lumber was played out, the land was sold off cheap for farms. You know, the soil is so fragile up here. But the immigrant settlers were lured by cheap land. They pulled out the stumps and built farms and had a few good years growing potatoes. It wasn't long before the soil was depleted and people started drifting away. Then some businessman from down south, maybe Ludington, bought up most of the land east of town and started what they called a sand mine. They hauled out millions of tons on the railroad. I think that lasted until sometime in the 50s. It tore up the terrain something awful, just like strip mining. That area is mostly overgrown now. It's worthless land. And almost nothing is left of the town now—a cemetery and a few old houses. There used to be lots of vacant houses, but they had some arson a decade or so ago. People said it was one boy, others thought it was a gang of them that liked to see things burn. Since they were unoccupied, pretty much worthless, I don't think anyone cared. Anyway, Sandville is little more than a ghost town. Sorry I can't tell you much else. We haven't been very good at writing down local history." Schaffer smiled sadly.

"On the contrary, you've been most helpful. Could I see Terry's records, and would you check and see if there was a request for the girls' records?"

"Yes. This will take a few minutes."

While she waited, Sue pulled her laptop from a backpack and typed notes about her conversation with Schaffer. Then she read through them, making revisions and corrections.

Finally, Schaffer returned, a little out of breath. "I have the folders for Caitlyn and her sisters," she said, settling back at her desk and opening the top folder. She shifted through the contents, then she did the same for the other two. She peered up at Sue over the top of her glasses and shook her head. "Nope, nothing. It doesn't appear that there were any requests for records. But like I said, that's not uncommon."

"So you've got the folders for Terry's siblings. I'd be interested in seeing Terry's school records, too."

"I'd planned to bring his, but..." She opened the top folder distractedly.

"But what?"

"I couldn't find his CA60, his file that is. It doesn't seem to be there."

"Maybe it was moved after he died?" offered Sue.

"We've never done that. We've always kept every class year together, A to Z. I'll do some more checking. I don't understand it."

"Do you have an address for the family, the Sandville address?" asked Sue.

Schaffer opened the top folder again and scanned with her finger. "Yes, it's 411 North Second Street. I doubt if there is still a structure there."

"You have my card," said Sue. "If anything else occurs to you about Terry or his siblings, please give me a call. And I'd like to know if you find his records."

"I'll look for them," she said, shaking her head again. "This is most peculiar."

4
~

Ray sat at his conference table, the 10 pages of a Missing Person Report laid out in two sets of five. Ray couldn't remember ever having any previous contact with the woman sitting on the other side of the table, but she looked vaguely familiar. She'd identified herself as Joan Barton, and appeared to be in her middle to late 50s. Her long black hair, streaked with gray, was pulled into a loose bun. A tight black jacket covered a maroon turtleneck.

"There's a lot I didn't fill in," Barton said, her hands grasped together in her lap.

"I understand. It's a generic form. Only a fraction of the information applies in this case." Ray looked at second page the form, "And you're Vincent Fox's daughter, Ms. Barton?"

"Yes."

Ray slid the first page of the report across the table. "Would you put your e-mail in the margin next to the phone numbers. We need to get this form updated."

"Can you read it?" she asked, sliding the form back.

"No problem, you have beautiful handwriting." Ray sat back and took a breath. "When did you last see your father?"

Speaking quickly, Barton said, "It was this past Wednesday. I took him grocery shopping and to the bank. Then we had lunch at the Last Chance. He loves their cheeseburgers and fries. That's not what I think he should be eating, but when you're pushing 90 it probably doesn't matter much."

"And you've had no contact since then?" he asked, noting the shade of her eyes, a mahogany brown.

"I call every day to check on him, but quite often I don't reach him. I don't bother to leave messages because he refuses to learn how to use voicemail, says he doesn't want to talk to a machine. I even got him a cell phone and he wouldn't use it." She shrugged, tugged at her collar. "So it's no big thing if we miss a day or two, sometimes three. Like I said, I was with him on Wednesday. He didn't answer on Thursday. We did connect on Friday and Saturday morning. But then I couldn't reach him Sunday or yesterday morning. I went downstate to visit one of my kids; my daughter's having a rough time with a pregnancy." She lifted her chin. "I help her with housework and look after my two very energetic grandsons. Then I called him several times as I was driving north this morning. And instead of stopping at my house in Traverse City, I just drove right up to his place. His little dog was there, cold and hungry. He almost never goes anywhere without her. His bike was there, too. That's how he gets around. And now that the snow is mostly gone, he's been using it again."

Barton was looking agitated. Ray smiled and said gently, "So you went to his house. Tell me what you did then, step by step."

"I parked in the drive. His dog came out and yapped at me—there's a dog door and a small fenced area off the kitchen. I don't know if I'm over-reading the situation, but the dog seemed more hysterical than usual. Dad's very hard of hearing, but the barking is usually enough to bring him to the door. I knocked and knocked, and when I didn't get a response, I let myself in."

"The door was locked?"

"Yes, he's very compulsive about that, keeping the place locked up. He's afraid of getting robbed," she scoffed. "Not that there's much anyone would want. I had a lock put on his door with one of those keypads about a year ago. I programmed his birth year as the entrance code, something he wouldn't forget. Before that, he kept losing his key and then the backup, which he would invariably forget to return to its hiding place in the shed. He'd go to the neighbors and call me and ask me to drive out and open the door. That gets old real fast."

"Why didn't you give the neighbors a key?"

"I did," she said, raising her hands in the air. "He would get that key, also, and forget to return it." She sighed and shrugged back in the chair. "So, like I said, I let myself in. By this point, I was getting scared, like what if he'd died a few days before and I'd stumble over his body. I don't like him living alone. For years I've been trying to get him to move to a senior apartment, but he's such a stubborn old coot. He insists on staying in that tumbled down shack. When my mother was alive, they had a cute little house in town. After she was gone, he moved to the cabin. It was his 'getaway in the woods.'"

Ray took a moment to type a few notes, letting her simmer down. "Any ideas about when he might have last been there?"

"I don't know. Hard to tell. Some of the food we bought on Wednesday was gone from the refrigerator. So I think he was probably around till the weekend."

"He doesn't drive?"

"Not in recent years. His driving was getting pretty scary, so I was happy when he let me sell his car before he got hurt or injured someone else. Like I said, in warm weather he uses a bike. It's a big old black Schwinn he's had for decades." Barton passed her hand over her forehead. "I take him on errands at least once a week," she said, almost whining. "And there's a neighbor down the road, who will drive Dad to appointments and things when I'm not available."

Ray nodded his head, encouraging. "And his name, the neighbor?"

"It's Henry Seaton."

"Did you check with Mr. Seaton about your father?"

"I stopped by there after I left my father's house. No one was home." Barton stood up suddenly. "And let me say one more thing: I looked in my father's house, then I checked the garage, and finally I walked around the perimeter. Everything seemed normal."

"Sit down, Ms. Barton. How about friends, someone he might have gone away with?"

"He used to have a lot of friends, but not so much anymore. They'd drink beer and play euchre at the Last Chance, or go to the casino when they got their Social Security checks. Most of them are gone now. There are still a few people around the village he spends time with. I'm not sure who they are, but I can't imagine anyone who he would take off with."

"How about relatives?" Ray asked.

"No, not up here. I mean, it's just me and my sister. And she lives down in Livonia. She only makes it up occasionally, mostly in the summer. I would know if she was here because she stays with me. We don't have any other relatives in the area."

Ray slid the second to the last page of the form in front of him and studied it. "Was there anything missing from his house?" he asked.

"Not that I noticed."

"Did your father keep any cash there?"

"Not any big money, if that's what you mean. Just 50 or 60 bucks, a hundred at the most. Grocery money, beer money, something for the slots."

"How about the bank? Does he have substantial assets?"

"No, he has a checking account, a small savings account, and a few CDs. I have power of attorney and look after that for him. He gets on quite well on Social Security and a small annuity. When he needs money, I get it for him."

"And there's been no recent withdrawal of funds?"

"No. I was paying a bill for him this morning. They all come to me, and I pay them electronically. Everything is in order."

Ray ran his fingers over the pages of the form again, then gathered them into one pile. "Now tell me about your father, the kinds of things that aren't here," he said, placing his index finger on the top of the pile.

"What are you looking for?" she asked, looking genuinely perplexed.

"I need a sense of the man. Tell me about your father as a person. Give me a sense of his character."

"Where do you want me to start?"

"During his working years, what did he do? Tell me about the connections that he has, or has had, with other people in the community."

Barton relaxed. "Character, that's the word. My dad is a character, a real storyteller. At times he embarrassed me," she laughed. "Then I just sort of accepted him for what he is."

"I'm not quite following."

"Do you know my father?" she asked.

Ray shook his head, thinking. "I don't believe so."

"Well, even though you don't know his name, I'm sure you've seen him around the village. For the last ten years he's been wearing his Native American costume—a buckskin jacket with fringe, usually over a flannel shirt and worn-out jeans. Those jeans are too long when they're new. He just grinds them away with the heels of his boots. He stopped getting haircuts years ago. One of his women friends showed him how to make pigtails. And he wears this big old felt hat with a couple of eagle feathers in it. In the summer he's got these old moccasins that run to his knees with some beadwork on them. In the winter he wears a pair of Bean hunting boots, the kind with the rubber bottoms and leather tops." Barton smiled across the table at Ray. "Now you know who I'm talking about?"

"Yes, from your description, I know who you are talking about."

"Did you think he was a member of the band?"

"No, I just remember the costume," said Ray. "Is he? A member of the band?"

"Not a drop of Indian blood." Barton grimaced. "My mother had some, not much, maybe a 16th from her mother's side, way back in lumbering days. What my father is, is a storyteller. He has been for as long as I remember. When we were kids—my sister and me—he would read us stories at bedtime, but he would change them; he put himself in the story as a knight, or prince, or pirate. It was terrific. We loved it. As I grew up, I could see that his stories were just part of his life, that he didn't separate fact and fiction very much. I mean, nothing malicious or bad, like he didn't cheat anyone in his business or anything, but he was always telling stories."

"What kind of business was he in?"

"He was a mechanic, a really gifted mechanic. For years he ran Vinnie's Import Auto Repair in Traverse City. Back in the day he was the only one in town that worked on the exotics. You know, for the summer people who would bring their Jaguars, Porsches and Mercedes up north. When they had problems, he was the only one around who could fix them. Dad was in the Army Air Force during World War II. That's where he learned mechanics. He was stationed in England." Barton paused and frowned across the table at Ray. "And here's a perfect example of what I'm talking about, the storytelling. When we were growing up, he always told us that he had been a bomber pilot, that he had flown dozens of missions over Germany. A number of years ago, his old unit had a reunion, it was down in Florida. I told him that I would drive him there—he doesn't like to fly anymore. He said he wasn't interested, but I sensed that he wanted to go. So I called the organizers to get some more details, thinking that I could persuade him. I knew he'd like it once he got there." Barton shifted in her chair, but kept her eyes on Ray. "But when I was talking to one of the organizers, I found out that my father had been a mechanic. The guy went on and on about how he was the best mechanic in the group, how he could fix anything. I asked if my father had ever been on a mission, had flown over Germany. He said that occasionally a ground crewman would sneak on an aircraft so he could experience combat. But he had no knowledge as to whether my father had ever truly participated on a mission.

"And his Indian get-up," Barton said, nodding. "It's just another story. And if you talk to him, he is not part of the local band. He is a descendent of what I like to call the movie Indians, Crazy Horse and Sitting Bull. And then there's Al Capone."

"Al Capone?"

"Yes. One of Dad's stories is that he was the driver for Al Capone, and not only in Chicago, up here, too. I've checked, not that I ever believed it would've been possible. The dates didn't match up. He wouldn't have been old enough. He did grow up in Chicago, that's his only connection. But he's got this great story of how he worked for Capone. When big Al was under pressure from the Feds, my father helped him hide millions of dollars in northern Michigan. In fact, he wrote a book about it. He's even sold a few copies."

"Let me have this again," said Ray. "Your father wrote a book about Al Capone stashing money in northern Michigan? When did he do this?"

"Just in the past few years. He said he wanted to write his memoir before he died. He took one of those life story classes at the library a few winters ago. My sister and I bought him a Mac. He loves that machine. He had no trouble learning how to use it. Occasionally he'd get in a bit of a mess, and we would sort it out for him." Barton laughed, this time to herself.

"When I started to read the stuff he was producing, I was amazed. It wasn't a real memoir. It was all about Al Capone. Of course, I confronted him, but he just laughed. He said the stuff he was writing was a lot more fun than what actually happened to him, growing up poor in Chicago. When he finished it, he found a woman who does this kind of thing, you know—helps people put together memoirs and family books. She formatted the book for him. Initially, he got 10 copies, print on demand. Dad buys a lot of stuff at that little bookstore in the village. He got the owner to take a copy or two on consignment. Turns out Dad has sold or given away a couple of dozen over the last six months. He's been having so much fun with this. I hope people don't start digging up the beaches…."

"Does he give locations? Are there maps?"

"No, nothing like that. But he hints at what the places look like. You know, sand and beaches, headlands, and islands." She laughed. "Almost everything around here fits that description."

Ray took another moment to make notes.

"Has your father ever gone missing before?" he asked.

"Never," she responded emphatically.

"How's your father doing cognitively?"

"What do you mean? Like is he getting senile? Alzheimer's?"

"Yes."

She shrugged. "Other than his rather bizarre fantasy life, he's pretty sharp."

"Has he ever had a stroke, anything like that?"

"No, not that I'm aware of. But he's close to 90."

"How about his spirits? Depression?"

"No. He's one of the happiest people I've ever met."

Ray nodded. He could see it in the daughter as well. "There's just one more thing. I need to clarify something, When you got to the house, was the door locked?"

"Yes, like I said. I used the keypad to get in."

"Did you check other entryways, the doors and windows? Any evidence of forced entry?"

"Quite frankly, I didn't look that closely. I think I was in panic mode by then. I wasn't thinking clearly."

"Do you have a photo of your father?"

"Not with me, but I can get you one. I'll put it in an e-mail as soon as I get home." She stood up again, slowly this time. "What happens now?"

"We will alert our officers and other police agencies to be on the lookout for your father. We can request help from the media. We usually get the best response from local TV news."

"I've seen those stories about some poor old soul who wanders away from a nursing home in their PJs. I don't think my father falls into that category."

"Something has obviously happened, Ms. Barton," said Ray, standing up as well. "Your father's unique style of dress will have put him on the radar of lots of people around here, even if they don't know him. I think we should request help from the public. The media is always ready to cooperate." Barton was silent for a few moments, staring at her hands, left over right on the conference table. She looked up at Ray. "Okay, let's do it. What else?"

Ray glanced at his watch. "I'd like to go over to your father's house, with your permission and in your company, to have a quick look around, and then make sure the place is secure."

"Yes. Then what?"

"First thing tomorrow morning, Sue Lawrence, our detective who does crime scene investigations, will carefully check your father's house and the surrounding grounds to see if there's anything that might give us a clue to his disappearance. I'll also organize a search of the immediate area, starting with a tracking dog, and then a search team. Give me about five minutes to write a press release. I'll send it out immediately, and later I'll add his photo to a revised release. If it starts running on the eleven o'clock news tonight, we'll be getting calls and e-mails from the public in the morning. How about your father's dog?"

"Big Al? I've got him in the car. He's pretty frantic."

"What type of dog is he?"

"He's a papillon mix who thinks he's a great Dane. He and Dad are so close, I can't…" Her eyes suddenly overflowed with tears.

5

S tarting her engine to get the heater going, Sue keyed 411 North
Second Street, Sandville, into her GPS. When the map appeared
on the screen, she pulled out onto the highway and headed south
toward the sparsely part of the county. Simone, the Cairn terrier, roused
herself from a fleece blanket and stood, her paws against the side window,
peering out at the passing countryside.

Cedar County was divided into four sectors by the department. The
northern part is a wooded and rolling landscape with miles of Lake
Michigan shoreline and many beautiful inland lakes—some quite large,
some little more than puddles. Away from the resort areas, cherry and
apple orchards and vineyards cover the gently undulating hills and valleys.
The southeastern part of the county has neither the topography nor the
fertile farmland that enables the rest of the county to prosper. Land that
was briefly farmed after the end of the lumber era had lain fallow for
almost a century. Scrubby forests of oak, pine, cedar, and maple slowly
reclaimed the territory. Once flourishing villages became nothing more
than crossroads — deserted cemeteries and a few dilapidated buildings
of a long-departed population. Of the hundreds of square miles in the
department's jurisdiction, only two deputies—road patrol officers—were
routinely assigned to the southern sector.

It took Sue less than twenty-five minutes to reach Sandville. She
parked briefly on Main Street and looked around, comparing the data
of the GPS with the current reality of the place. Her computer screen

displayed a six-by-six grid of streets, the county line running down the center of six blocks of a paved two-lane road, also known as Main Street. From her parking spot, it appeared that the only houses remaining were in the most central area of the town. The largest structure was a vacant, two-story cinderblock building. Two display windows, one of which had duct tape running along the lines of a bad fracture, faced the deserted street. The window in the entrance was boarded over with a piece of plywood, the blackening top layers delaminating at the edges. Across the street was another cement building, low and square, its windows and doors also boarded over. A faded sign over the entrance read, "Groceries and Hardware."

Sue put the Jeep in gear and followed the onscreen directions until she reached 411 North Second Street. Much of the lot was still covered with snow, with some grey weeds and grass becoming visible along the margins. All that remained was an enormous, gnarled oak. Getting out of her vehicle , she carefully walked around the area, finding the crumbling remnants of a sidewalk and the home's foundation. There were several remaining houses on the block—mostly abandoned and badly sagging, their naked dark siding without a hint of paint. Based on the size of the foundation and the fact that the surviving homes were all two-story, this had been a substantial structure in its day. Sue paced off the foundation and estimated that each floor probably was about 1,000 square feet. When she returned to her Jeep, Simone had moved to her side of the car and attempted to scramble out as she opened the door. After attaching a leash, she walked the perimeter of the block with Simone before lifting the dog back into the car.

Ray followed Joan Barton out to her father's home where he did a quick walk-through of the premises, taking care not to disturb anything in the small building's interior. Then, accompanied by Barton, he checked the shed-like garage and walked around the yard. Although nothing seemed particularly out of place, Ray planned to have Sue Lawrence carefully go through the scene the next morning.

As Ray began to say his goodbyes, Barton asked him to accompany her to a small lake about a mile up the road. She explained that her father's greatest passion was fishing. Because of its proximity, this lake was a place he visited almost every day, either riding his bike or walking, depending on the conditions. Barton led the way. They parked on the shoulder of the road and Ray followed her down a narrow trail that ended at the shore. Open water extended from the shoreline for several yards to join a thin layer of opaque white ice.

"Dad comes here all year long. He's on the ice in the winter, and he uses that dinghy the rest of the time." Barton pointed toward a small, overturned aluminum boat a few yards off the trail, most of it still buried in the snow.

"It's between seasons," Ray observed.

"Yes, I'm aware of that. But what if he had a small stroke, or something, and gets a bit dotty? I was just thinking about things that he might do if his rationality was slipping away." She shivered and pulled at the collar of her coat. "This is one of his favorite places. I thought it might be a place that he would wander off to. I didn't want to come here alone."

Ray remained with Barton a full ten minutes, silently gazing out at the frozen lake.

After picking up some groceries, Ray stopped at the local bookseller, a cozy place managed and owned by a British ex-pat. The building, originally a pharmacy, dated from the 1880s or 1890s, and was one of the last original structures in the two-block long commercial district in Cedar Bay. The interior had not been changed much over the years. The maple flooring showed wear from generations of shoppers who had pushed through the heavy front door with its thick, plate glass window. Above, the tin ceiling was mostly intact, only slightly damaged by some less than skillful modifications when electric lights were added in the 20s. Books were displayed on tables appropriate in age and design to the building's interior and on shelving that covered the walls.

"Nice tan, that," said Phillip Noble, getting up from his hidey-hole behind an antique display case and counter. "I've got the volume of Robinson Jeffers you wanted. I didn't know anything about him, and your request got me started on some background reading. Interesting man. The things I read off the web suggest that he fell out of favor for his politics. You Yanks don't seem to like pacifists much."

"Especially during the run-up to war," said Ray. "But they probably weren't too popular in the UK either when the Luftwaffe was making daily visits."

"Right, but pacifists were tolerated. We're a small, densely populated island with vastly different political and social views and a whole lot of eccentrics. We probably were forced into tolerance so we could all occupy the same space. In point of fact, I was reading a letter to the editor today in The Record-Eagle. The author, a woman who I would guess to be rather elderly, suggested that people who did not share her views were not real Americans, whatever that is, and she went on to intimate that they were deserving of some major violence. Quite frightening, actually."

Ray nodded his head. "I worry about another homegrown Tim McVeigh, who might decide to take out the local police agency because in his fantasy world we're conspiring with the UN and God knows who else to take over the country. There's a lot of lunacy out there on the Internet and talk radio. But getting back to Robinson Jeffers."

"Yes, he's quite good, actually," said Phillip. "I certainly knew the name, but I have to admit that I was unfamiliar with his work. I started thumbing through your book after it arrived—hope you don't mind, white gloves on, of course—and it is sort of the prerogative of Ye Old Book Shoppe to understand the literary tastes of our customers. To better serve you, I actually read most of the book. I hope you want me to continue to look for more of his work. I've become quite a fan."

"Sure. Find out what's out there. Most will be in the used book market. Get some prices and we'll talk. Right now I need to know about something else, a book by a local author, self published."

"And the title is?"

"Al Capone's Michigan: The Secret Lost Treasure by Vinnie Fox."

"It should be right here with the locals." Phillip came around the counter to a bookcase in the front corner of the store. "That is, it should be right here if it hasn't been nicked yet."

"Nicked?" ask Ray.

"Strangest thing, actually. I seldom lose anything. It's a small store, and I can see what's going on. Although, I did have a problem with audio books a few years ago. Far too many left the store without going through the cash register. As soon as I stopped carrying them, the problem went away. But this Capone book is becoming a real nuisance."

"Tell me about the author, Fox," said Ray.

"Vinnie comes in every few days, especially during good weather. I don't see him quite as much in the winter. He is a reader, and he has money to buy books. A very good thing, especially when the tourists aren't around."

"And his literary tastes?"

"Quite astounding, actually. He likes action-adventure, the kind of books that usually appeal to adolescent boys—Ivanhoe, Captains Courageous, Two Years Before the Mast. Old stuff, the classics of the genre. He's also big on Native American history. Deems himself quite an expert on the topic, although I've never been able to figure out exactly what his heritage is. A bit vague there."

"What about his book?"

"Yes, the book. Vinnie came in sometime last fall, asked me if I would stock it." Phillip paused and made a little pout. "This happens about once a month, sometimes more, and it often involves a regular customer. People who like books seem to want to write at least one during their lifetime." He sighed. "Puts me in a bit of a tight place, actually. This is a tiny shop. To stay alive I've got to be exceedingly careful about what I stock. That said, I don't want to antagonize valued customers. But most of the self-published stuff doesn't sell. Some of it's not that terrible, but there just isn't a market. I told Vinnie I'd keep two copies on consignment and see if they sold. Much to my surprise they went, so I got two more. Within a fortnight, those were gone, also. Heading into the Christmas season I stocked four copies. Two went through the till, the other two were nicked. Must've happened when I had unusually large crowds in the store. I couldn't believe it. And then Penny from the library comes in—she's good enough to order most of her books from us—and she told me she'd experienced the same problem. Vinnie gave the library two copies, and they both disappeared." Phillip pulled a book from a shelf and handed it to Ray.

"Is this the only copy you have?"

"One more behind the counter. Vinnie dropped them off a week ago. I put one out and kept the other back there."

"Phillip, Vinnie Fox is missing. It'll be on the eleven o'clock news."

Phillip's eyes grew wide. "You don't think it's connected to this?"

"I don't know what to think. We are just beginning to investigate. His daughter told me about the book, and I thought I should look at it. Any idea who might have stolen the books?"

"I have two different sorts of customers," he sniffed, "the locals who I know by name and see on a regular basis—that includes summer people who return year after year—and the holidaymakers, the tourist trade. Among the locals I know who's a bit dodgy and needs watching, the others…well." Phillip turned to gaze out of the front window toward the harbor, then swung back to Ray. "If they had only charged their stolen books with a credit card, I could get their names for you." He chuckled at his joke.

"How about Vinnie's book?" asked Ray. "Have you read it?"

"Yes. Not a bad read—needs some editing and proofing. It's quite remarkable, actually, given his age, and this is the first time he's ever done anything like it."

"And the contents?"

"He says it's all true, but I think other than the landscape, it's all fantasy. He'd have you believe that he was Al Capone's driver. Old as Vinnie is, he isn't old enough. He was still in nappies when most of this went down. But it's a great story about Big Al being under pressure from the FBI—Elliot Ness and his mates—and how Al works to insure his retirement by burying bags of gold coins along the shore and out on the islands. Everything always happened on moonless nights under great secrecy. He just followed directions, never really knew where he was—the maps were kept by the bosses. According to his story, at the end of the day no one who knew about the treasure was left. Capone's brain was destroyed by syphilis and his lieutenants were killed in gangland wars or died in prison."

Ray handed a credit card to Phillip.

"I hope Vinnie's story has a happy ending," said Phillip as he processed the sale.

"I do too," said Ray, picking up his book.

"Would you like that copy of Vinnie's book, my compliments?"

"Sure," said Ray. "I'll read it tonight."

6

Ray had uncorked a bottle of Beaujolais and was scanning the opening chapter of Fox's book when someone knocked loudly at the front door. Before he could get up, Hannah Jeffers, a local cardiologist he'd met during a case the last winter, pushed her way into the kitchen.

"How is it that you just arrive like that?" asked Ray, putting down the book.

"Does it bother you?"

"No, I'm just curious."

Hannah tore off her coat and flung it toward the sofa. "There's no one else I can do this to," she said, getting a glass from the cupboard and helping herself to a Diet Coke from the fridge. "I don't know a lot of people up here. And I can't drop in on the other men I know because they're all married or living with someone. Anyway, I like your company. We do interesting things. Most importantly, you don't put any demands on me." She said this without looking at him. "I need a buddy, and that seems to be okay with you. And ..." She paused.

"What?" Ray pursued.

"I know I can always get a decent meal here. I hate to cook, and I don't like most restaurant food."

Ray laughed. "The menu isn't too inspired tonight. Most of it will be out of the freezer."

"Do you have enough for...."

"No problem."

What can I do?" she asked.

"Wash and spin the salad. Grate the Parmesan. I'll do the main course."

"Which is?"

"Ricotta cheese gnocchi in browned butter. I hope you're not dieting."

"The nice thing about being super hyper is I burn it off." Hannah began to work on a head of romaine. "By the way, weren't you involved with someone when we first met? I remember a very pretty woman who visited you in the hospital."

"Yes." In fact, Ray had been thinking about Sarah earlier in the day.

"What happened to her?"

"Her job up here was going away; she had a terrific offer with a large law firm in Chicago."

"Are you two still talking?"

"Occasional e-mails."

"There's a wistful tone to your voice."

"The timing wasn't right."

Hannah put down her knife and cocked her head until he looked at her. "C'mon, Ray."

"All right. She is a very pleasant person. I enjoyed spending time with her. Unfortunately, during our brief relationship, I was injured twice. I think she found that quite frightening, perhaps more than she could deal with—even though over the course of my whole career, I've only been injured once before. And, then, I was working all the time. That goes with running a small police agency with minimal staffing. And probably it's a personality thing on my part."

Ray turned back to the stove. "Early on I thought she'd come back for weekends, or I'd go down there—I'd like a bit of an inducement to get to the Lyric Opera more often. It never seemed to happen. And then she quickly fell into a relationship, someone in her apartment building. We were in different places."

"Yes?"

"I seem to be working all the time," Ray said, facing her. "I guess I'm a workaholic. At the end, she was questioning whether I had the capacity to make time for her. Not just *time* time, but the emotional time."

"What do you think?"

Ray waved his spoon in the air. "I don't know. I haven't been in a serious relationship for years. I'm used to being alone. When I'm not working, I'm kayaking, skiing, reading. I fill every moment. Perhaps I've forgotten how to make time for someone else." He shrugged.

"I'm sort of the same way," Hannah said, picking up her knife and beginning to slice the lettuce leaves from their stem. "When I'm not working, I'm being my hyperactive self. I once told you that I came up here to reconnect with a guy I had a relationship with in medical school. I had a silly idea about finding some kind of normalcy, part of my therapy to get beyond the war experience. I must have missed the fact years ago that he was sort of wacko. That's the problem with hormonal relationships." She laughed. "Sometimes you miss the really important stuff about a person, at least for awhile."

Ray nodded as he worked on browning butter without burning it, his focus on the contents of a stainless steel pan. Hannah, too, settled into wordless concentration of washing, drying, mixing, arranging.

"How's the world of crime?" she asked after they settled at the table and began their meal.

"Nothing too awful seems to be happening right now, fortunately. It's funny, but when I started up here there would be long stretches where things would be routine, especially during the fall and winter. But in the last year, it's been one thing after another." He considered. "I do have one case that's concerning me."

"What's that?"

"An elderly man has gone missing."

"From a nursing home?" Hannah asked.

"No, he lives independently. Most of these cases with old people don't have a happy ending."

"I can imagine—heart failure, stroke, hypothermia. Our bodies fall apart, our brains turn to mush. We become increasingly vulnerable. And if you wander away somewhere and don't get immediate medical attention …." She paused. "Maybe that's not so bad, to die quietly. How many times have I watched, sometimes participated in, an attempt to resuscitate an elderly person. Our best efforts to keep someone going can be violent. She looked directly at Ray, holding his eyes in her gaze. "I've often thought it would be so much more humane to let them die quietly." Hannah smiled. "But you usually have the hysterical family there wanting you to do everything for Grandpa."

They fell into silence for several moments. "I spent time with his daughter this afternoon," Ray said. "She told me that her father's a real character. He's recently written and published a book on his years as a driver for Al Capone. He says he helped Capone bury his treasure up here."

"For real?"

Ray left the table, retrieved the book off a nearby counter, and passed it to her before settling back into his chair.

"As you can see, the book is for real, and the author would have his readers believe that it's all fact, not fiction. According to his daughter, however, Fox has a rich fantasy life."

"How about the Capone connection?"

Ray chuckled, "Another urban legend that has been around for decades. I used to hear about Capone as a kid from the old-timers. It's one of those stories you can tell and continue to embellish because no one can disprove anything you're saying. Big Al supposedly had two or three hideouts up here. For example, there's a house in Frankfort that reportedly has a tunnel that runs toward the beach. Story is that Al's boys would come up in speedboats on moonless nights and drop off loads of hooch. But speedboats all the way from Chicago in the '20s? And why would you bother to dig a tunnel where there are hundreds of miles of deserted beaches and dozens of remote road ends. The storytellers were mixing legends and yarns. Along the Detroit River, smugglers were running booze into this country with speedboats, an easy trip across a narrow band of water. And, yes, there were lots of tunnels and boathouses along the river. Most of the booze that got up here probably came in trucks or cars from Detroit."

"How about the police?"

"This was a very rural county. People stayed out of other people's business. I would bet there was little effort to enforce the Volstead Act locally. My grandmother told stories of her father brewing beer and the sheriff dropping by in his Model T to share a few bottles."

"So what about the buried treasure? Any truth to that?"

"I've just skimmed the first few chapters. According to Fox, Capone amassed a huge amount of money, most of which he converted to gold coins. This was going to be his special retirement fund. Not trusting Bank of America, he and the boys buried barrels of gold all along the Lake Michigan coast with the plan that they would retrieve it as needed. Alas, the wages of crime caught up to them." Ray flipped the book over to show Hannah the back. "The best thing is, if you look on the author's note, Fox says the book is an invaluable guide to finding the Capone treasure."

"So what happens now, a summer of digging up beaches?"

"Probably. Many of them are in the National Shoreline. It will give the rangers something else to worry about besides the nude sunbathers."

Hannah stood up with her plate and reached for Ray's. "I've got my boat on the car...."

Ray yawned. "It's too late, and I'm too tired. How about a short hike? Then I want to crash."

"You're on," she said. "Let's do the dishes."

7

Sue had backed into Vincent Fox's gravel drive and was standing at the open tailgate of her Jeep organizing her gear when Ray arrived.

"That was fast," she said over the noise of Simone, yapping her greeting from the front seat.

Ray opened the door and accepted the kisses of the dog's enthusiastic welcome. "I was already rolling when your call came."

"I'm getting ready to cast a couple of tire prints. But I didn't want to start on the house until you saw it. You can tell me what things looked like yesterday. And before we go in, I want to check the exterior for footprints, especially the area around the back door. That appears to have been the point of access."

"So you're telling me to hang back and not mess anything up?"

"Boy, are you fast," Sue said, dryly.

Ray set Simone back in the car and closed the door. "You're a bit touchy this morning," he said.

"I'm a little ticked at myself. I should have been here yesterday and looked the place over. But it was late in the day, the search warrant wasn't ready yet, and..."

"I didn't expect you to be here yesterday, Sue. Didn't I say that in my e-mail?"

"Yes, okay, but I would have normally come over and checked the place out. Shot some photos, looked for anything that might have shed some light on this man's disappearance. I would have secured the place to come back to do a more thorough search, if it seemed necessary. But it was close to six o'clock when I got back from Sandville. And if I had started, I would have spent most of the evening here. I'm trying to figure out how to get a life. We've been working crazy hours for months."

Ray waited for Sue to look at him, but she continued to fuss with her gear. "It's okay, Sue," he finally said. "Yesterday this wasn't a crime scene. You did the right thing. When I requested that you look the place over, all I was thinking was that you might spot something that would give us a hint at why Fox went missing. You're so good at that." Ray paused for a long moment. "And you deserve a life, I recognize that."

Sue faced Ray and crossed her arms over her chest. "I'm not putting this on you, Ray. It just happens when we are in the midst of an investigation. And, well, we are both like bulldogs. We keep going until we solve the crime. But I still need a life. I haven't made it to yoga in months. I seldom spend any time with friends. I know it's been the same for you." She turned back to the Jeep and lifted out a bag of Traxtone, a powdered casting material. Then she said quietly, "I photographed the tire prints already and hope the castings will provide a better impression of the sides. I'm not sure there's enough on the treads to give us any real evidence. If this is the perp's ride, he's driving on a couple of real bald eagles."

Ray watched as Sue knelt and measured some warm water from a thermos and poured it into a plastic bag. Then she added the Traxtone. As the water came in contact with the cement, colored pellets appeared. She kneaded the material until the color disappeared, then carefully poured the mixture into each of the two tire prints. Ray stood by quietly. He knew that Sue liked to focus on her work without the interference of a conversation.

Suddenly she stood up and once again faced Ray with her arms crossed. "And I started seeing someone," she said. "It would be nice to have weekends off, most of the time, and sort of a normal life."

"Anything else?" Ray asked, matching her serious expression.

"Simone. I think we should have joint custody. I would like to be able to go away for a few days and not board her. She really likes you. I think it would be good for you, for her, and for me."

"It almost sounds like we're negotiating the terms for divorce."

"It does," she responded, half laughing. " And we've never had the joys of a marriage, let alone the pain of separation." Sue's tone changed. "I really like you. If you weren't my boss and a bit too old, I could go for you. You're a prize, Ray Elkins, a truly nice man who's one hell of a cook. Even though you don't seem to do shirts or windows, you'd be okay. So how about joint custody?"

"I can probably manage that."

"Now let me show you the house." Sue was back to business. "We'll start at the front. Whoever broke in last night didn't bother with the front door. They probably scoped out the place enough to see that it was fairly substantial. The back door, however, is little more than an interior door. Something they could easily kick in."

Ray followed Sue through the open front door and stood motionless for a few moments, allowing his eyes to become accustomed to the dark interior. "Unbelievable," he said.

"Bit of a change from yesterday?" asked Sue.

"Someone really tore the place up." Indeed, the house had been thoroughly ransacked—furniture upended, drawers dumped, books pulled off shelves, cupboards emptied.

"What were they looking for?" asked Sue.

"Did you read my notes from yesterday?"

"Yes."

"Did you see the line on Vincent Fox's book?"

"Yes," said Sue. "You noted the book's title, something about Al Capone."

"I scanned it last night. According to his daughter, it's all fiction, but Fox presents his story as fact. Here's the condensed version: Fox writes that he was once Al Capone's driver and that Capone hid millions of dollars in gold coins up here during the 1920s and '30s. He hints at the locations, but says with the passage of time things look different and, also, his memory is starting to fade so...."

"You think the trashing of his place...."

"Yes, and maybe even his disappearance, is connected to the book." Ray carefully studied the interior. "It's gone."

"What's that?"

"His computer, a desktop model. It was there, to the right of the printer."

"So if we go with the theory that this break-in is connected to his book...."

"Exactly," responded Ray. "Someone was looking for more information on the buried treasure. Maps, diaries, whatever. If what his daughter says is true about the story being total fiction, it must have been a frustrating search because there isn't anything here. He wrote the book on the computer, so a quick glance at the directory would probably show file names related to the book. Maybe the perp was hoping there would be other material stored on the drive, so taking it would make sense."

"New ring tone?" said Sue.

Ray nodded as he reached for his phone. He listened, looking at Sue. After thanking the caller, he switched off the phone.

"What's up?" she asked.

"That was central. They just had a call from one of the security people at the casino. One of their employees noticed the piece on Vincent Fox on the early news and remembered seeing him at the casino over the last few days. When he got to work he checked a recently archived video. He's got Fox and several people that he was with on tape. And, get this, Fox had a big win on Friday. Six thousand bucks on the slots!

"So, maybe, after all, it was just someone after the money he won?"

"How does that explain the computer?"

"A useful and somewhat easy item to turn into cash?"

Ray gave the small room another thorough look. "I'm not seeing anything else. Why don't you finish up here, Sue? I'll run up to the casino. Let's plan on meeting in the late afternoon. Anything else?"

"The new ringtone," said Sue. "I taught you how to download them and now you seem addicted."

"A cheaper obsession than playing the slots," he responded.

8

~

Ray waved his way past the greeter and headed toward Bear River Casino's security department. Passing through the central room in the building, he paused to take in the rows and rows of slots, the noise and confusion generated by flashing lights and the jingle-jangle of whirling cylinders and techno beat. The air was redolent with cigarette smoke. Occasionally there was a loud orgasmic cacophony celebrating a jackpot. He looked at his watch. It was only a few minutes after 10 a.m. and the place was already bustling. Most of the players appeared to be retirees.

A stainless keypad was mounted under the doorknob of the steel security office door and a *Non-Smoking Area* sign attached at eye level. Ray knocked, and, after a long moment, the door swung open. Donald Sterling, a former Chicago detective he had met during a prior case, stretched out his hand.

Sterling escorted Ray through a maze of surveillance tech screens monitoring different parts of the casino. "Like I told one of your dispatchers," he said, pointing at a display away from the main action, "I saw Fox's picture on early news this morning. I knew I'd seen him in the last few days. He's a regular, not a daily like some of our guests, but at least once a week. And given that weird costume, he's hard to miss." Sterling chuckled. "Nice old guy, though. I've talked to him a few times over the years. Once he found out I had been a Chicago cop, I got a lot of Capone stories." Sterling pointed at the screen, "Here he is coming in on Friday morning. He's with a man and woman, the people I usually see him with. There used to be four or five in his group, but these seem to be the only ones left. And look at that old boy on the right, he's carrying his oxygen bottle. Not long for the world. And that woman…"

"What about her?"

"A real character. She's the driver—a scary thought. She's got this big old Town Car, white, with suicide doors. When did they stop making those? I'm sure you've seen that vehicle around."

"Mildred Hall," said Ray. "She's in her early 90s and keeps passing her driver's test. "

"She's a character."

"She used to teach math and physics at the high school. I don't think she retired until she was about 75."

"That explains a lot," said Sterling. "We used to keep her under surveillance."

"Mildred Hall?"

"Uh huh," responded Sterling. "She was a regular for a while, three or four times a week. Always played blackjack and always won. Not a lot, but she'd get 50 or 100 bucks ahead and cash out. Obviously, she was counting or had some system. Some of the suits in the front office got excited, thought she should be banned."

"But she wasn't."

"Nope. Like you said, she's well known in town. They worried about bad PR. And then, the problem just went away. She stopped playing. My guess is that she wanted to see if she could beat the system, and once she did there wasn't a challenge. But she still brings in her group of buddies. Seems to like the company. Only now there's just the two: Fox and Tommy Fuller." Sterling pointed to the screen again. "Fuller's the guy with the World War II hat. If you talk to him for more than two minutes, you'll learn that he was in the Battle of the Bulge. Nice old guy, but not long for the world. And a walking menace. I'm surprised all these smokers with their oxygen tanks haven't blown the place up."

Sterling let the video run briefly, then said, "I've collected other video with the three musketeers. All from Friday. Do you want to see it all, or do you just want a summary?"

"A summary would be fine," Ray said, nodding.

"So, they come in around 10 a.m., play the slots until about 11:30, have lunch, and go back to the slots for half an hour or so. Then Fox hits a big jackpot."

"How much?"

"Six grand. All the lights, bells, and whistles. The racket gives hope to the other folks in the place. Keeps them playing. Right after that, Fox cashes out and leaves. You're not supposed to do that," Sterling said in a mocking tone. "You're supposed to stay around and reinvest in the company."

"Anyone else with them, anyone tailing them?"

"I've got exit and parking lot video," Sterling said, tapping the top of the monitor. "You're welcome to view it yourself, but I didn't see anything unusual; just the three of them leaving, going to the car, and, oh, so slowly, driving away." He shook his head sadly. "Man, I hope nothing bad's happened to Fox, but I don't like the sound of it. My wife says all police officers are pessimists. I guess maybe that's true. Can I buy you lunch, Ray? We've got a great new executive chef. He trained at the CIA, then studied in Paris, then went to Vegas and made a name for himself. I'm always amazed at what money can buy."

Ray joined in the joke and took a long moment to decide, considering Sue's comments on having a life. "I'd love to," he said, finally, "but you know how it is. Can't take the time right now."

"Been there, done that," said Sterling, slapping him on the back. "You walk the walk and talk the talk. Duty calls."

9

The ordinary two-story frame home dating back to the lumbering days sat on a quiet street four blocks away from the bay. Mildred Hall had been born in the house a few years after the end of WWI, one of the several hundred home deliveries performed by Old Doc Wade over his long career. It was one of the oldest houses in the village.

Ray pulled into the drive, parking behind the Lincoln. He knocked, using the bronze ring in a bronze lion's mouth. Classical music blasted from the interior. He knocked again more vigorously. The volume dropped and shortly after, the door swung open.

Mildred Hall, in jeans and a blue sweater, was smaller than he remembered, but surprisingly wiry and vital for her years. "Ray Elkins, what brings you to my house? Come in, come in. I've just made some tea. Will you have a cup?" Hall didn't wait for an answer. She just marched off to the kitchen. Ray followed her through the living room and dining room. With the exception of a television, the home was furnished in antiques, mostly original to the house he guessed. The smell of lemon and lavender hung in the air.

"Sit here," Hall ordered as she placed a second saucer and cup on the kitchen table." She pulled a knitted rooster off the teapot and filled both cups. "Sugar, honey, a little milk?"

"I'm fine," said Ray.

"The honey is local. Raw. It's got pollen in it. Keeps your immune system tuned up. Helps with allergies and hay fever." Hall halted her rapid-fire delivery and examined Ray for a long moment. "I'm not used to visits from the local constabulary."

"Vincent Fox," said Ray, "He's been missing for several days. Reports of his disappearance ran last night and this morning on the local television news."

"Oh my, oh my, oh my." she said, her hands rising to her cheeks. "I don't have a TV anymore. I just didn't know. Well, I have one; I mean I keep some African violets on it. When the television people made that change…. Tell me about Vincent. What's happened to him, do you think?"

"You were with him on Friday, at the casino?"

"That's true, Saturday too, not at the casino, but I was with him."

"We need to establish when he was last seen. I think you can help me with that. Tell me your history with Vincent. Then focus on the time you spent with him in recent days. What you did, where you went." Ray took out a notebook from his coat pocket and flipped the pages slowly until reaching a blank one. Mildred Hall was staring into space. "Start at the beginning, Ms. Hall," he urged her.

"Well, I met Vincent Fox five or six years ago at the Friends of the Library book sale. I was in charge of the cash box, and he was assigned to help me. After that he called me a couple of times. I think he sort of invited me out. I certainly wasn't interested. Then he called and wanted to know if I would go to the casino with him. Well, Ray, it's just up the road, been there for decades, but I'd never made a visit. Turns out, what Vincent really wanted was for me to drive him. Seems his kids had taken his car away, much like mine would like to do," she said with a scowl. "But, I ended up taking Vincent and his cronies to the casino. Those old boys just loved it, especially the slots. Just toss the chip in and push the button. I tried to explain to them about B.F. Skinner and how they would assuredly never win anything. They weren't interested. They were paying for the entertainment. I just don't understand how losing money is entertainment."

Hall attempted to refill their teacups, but the pot was empty. She went to the sink to fill the kettle, then set it on the stove, a curvy model with chrome, probably one of the first electrics made.

"I can't say I liked it, though—too much smoke and noise. But I got to wandering around the place and found the blackjack tables. They were off to the side in their own room. It was so much quieter in there. The first few times, I watched. Then, I got a book on how to win at blackjack at the library. It was decent, but it was too sketchy for my taste, so I ordered some others through an interlibrary loan. I spent weeks figuring out the system."

She turned around to check the kettle. "Oh my, I forgot to turn it on. Let's see. At first I lost money. Never more than 10 bucks; that was my limit. Boy do I hate to waste money. And then I started winning. Not much. I read about how they keep an eye on you. If you win too much, they ban you. Anyway, after a while it wasn't fun anymore. But I'd gotten to like spending time with the boys. And they have uncommonly good food there, cheap too. So it just became my social outing of the week. Alas, there are only three of us left now, and I don't think Tommy Fuller has got much time. Now you say Vincent is missing. I don't quite understand. What does that mean?"

"Fox has a daughter in Traverse City. You probably know that."

"Yes."

"She talks to her father almost every day on the phone. When she was unable to reach him, she drove up to his home. Not finding him, she contacted us." He paused to make a note. "So you were with Vincent on Friday, and you also saw him on Saturday?"

"Yes, I picked him and Tommy up at the library about 9:45; that's our usual meeting time. We were at the casino by 10 o'clock. The boys played the slots for a while and then we went to lunch. I told them at lunch I couldn't stand the place much longer and gave them a half an hour more. Just about the time we were leaving, Vincent hit a big pot. He wanted to stay around and play some more, saying his luck had just changed. I told him not to be a damn fool. He should take his money and get out of there. He wasn't too happy, but he did what I told him. That was it. I drove them back to the library."

"How much money did he win?" asked Ray.

"Six thousand dollars in that one pot. I don't know what he might have won or lost before that." When the kettle began to whine, she lifted it off the stove and poured the contents over the old tea leaves. "But you know," she said, "the strangest thing happened. I'd completely forgotten. On the way back Tommy said he wished he had won that big pot. Vincent asked him why and Tommy says he has a friend outside of Miami, one of his war buddies. He says he'd like to see the guy while there was still time. Vincent asked if $4000 would be enough. Tommy said that would be more than enough. So Vincent, who was sitting next to me, counted out four grand and passed the money back to him. Isn't that extraordinary?"

"Then I asked Tommy how he was going to get to Miami. He said he thought he should fly, but he had no idea how to make a reservation or anything. We went into the library and I used the computer to make a reservation for the next day, Saturday. I used my credit card, and Tommy gave me cash. The next day we met at the library again, and...this is the part I shouldn't tell you, I drove Tommy and Vincent to the airport."

Ray looked up. "Why shouldn't you tell me that?"

"I've promised my kids I'd only drive around the village—just to the grocery store, the library, church, and the doctor's office. They don't know about the casino, but that's only up the road a bit. I never get to go to Traverse City. And they've got a beautiful new terminal at the airport. After we dropped Tommy off, Vincent and I went to the mall and had some lunch. I tried to do a little shopping at Macy's, but it's not the store that Hudson's was."

"Then what did you do?"

"We drove home. I took back roads. People drive too fast on M-22, even in the winter." Hall poured tea into both their cups. It was the color of a sandy lake bottom.

"So when did you last see Vincent Fox?"

"It was some time after 3 o'clock. I dropped him off near the library."

"Did you see him go into the library?"

"No."

"Did you know where he was going next?"

"No."

"Why didn't you drop him off at his home?"

"I never do that," she said firmly. "I never go to their houses, never let them come to mine. We always meet at the library. This is a small town. I didn't want to start any talk. And I certainly didn't want to start running a taxi service for a bunch of geezers."

"So you didn't see him or talk to him again after about 3 o'clock on Saturday?"

"That's right."

"When you were at the casino, did you notice anyone hanging about? Was there anyone who seemed to take special interest in Vincent's winnings?"

"I don't remember that. Nothing comes to mind."

"Do you stay in contact with Fox on the phone?"

"I talk to him occasionally. I don't really know him well, not really. We've just had conversations over lunch."

"Was he carrying a lot of cash on Saturday?"

"I don't know. If he was, he wasn't flashing it around. But he wouldn't have anyway. That wasn't like him."

"How about his mental state?"

"What are you asking? Do I think Fox was going a bit dotty?"

"Essentially, yes."

"No. He's still all there. He has some trouble with names, but don't we all? And he told a lot of stories that were awfully far-fetched, but I think he was just having fun. I can't imagine that he would suddenly wander away, not knowing who or where he was. Not unless, of course, he had a stroke or something. When you get to be our age, all the statistics are running against you."

Ray closed his notebook and slipped it into his coat. "I'm surprised no one called you about his disappearance. It's gotten a lot of coverage on the news."

"There's no one left to call, Ray. The lights of my generation have almost all gone out."

10

Mackenzie Mason stood in the great room of her recently acquired home and surveyed the scene—white walls, thick white carpeting, black granite on the countertops and the fireplace surround. Built on a small spit of land that extended into the bay, the contractor's trophy-home intentions were limited by the buildable area of the lot. More by accident than aspiration, he had managed to build a structure appropriately sized for the setting, his efforts enhanced by the work of a skilled young architect. The final product was a home of modest proportions with luxury accoutrements—exotic woods, pricy fixtures, and high-end appliances. A great room—high ceilinged, glass walled, and occupying half of the building's footprint—was the focal point of the structure. It provided spectacular views of the bay and the orchard-covered hillsides beyond. A large master suite, a second bath, and two tiny bedrooms completed the house.

Mackenzie had found the listing online. The real-estate agent told her that the house was completed just as the economy tanked. The builder's company went into receivership and the bank was left holding the bag. The bargain property was then picked up by a Bloomfield Hills orthopedist as an investment. Less than six months later, he walked from the mortgage as his own financial house of cards came crashing down.

When Mackenzie offered $100,000 less than the asking price, she was amazed at how quickly the bank snapped up the offer. She chided herself for not going lower. *So much for toxic assets,* she thought out loud as she looked around the room. She'd had spent little time or effort redecorating. The house was furnished with only the essentials needed for the next few months. She had, however, upgraded the security system with cameras, monitors, additional motion detectors, and a wireless uplink to the alarm company's headquarters.

Mackenzie walked to the front of the room and stood near the wall of glass that faced the bay. Small patches of snow were still visible on the opposite shore, and cold drizzle blurred the already formless landscape. After spending more than two decades in the west, most of it in California, she was having trouble adjusting to the cold, gray, March weather of northern Michigan. Sliding into an Aeron chair, she wondered, *Is this just madness?* Her eyes ran along the bleak horizon. *Why am I here?*

Mackenzie Mason had left her senior vice-president position in a high-tech company on December 31. She and three other top-level executives walked away with severance packages equal to a year's salary with the customary bonuses—a generous parting gift for the fortunate few. Based on their rank in the hierarchy, the other employees got from three months to two weeks wages as the once highflying dot.com slid toward insolvency.

January 1 found Mackenzie at loose ends. But the search for a new job was the least of her concerns. Headhunters had started harassing her as soon as rumors of the company's demise went public. More than one had made the point that she was the dream client: young, bright, articulate, the right education from the best places, and a solid track record of accomplishment. What they didn't say, because it might be considered inappropriate, was that she was also funny, beautiful, and very sexy.

For Mackenzie, the end of a long-term relationship was more problematic than the employment situation. Although she was the one who had insisted on it, she still woke up at night with the fear that she had made the wrong decision. Which was why she'd decided to come back to Michigan. There was something she needed to know, investigate, understand, and perhaps resolve before she could move on with her life.

Even as she admired her now sumptuous surroundings, she could still remember being poor and hungry and vulnerable. For years she had done her best to avoid the painful memories of childhood and the trauma and sadness of her brother's death. Those memories had intensified the day before, when she drove to the south end of the county to look at the village where she had spent two desperately unhappy years.

Mackenzie was shocked at how the town, Sandville, had almost vanished over the past several decades. Any thoughts of taking a closer look at her grandmother's old garden, or perhaps searching the cemetery for her brother's grave, quickly evaporated when she saw a sheriff's car parked on the road. The deputy, a young woman, had a small dog on a leash, and they were walking around the lot where the house formerly stood. Mackenzie slowed enough to take in the scene; she circled the block, then left, not wanting to attract attention to herself.

What was that all about? Mackenzie thought as she drove north. She ran several scenarios that would explain the deputy's presence at her grandmother's house, but couldn't generate anything more plausible than a chance happening. Perhaps the dog needed a walk. She reassured herself that it would be silly to read anything into the event.

Mackenzie picked up an iPad and flipped through the apps. She opened a project planner and looked at her early notes. Scrolling through the first draft, she was struck by the disorder of her stratagem. She had been doing project planning for years and was known for the precise and skillful way she could focus the work of hundreds of people and millions of dollars to achieve timely, profitable results. But here she was stymied. She hardly knew where to begin.

In frustration, she got up and began switching on the lights, making the room as bright a contrast as possible to the end of winter gloom. Then she unlocked the hinged covers of the two stainless steel shipping cases she had collected a few hours earlier in Traverse City. She had been apprehensive about the pick-up, but everything went without a hitch. Ken Lee Park, a sometimes boyfriend, Taekwondo instructor, and expert in computers and corporate security, had assured her that everything would come via FedEx Ground without inspection. FedEx had further helped her by putting the trunks on an aluminum hand truck, rolling them to the parking lot, and lifting them into the back of her Subaru.

She lifted a layer of dark gray foam from the first case, exposing the precisely engineered interior. The contents had been carefully packed, foam cut to surround every component. She removed a large computer display and set it on the desk. After pulling out more of the packing, she found the tower for the system and positioned it beside the display. From the second case, she lifted a small laser printer and a box of wires. Each cable and cord had been marked with colored stickers for easy assembly.

In a few minutes, the computer was running. Mackenzie plugged in a thumb drive she'd brought with her from California and opened an encrypted text file, working her way through the elaborate security system Ken Lee had installed to protect the contents of the hard drive—the normal array of business application programs plus a collection of sophisticated intercept, surveillance, and hacking software.

Returning to the second trunk, she lifted away another layer of foam and began unpacking several articles of clothing, all black, each packaged in a sealed plastic bag. There was also a bag of special soaps and shampoos. Without opening them, she stowed the bags in the large walk-in closet of the master suite and put the toiletries in a cupboard in the bathroom. The last block of foam came apart in two halves, revealing meticulously hollowed-out spaces. Ken Lee, well aware of her competence in the martial arts, had stressed the importance of weapons for self-defense. He had selected and trained her to use the two pistols, a Glock 19 and a Rohrbaugh R9. Each was tucked into a holster. The Glock was to be carried at the hip, the Rohrbaugh inside the left ankle. In addition to extra magazines for each weapon, there was also a small, high-quality LED flashlight and a bear claw knife.

At the desk, Mackenzie stacked the six boxes of Winchester PDX-1 shells she'd purchased earlier at a Walmart, then loaded three magazines for each pistol. That done, she opened the safe hidden behind a panel in the built-in shelves in her bedroom and carefully placed the guns in the interior, along with the extra shells. She started to close the door, then stopped, retrieving the small Rohrbaugh, its holster and magazines. Sliding one of the magazines into the pistol, she put it in a drawer next to the bed, along with a flashlight.

Ken Lee had overcome Mackenzie's ambivalence, stressing that her skill at close-in fighting could be worthless against an armed and determined assailant. Although she had misgivings about the guns, she looked at them as necessary equipment to carry out her current mission.

Slipping back into the chair, she decided she felt much better about her plan. The two-part mission statement at the top of planning draft read:

Find the boys responsible for Terry's death,

Facilitate convictions and life sentences for: Richard Sabotny, Zed Piontowski, Jim Moarse, and Chris Brewler.

She looked at the list. Then with her finger she highlighted Richard Sabotny's name and chose the bold option from the toolbox. There. **Richard Sabotny.** That's the man she wanted, the bully and ringleader, the one most or wholly responsible for her brother's death. Not the brother of Mackenzie Mason's for that was pure fiction. Terry was Caitlyn Hallen's brother. Her brother.

11

~~

Sue Lawrence responded to the call first. Ray reached the scene 15 or 20 minutes after her. A Cedar County Road Commission truck, flashers blinking in the misting rain, was blocking off the road to northbound traffic. The driver, Hank Pullen, stood in the center of the road behind the truck, a reflective vest over his jacket, turning cars around.

Ray waved as he guided his patrol car around the truck and parked on the far shoulder behind Sue's Jeep. He could see a second county employee standing at the intersection 50 yards up, keeping traffic from entering the road.

Sue looked up at Ray as he approached. Camera in hand, she was crouched on the shoulder of the road. The ditch below was swampy and filled with water. A partially submerged body lay just below the embankment. "The ME is on his way," she said.

"Did you tell him to bring waders?" asked Ray, referring to Dr. Dyskin, the semiretired pathologist, who contracted as the county medical examiner.

"No, but I told the EMTs to bring their hip boots. No point getting Dr. Dyskin mired in the mud."

"Who spotted the body?"

"Hank Pullen called it in. He and Dan Beeson were riding around patching chuckholes. I need to talk to them again, but I think it was Dan who saw the body. He was riding shotgun."

"They didn't see who dumped it?" asked Ray.

"No such luck. And given the body's location, you could probably only spot it from the height of a truck cab. It might not have been found for days or even weeks."

Ray stepped as far as he dared to the edge of the bank and peered down at the corpse. "Not much doubt about who it is, or was. Looks like he was just thrown out."

"That was my thought," said Sue. "The poor old guy tossed along the road like a beer can or a fast food bag."

"And he's missing a boot."

"I noticed that. Brett is on his way. After the body is removed, we'll do our best to look for other possible evidence. Perhaps the missing boot is submerged in the water."

Their attention was pulled from the ditch by the arrival of an EMT unit and Dr. Dyskin. "Where's the body?" he asked.

Sue pointed over the embankment. Dyskin walked to the edge, gazed at the body for a long moment. "Well let's get him up here and see what we can see."

Sue directed the actions of the EMTs, two young men. After pulling hip boots over their orange coveralls, they carefully approached the corpse, gently scooping it into a metal rescue litter that they carried back to the surface of the road.

Dyskin knelt at the side of the litter and started his examination, working from the head down, running his hands along the skull, then the neck, continuing all the way to the feet. He moved extremely slowly, taking everything in with his eyes and hands. Dyskin asked one of the EMTs to help him rotate the body. Then he continued his investigation. He studied the bottom of the bare right foot for a long moment. Next he removed the boot and sock from the other foot, pitching them on the pavement. He held both feet, one hand under each heel, lifted them gently, and carefully studied their appearance. "Bring your camera over here," he said, gesturing with his head to Sue. "I want a picture of this."

She knelt at his side and shot a series of photos, the strobe throwing an eerie glow in the drizzle.

Dyskin gently laid the feet back on the litter and stood. He brushed his hands, one against the other. "I think we're done here," he said.

"What did you learn?" asked Ray.

"Is this the man they've been talking about on TV, the one that went missing?"

" Yes, his name is Vincent Fox."

"And where did he disappear from?"

"He lived a couple of miles outside of Cedar Bay, probably about 20 miles from here."

"Well, you know that happens with old people, especially when they have some sort of dementia. They just go wandering away, and sometimes they get pretty far before they are found. That said, I don't think that's what happened here. When did you say he was last seen?"

"Saturday, but he wasn't reported missing until Monday," answered Ray.

"He's been dead for several days," said Dyskin. "I can't find any injuries to the body, no wounds or fractures. Nothing of that nature. But there's something really curious about the bottom of his right foot. It's been burned. It looks like it was held against something hot, like a wood stove. And I can't imagine that it's self-inflicted or accidental. After you have the body identified, it should be sent to Grand Rapids for an autopsy. We'll know a lot more when we get the results. Something's not right."

Ray raised his eyebrows at Dyskin who was reaching for his fleece jacket, noting that instead of the usual rumpled suit, he was wearing a nylon workout outfit and looked fifty pounds lighter. "On your way to the gym?" Ray asked.

"Looks that way, doesn't it," said Dyskin. "Had a little wakeup call just after the holidays. My wife, in collusion with a cardiologist, has put me on a strict diet and a regular exercise program. Sonja even hired a personal trainer. Me with a personal trainer! The planet is spinning off its axis."

"How about the cigars?" asked Sue, laughing.

"Verboten."

"Going through withdrawal?"

"I did for a bit. Now I can't believe I ever used those things. Think I was just trying to kill the smell of my workplace." Dyskin smiled, and Sue and Ray laughed again, more quietly.

Watching Dyskin pull a three-point and head back to town, Ray asked, "Are you going to be more tolerant of the good doctor now?"

"He's still into Old Spice," Sue shrugged, "but without the tobacco it's not so bad." Ray squatted and leaned over to look at Fox's feet again. Sue knelt beside him. "What are you thinking?

"Piñatas. Like when we capture the bastards that did this, we pull them up by their heels and beat them with baseball bats, the aluminum kind they use in Little League, the ones that make that satisfying pinging sound every time you get a good skull whack in. That would offer a certain satisfaction."

"Is that all?" Sue gasped at her boss's rich fantasy life.

"We could meet this evening," said Ray, grasping Sue's elbow and pulling her up to face him. "We could go over the events and think through who might have done this, our resident bad guys, someone who has just been paroled…."

Sue shook her head. "It can wait till tomorrow, Ray. Tonight I need to hang out with my dog, go to yoga, stop off at the bar with the girls for a couple of glasses of wine, take a long hot bath and sleep for 10 hours. Then I can think about this case again. And I'm coming in late tomorrow—using a couple of hours of comp time." She gave him a long, measured look. "And you better get in a kayak before you explode, while there's still some light. I'm going to start processing this scene."

Ray stuck his hands in his pockets and took a step backwards. "What's your plan with the media?"

"I'll send a one- or two-sentence press release," Sue said, heading back to her Jeep and back to business. "Something to the effect that the 'body of an elderly man believed to be Vincent Fox has been found. More information will be available after formal identification.'"

"That should be enough to get us through several news cycles. I'll contact his daughter and have her identify the body. Then I'll have it sent to Grand Rapids for an autopsy."

"Thanks," she said, and walked away from him to let the EMTs know the body was ready for transport.

12

Ray sat in his car and watched Brett and Sue begin to process the scene. Then he pulled on his seatbelt and slowly drove away. He knew that Sue was right. Spending the evening in the office trying to puzzle out who might be responsible for the crime, especially when they were both exhausted, would be a waste of time. He headed home.

When he reached the top of his drive, there was Hannah Jeffers waiting for him. His kayak was already secured to the roof of her Subaru wagon. They exchanged a friendly embrace.

"How did you get into the house?"

"The side door of the garage was unlocked. Your place never seems to be secured. You're either very trusting or extremely careless," she said, chuckling. "Doesn't your department do those homeowner security workshops?"

Ray just shook his head, making no other response.

"Of course, you don't have much that anyone could fence. Your 12-inch flat screen wouldn't bring much, and no one wants books or classical CDs. But you do have an iPad; that's worth stealing." She gave him a poke in the chest. "Get into your dry suit," she said. "We don't have many hours of light left."

Ten minutes later, Ray tossed his gear bag and two paddles in the back of Hannah's vehicle and settled into the passenger's seat. But she didn't start the engine.

"Bad day?"

Ray did not turn to meet her gaze. "I thought we had an agreement to never talk about our work days, especially when we are on our way to the lake, on the water, or après kayaking."

Hannah started to laugh. "Where did that come from? You're making it up." She reached over and felt for a vein on his neck. "The good news is you've got a pulse, but it's a bit too rapid. I'd like to take your blood pressure. You seem hypertensive."

"Come on, Hannah," Ray said, pushing her hand away gently, "get this crate in gear. Once I get out on the water everything will be okay. Cut straight across to 22, then head south. There's something I want to see."

They drove for a while in silence, the windshield wipers providing a slow and slower tempo as the drizzle turned to mist.

"So you had a bad day?" Hannah asked again.

Ray took a deep breath, exhaled. "One of the worst." He turned in his seat to face her. "I told you about Vincent Fox the other night?"

Hannah nodded, glancing at him. "Yes, I remember. The old guy who wrote about the Capone treasure."

Ray told her about recovering Fox's body, and the charring on the bottom of one of his feet. "It reminds me of something I saw in France."

"What's that?"

"When I was in the army, stationed in Europe, I toured a historical farm somewhere in France. The outbuildings had been restored to how they appeared in the 16th or 17th century. There were wonderful descriptions on everything, with translations in English, German, Spanish. One display talked about some outlaws of the time, La bande d'Orgeres, who attacked wealthy farmers and held their feet to the fire until they disclosed where their gold and valuables were hidden. My memory is that this kind of extortion took place shortly before the beginning of the French Revolution, and that these activities were a precursor to the bloody events that followed."

"You think that's what happened to Fox?"

"Who knows?" Ray said. "It's such an old technique, been around since medieval times, probably before. And now, possibly right here in Cedar County. Hard to be optimistic about human progress." Hannah snorted. "So, what would be the physiological effect of that kind of torture?" he asked.

Hannah's eyes were locked on the twisting county road in front of her. "You don't need a medical degree to figure that one out. Elderly man, high-stress situation. Heart attack, stroke. By his age lots of things are just waiting to fail. The autopsy will probably provide a reliable answer." She grimaced. "Medieval, that's the perfect word. It's hard to imagine the horror they put this poor man through."

The mist had faded to almost nothing, and Hannah turned off the wipers. Again they were silent as the orchards faded away to piney scrub and marsh. "I understand you're upset," she said at last. "My question is, is our destination connected with this case?"

Ray chuckled. "Maybe. I'm not sure. Given all the money involved, Fox probably got himself involved in something drug-related." He told her about Ma French finding the large stash of cash on the grounds of the Hollingsford Estate and explained he wanted to paddle to the estate from the Lake Michigan side for a look around.

"It's really isolated," he said. "Of course, in the summer you can get there by crossing a small lake—Lost Lake, that's what it's called—in a boat or a canoe. In the winter it's skis, snowshoes, or a snowmobile across the ice. These days, the ice is probably too thin.

"Why not hike in? Can't you just go around the Lost Lake?"

"Most of the surrounding area is marshland and swamp. There are places where you can slip into mud up to your waist. No thanks."

"Looks like we have some chop," Hannah said, pulling into the parking area.

"Not too bad," Ray responded. "And given the direction of the wind, we will be protected by that headland for launch and landing. There's a storm coming in tonight, but we should be off the water long before it comes onshore."

Hannah parked the Subaru in the launch and they both got out to offload the boats. "Do we need lights?"

"Wouldn't hurt."

"I don't think the batteries in this thing are any good," she said, fiddling with the navigation light attached to her life vest.

"I can't help you out. I don't have any in my gear bag," Ray said, pulling on his gloves. "They're really only for visibility, but this time of the year there's never anyone on the water. Mine works, and I'll put a flashlight in my day hatch."

They paddled north for more than an hour along the miles of empty shoreline, beach. and low dunes without a single cottage. They landed on the south side of the small stream that emptied from Lost Lake.

Hannah pulled off her PFD and spray skirt, and tossed them into the open cockpit of her kayak. "What are you looking for?" she asked.

"There is supposed to be an old cemetery up on that bluff overlooking the lake. That's where Ma French found the cash. My best guess is that whoever is connected to the money is accessing the area on a snowmobile or ATV. Probably coming from the north."

"Why didn't we…?"

"The put-in would have been more than twice as far, and we wouldn't have had enough daylight. We barely have enough as it is. We better get going."

Ray led the way over the beach and up the hill, stopping near the remnants of a wrought-iron fence that marked the perimeters of the cemetery. They walked among a small collection of headstones, some standing, others fallen flat over graves.

"Rex, Star, Lady…looks like mostly pets in this section," Hannah said. "And on the human side, the ones I can read go back a hundred years."

"This is probably the newest one." Ray pointed at a monolith of gray granite, the largest headstone in the cemetery.

"What are the rules on cemeteries? Can you make one anywhere?" asked Hannah.

"Not now. There are zoning and environmental rules. In the early days, though, you could pretty much do what you wanted."

They walked around, looking at head stones, at times stooping and brushing off the surfaces of the markers to read the inscriptions. Eventually they met each other. "Did you find what you were looking for?" Hannah asked.

"I came here mostly to get a sense of the place. I wasn't anticipating any major discoveries." He nodded toward the lake. "We better get going. I want to get back before it's completely dark. Looks like the wind's come up."

The surf had started to build while they were on land. After getting their gear back on, Ray helped Hannah launch into the breakers. Then he climbed in his boat, secured his spray skirt, and pushed into an oncoming wave with his hand. His bow was immediately shoved parallel to the shore. He struggled to get it turned back into the surf, and finally, he was able to break free of the beach and the pounding waves. Together, they paddled out about a 100 yards , beyond the second sand bar, where the rolling action of the waves was a bit less intense.

The trip out had been relaxed. The return was tense—the wind and waves building as the light diminished. They had to paddle hard through the troughs, bracing at the tops of the waves on the windward side to keep from getting rolled.

Ray didn't see Hannah capsize. They were often on opposite sides of five-foot crests. But as he moved into the next wave, he saw the white bottom of Hannah's kayak turned skyward. She rolled up, only to be knocked over by the powerful crest of the next wave. When she rolled up, Ray was relieved to see her brace against the following wave and quickly settle back into a muscular stroke.

They pushed on. Ray checked his watch and worried about Hannah getting too cold. He estimated that they had about 20 minutes more of hard going before they would come under the protection of the headland. In the roaring wind he didn't hear the shriek of the Jet Ski engine until it crashed over the wave in front of him, coming between his boat and Hannah's. It disappeared out into the lake for 20 or 30 seconds, then returned, splashing across Hannah's bow and crossing Ray's a second time. Then it was gone. Ray tried to remember the details as they paddled toward calm water.

"I thought you told me there were never any boats out here at this time of year," yelled Hannah as they approached the shore in the protection of the headland.

"There aren't," said Ray.

"Then, what was that all about?"

"Come on Ray, what was it all about, that Jet Ski?" Hannah asked. They were back in Ray's kitchen, having endured a stricken paddle to the shore and a tense, silent ride home. Hannah had found solace in the inner workings of an espresso machine.

"How is it that you have two of those?" Ray asked.

"Don't change the subject." She gave Ray a look. "It's a long story. A certain someone dropped off a machine that I never thought I'd see again. I had already bought a replacement. And it's not that I don't like your French press, it's just that I like cappuccino so much better. You needed one." She walked him through the process of pulling a good shot, explaining that if the grind is right and tamped with 30 pounds of pressure in the portafilter, a lovely crema will form on the top of the coffee. When they were seated at the table with their cappuccino, she sighed deeply.

"All right. I don't know. Someone was giving us a look. Maybe trying to scare us," Ray said.

"What are you going to do about it?"

"Technically, he was getting too close and running without navigation lights. Other than that, he didn't do anything that was illegal."

"Yes, but don't you want to talk to him?"

"If I know who he was, sure, I'd like to know why he was out there. But he's not going to be easy to find. I didn't see a registration number on the boat, not that there was much light. It might have been there."

"I needed your flare gun for protection. And I hate those things. Jet Skis."

"I don't like them, either. Maybe when gas goes to $10 a gallon most of them will disappear."

"Did you see me capsize?" Hannah asked, sipping.

"No, I only saw your white hull and knew you were over."

"I was trying to brace, and I missed the top of the wave. Bingo, I was upside down. Then I rolled up and got nailed a second time. In the dark water and the low light, I had trouble finding the horizon. I was really disoriented. I love to roll, but I didn't like that. I was out of control." She shivered.

They sat in silence for several minutes, attending to their coffee and reflecting. "You know what I'd like to do?" Hannah said, pushing away her empty demitasse.

"What's that?"

"Raid your refrigerator for the remnants of your last box from Zingerman's, open a bottle of Mawby, mess around awhile, and spend the night." She stood up and was by Ray's side, bending over and kissing him hard on the lips. Then she picked up their cups and set them noisily in the sink. "But," she said, "I'm on call tonight, so our friendship can remain blissful and uncomplicated."

As they kissed again, Ray pulled her close. "I think we have broadened the definition of speed dating," she said on her way out the door.

13

Ray wandered around the house after Hannah's departure. After finishing with the kitchen, he hung his PFD and spray skirt in the mudroom and carefully balanced his mukluks, the open side down, over a floor vent. He draped his dry suit, inside out over the shower curtain rod in the guest bedroom, along with the fleece jumpsuit he wore under it.

Although physically exhausted, his mind was still buzzing from the events of the day. He retrieved his journal and a fountain pen and stood for several minutes looking at a blank page. Finally, he unscrewed his pen and brought it to the top line of the verso page. He moved the point in an upward sweep, and the line of brown ink went from thin to invisible. Ray pulled a small pad from his desk and tried the pen again, making gentle circles—a few more blotches and then nothing. He refilled the pen, wiping the tip carefully and returning the inkbottle to its cubbyhole.

Starting again, he wrote about Vincent Fox, the man in the worn buckskin jacket with the fringes, the old guy with the long gray hair in pigtails he had seen occasionally shopping in the market. The character walking along the side of the road with a weathered, leather backpack. He thought he also remembered seeing Fox on his old bicycle, maybe a Schwinn.

Real and false memories occupied his thinking for several minutes.

Did he actually remember seeing Vincent Fox on a bicycle or was that just an invented memory, an imaginary connection his brain made seeing the bike or hearing Fox's daughter talk about her father?

The scene with Fox's body flashed across Ray's memory. He reflected on the hardest part of police work, crimes against the most vulnerable members of the community, usually the young and the old. Ray wrote about controlling his rage as he viewed Fox's body in the water and his revulsion as Dr. Dyskin pointed out the charred area on Fox's foot. Then he recorded his conversation with Sue about the aluminum bats, adding a few lines about a colleague from his first year of police work, an avid tennis player, who had a steel racket he repeatedly slammed into a large canvas beanbag chair as a way of unwinding after a particularly rough shift.

April is the cruelest month, he said out loud, repeating each word again as he wrote it, two lines high in his careful cursive. He put in a long slash mark after *month* and wrote, *And it's not even April yet.*

Ray thought about the line and the poem. *April is the cruelest month, breeding Lilacs out of the dead land, mixing Memory and desire, stirring Dull roots with spring rain.* Then he penned, *Memory and Desire,* also using two lines. He sensed a melancholy in the phrase.

He remembered the class where he first studied the poem, an undergraduate course in 20th century British and American poetry. He started filling lines, then several pages in the journal about the class and the teacher, Alice Bingley, a fragile-looking woman who was quite brilliant, but routinely brutalized her students because they were not.

He remembered how the class of 20-some had shrunk to four by the end of the semester: a beautiful and distant girl who often talked to the professor in French and Italian; a tall, thin black woman who articulated most of the best answers to the professor's probing questions and then Ray and his friend, Zeigler.

The first day of class in early January, Zeigler showed up late and seemed to immediately earn the instructor's enmity. He was wearing athletic department sweats and a stocking cap. Ray recorded the dialogue as he remembered it.

"Are you a football player, Mr. Zeigler?"

"Yes ma'm."

"And what position do you play, Mr. Zeigler?"

"Defensive tackle, mostly, ma'm."

"And why are you taking this class?"

A long silence followed as Zeigler considered his answer. "My advisor, Professor Foster, recommended the class, and you."

"Really, I must have a word with Milton."

Ray then recorded how he and Ernie Zeigler became friends and study partners. Ray reflected that he had come to college from an exceedingly modest home, but Zeigler had come from real poverty. His mother had died in his infancy, and his father—alcoholic and mostly unemployed— did his best to palm off young Ernie for weeks, sometimes months at a time, to family members, sympathetic neighbors, and girlfriends.

Fortunately, by junior high his size and athleticism had drawn the attention of the coaches, and other teachers found that the huge kid in tatters was enormously likeable and exceptionally bright. Ray based this part of his commentary on things Zeigler told him during their many rambling conversations. Ernie came to college with the clothes on his back, nothing more, not even a suitcase. He didn't have an athletic scholarship, and he wasn't a starter. But the equipment manager and some of coaches found him clothes, shoes, even a place to live. Fortunately, it was also a time when the citizens of Michigan were still funding their universities at a level where students of limited means could cover their tuition costs with part-time and summer jobs.

One of Professor Bingley's first assignments of the semester was the close study of T. S. Elliot's "The Wasteland." Ray recorded how lost he was the first time he tried to read the poem. He couldn't begin to decipher the meaning of the text. He and Zeigler spent hours in the library pouring over scholarly guides, and they both struggled to answer Bingley's classroom interrogations, which seemed designed more to inflict pain than to elucidate the text.

From that point forward in the semester, Zeigler would say, "Hey, Elkins, April is the Cruelest Month. That's when she's going to flunk our sorry asses." There seemed some truth to that possibility. They both got C minus on their midterms. Ray had three minuses on his bluebook after the C, and Ernie had four. They laughed about the minuses over a pitcher of beer. But in the end they'd both managed to survive Bingley. Ray remembered how startled he was to find a B, no minuses, when he opened his grade report.

Months later, in the fall, he ran into Zeigler crossing campus. "You won't effing believe this!" Zeigler blurted out loudly from 20 or 30 yards. "She gave me a B."

The memories had managed to brighten Ray's mood. *And maybe in England, April is the cruelest month,* he thought, *the beginning of spring. In Michigan that would be late May or June. March is the cruelest month here because spring doesn't seem possible.*

14

~~

Mackenzie woke with a start. There was a sound, a new noise that she hadn't heard before. She lay for several minutes listening, trying to determine the source. Finally she decided that it had to be rain hitting the skylight or perhaps dripping off the long overhangs onto the deck.

She was uncomfortable in the bedroom. It was far too large for her tastes. The king-size bed looked minuscule on the expanse of white carpeting. The six-drawer dresser—three sets of two drawers, a long low modern piece—did little to absorb the available space. And the vaulted ceiling added to her feeling of unease. The room was just too big, too open. Her decision to take the master suite was based on the convenience of having the adjoining bathroom. She now considered switching to one of the other guest bedrooms.

Lifting her left arm above her head, she gazed at the luminescent face of the military style watch, 4:47. Rolling over on her side, she tried to find a comfortable position, pulling one pillow under her head, pushing another between her knees. She couldn't remember a time in her adult life when she had been so filled with misgivings.

This project was different from anything she had ever encountered. And it was heavily loaded with memories and emotions. Mackenzie was better at dealing with data; feelings were not her strong suit.

Years before, Mackenzie had traced her mother, not that she ever desired to have any contact with her. Sally Hallen's trail had been easy to follow, littered as it was with numerous arrests for petty crimes, the occasional incarceration, and ending in a late-night motorcycle accident where she and her companion were killed in a high-speed collision with a pickup truck.

She had also used her considerable technical skills to see if anyone could find anything on herself and her twin sisters, all three who had left Sandville decades ago in the company of two elderly relatives. There was nothing. She wondered if it would still be possible today for three children from an impoverished background to completely disappear without a paper or digital trace. She doubted it. But she had long believed that her mother was relieved that the children were gone. How many times had her mother had told her and her sisters that they were *only a burden*.

Giving up on the possibility of falling back to sleep, Mackenzie crawled out of bed and pulled on some fleece sweats. After switching on the coffee maker, she settled on the couch with her iPad and did a quick check of her e-mail.

Next she opened the planning document and flipped to the *Threats* page. The first item on the page was labeled *Possible Identification*. She clicked on the link and another page appeared. On the left was a picture that she had taken the day before. On the right was a photo she'd carried with her for years, the last class picture from Consolidated High. She had scanned it into a jpeg while still in California. She held the iPad up to look closely at the grainy black-and-white image of a young teen whose eyes looked almost too large for her narrow face. The girl had short hair—a jagged cut, inexpertly done with kitchen scissors by her mother or grandmother. The thin smile displayed buckteeth beneath an asymmetrical nose, the result of a fall from a tree a year or two before. There was never money for a visit to a doctor. Her grandmother had straightened it as best she could and packed it with cotton until it stopped bleeding.

Mackenzie looked at the face on the other side of the screen, 20 years older, perfect teeth, and a *retroussé* nose—her first substantial investment after she entered the world of work. Her hair was luxuriant and carefully styled, and her once soft blue eyes were now green. The little girl voice had disappeared years ago; intense voice training starting in high school had enhanced her rich contralto. And there would be no recognizing her diction, now educated, cosmopolitan.

For this project, she'd thought it essential to hide her identity. Even before the physical transformation, she'd been fortunate on that issue:

she'd been given a new identity long ago, when her great aunt rescued her and her sisters from her alcoholic and feckless mother. As she passed back and forth between the before and after photos, Mackenzie concluded that it would be difficult for anyone to make a visual tie between her and that delicate little girl of 20-some years ago.

The second link on the page was *Be Invisible*. She clicked on it and looked at her notes. Mackenzie was well aware of the impossibility of anonymity in a small town. Small towns are not like New York or San Francisco or other major cities where it is so easy to be just one of the crowd. Other than the realtor who sold her the house, Mackenzie had done her best to avoid local businesses. She did all of her shopping in Traverse City. She'd bought the most commonly seen vehicle on the road, a two-year-old Subaru. Her red Beamer convertible, an attention grabber, was safely tucked away in the garage of her condo in California.

Local Law Enforcement was the third entry on the list. She scanned the few lines of notes. Cedar Bay village had one policeman who worked a nine to five, 40-hour week; Mackenzie's home was just beyond the village limits. The Cedar County Sheriff's Department provided most of the police protection for the region. In her survey of newspaper articles, she had determined that the department was, along with the other units of local and state government, underfunded and understaffed. Ray Elkins was listed as the sheriff. She typed his name into Google. There were dozens of entries, most from the local paper, and most from stories concerning local police matters. She read through the entries on the first and second page and looked at a couple of pictures of Elkins. *Just another middle-aged cop*, she thought.

Finally, she thought about Richard Sabotny, the biggest threat, and the reason she was here. She had been searching for him for years, wasn't even sure he was alive. And then suddenly he was back in Cedar County, a decorated veteran and reputed soldier of fortune living very publicly in a trophy house on the bay, his driveway running off a major highway.

Putting down the iPad, she leaned her head against the couch. The black early morning was fading to gray. She could just begin to see the white caps rolling toward the far shore. She was filled with angst, not knowing where to start, but feeling an overwhelming need for action.

15

~

Ray was in his office before 8 a.m., first attending to routine paperwork and then perusing *Al Capone's Michigan: The Secret Lost Treasure,* as he sipped from a large insulated mug of espresso and hot milk. He thought he had followed Hannah's instructions on how to use the espresso machine exactly, but found with the first few attempts he wasn't getting the crema to form on the top. He poured all of the failures into his travel mug, topping them with four successful shots and a large quantity of hot milk from his feeble attempt at making micro foam. He added four spoons of raw sugar that had come in the box with the espresso machine.

Vincent Fox's book was a fast read. The opening chapter dealt with his growing up in Chicago. He described his neighborhood and Catholic grade school education—including a few detailed accounts of run-ins with the nuns, yardstick-wielding Sisters of Holy Mercy charged with civilizing and Americanizing the children of immigrants. Ray noted that most of Fox's text was vague and generic, containing experiences common to the lives of most people living in America's industrial cities early in the century.

In the second section of the book, Fox explained he was a kid of the streets when Capone first spotted him. He began by running errands for Big Al, and soon, while still in his teens, he became one of Capone's personal drivers.

Ray googled "Capone" to check the dates. As his daughter had already mentioned, Fox was far too young. But it was engaging fiction. Fox was a skilled storyteller.

In the final section of the book, Fox described how Capone came under increased scrutiny after the St. Valentine's Day massacre. With the coming of Elliot Ness and the Untouchables, Capone began to worry about the possible destruction of his empire. In an effort to protect his immense wealth, he started to collect gold coins, not trusting paper money. And not trusting banks—which were, of course, subject to thievery from both bank robbers from the outside and employees and managers on the inside. He devised a plan to bury his fortune in a number of locations along the shoreline of upper Michigan, from Frankfort to Petoskey, including the offshore islands. Fox went on to claim that most of the gold was buried north of Frankfort and south of Leland, as well as on the Manitou Islands. He provided a blurred vision of 11 treasure sites where he had participated in burying bags of gold coins, explaining that they had always worked at night, usually coming ashore from boats.

Each of the 11 sites was given several pages, but Ray quickly noticed that the first one was a template for the next ten. They were all variations on a theme, a word processing file worked and reworked in a less than convincing fashion. The descriptions, as Fox's daughter had suggested, were indistinct. Almost any piece of coastline could fit: sand, trees, dunes, small streams. The place to start digging would be more from the imagination of Fox's readers than anything he provided in *Al Capone's Michigan: The Secret Lost Treasure*.

Ray was still pondering the possible effects Fox's fiction might have on readers when Sue Lawrence arrived, thunking her travel mug on the conference table and dropping Simone into the one upholstered chair in the office. Simone immediately jumped out of the chair and ran to Ray, demanding to be picked up.

"I thought you were coming in late," Ray said, looking at his watch.

"Simone doesn't like sleeping in. She's used to getting up at 6 o'clock, having her breakfast, and going for a walk. I tried to pull her back into bed, but she'd have none of it. Plus, there was something going on outside, a deer or some other animal, so she was clawing at the venetian blinds and barking. Thus our day just started like usual, only we took a longer walk. Simone was doing more hunting than attending to business."

"I got here early as well. My motor was running."

"When are you meeting with Fox's daughter to I.D. the body?"

"Late this morning."

Sue pulled off her coat, threw it on the chair, and sat heavily. "So what did you do last night, get out in your boat?"

"Yes." He ran his thumb over the pages of Fox's book. "The plan was to go home, cook pasta, kick back, listen to music, and read."

Sue jumped up to retrieve her coffee. "What changed your mind?"

"Hannah Jeffers was waiting for me. She already had my kayak secured to the roof of her car."

"So someone new has a key to your house?"

"I forgot to lock the garage," he said. "She'd texted me earlier in the day about going out. I'd completely forgotten."

"Texted?" Sue laughed out loud. "I didn't think you did that kind of thing."

Ray ignored her. "We paddled to the Hollingsford Estate. I wanted to have a look around."

"And?"

"I found the private family cemetery, just like Ma French told us. Of course, in the last few days with all the rain, the snow is gone."

"Find anything?"

" Nothing that shouldn't have been there. Just sand and old headstones. I would have liked to look around the estate, but I was concerned about having enough light to get back to our put-in point. That, and a front seemed to be coming in faster than NOAA'd predicted."

"But you and the Doc obviously made it without too much difficulty."

Ray reflected on her tone a few moments before answering. "It was getting choppy. Hannah doesn't seem to be bothered by weather, she likes to paddle in conditions. But something interesting did happen." He told Sue about the Jet Ski.

"What do you think?" she asked.

"I'm still wondering. We didn't hear or see anyone on the water on the way out. It was so rough on the way back; I only became aware of the Jet Ski when it was too damn close. That said, the operator must have been aware of us. He'd probably had his boat beached along the stream that empties from Lost Lake. And when he circled, he had a better view of us then we did of him. We were right down there in the wash—he was three feet or so above us. Anyway, I don't think we looked like anything he was expecting."

"Did you get his registration number?"

"It was dark. If it was there, I didn't see it. When we get the Fox investigation under control, I want to go back and see if we can figure out what's going on."

Sue nodded and stood, picking up her coat and folding it over her arm. "I'll get all the material organized. But as you know, there are no obvious leads."

"So what do we know?" asked Ray, pulling down a whiteboard from the ceiling. He wrote *motive* in the first column on the left.

"There's only one that we've identified," said Sue. *"Money."* She paused as Ray added the word with a blue marker. "What about the family? Possible inheritance…?"

"I don't see it. No. It's all about the pot of gold Fox put out there in his book or the cash he won at the casino." Ray walked back to his desk and sipped at his coffee, thinking. "Last night I had trouble sleeping. I even got up at one point and tried to conjure a list of our known bad guys. No one fits."

"I agree. I can't put a face to this crime with anyone we know from the region."

"How about the Watonda sisters?" asked Ray. "They were willing to do most anything for dope or money."

"Or love," said Sue, "Last I heard Darcy was in a slammer somewhere in the south, maybe Tennessee. She was caught bringing dope to her boyfriend on a jail visit."

"I sort of remember that. How about her lovely twin, Marcy?"

"Rumor has it she's becoming a big porn star in Eastern Europe. Her newest flick, *All the way with the NBA,* is getting a lot of critical attention. Probably will be an award winner at Telluride and Sundance, maybe even TC."

"Where do you get this stuff?"

"You need to go to yoga with me, or at least to the bar after. When one of the local gals or guys makes good, it's something to talk about. And, according to my sources, the Watonda girls have been providing great gossip since they were in eighth grade."

"Okay, getting back on task, can you think of any of the usual suspects that we should check out?"

"No, not a one. We've got our share of lowlifes, but I can't paste this on any of them," Sue answered. "But we're living in such hard times. Maybe someone went over the edge. Maybe it's someone new to the area."

"We have to go back to the bookstore and library, see if Phillip or the librarian remember anything. I'd like to do that as soon as I get back from meeting with Fox's daughter at the Medical Center. Anything else I should know about?"

Sue put her coat back on the chair. Simone immediately jumped up and scratched out a bed. Sue sighed. "Well, we've had another theft of produce from one of the CSAs."

"What this time?" Ray got out a notebook.

"Potatoes and carrots from one of their storage units. Last week 500 pounds of potatoes went missing from Gourmet Boutique Farms. The Cedar County Gleaners has also reported some losses."

"Remind me when this started exactly."

"The first one was a few weeks before Halloween. A farmer near Inland Corners thought that he had some pumpkins stolen. I met with him and took a report. Let me get his name." She slid into Ray's desk chair. He waited as she keyed in a search command.

"John Dirker, an old guy, late 80s. I didn't think much about it at the time. There were hundreds of pumpkins in fields, near the barn, and loaded in two trucks. He was a little fuzzy on how many were missing, but insisted that it was the small ones, the pie pumpkins and the Wee-Be-Little, that disappeared. Nice old man. I learned a lot about different pumpkin varieties.

"I asked him if he had an inventory system, or a count, some way he could determine numbers and estimate the value. Dirker couldn't do it. Said he'd planted the Wee-Bees mostly for his great-grandkids and their friends, but he had a couple of commercial customers who'd also ordered several hundred, and he couldn't fill the order because most had gone missing. He couldn't tell me precisely when they disappeared. Could have been any one of several nights."

"And that was the end of it?" asked Ray.

"I listened to him, wrote up a theft report, had him sign it. Yep, that was the end of the pumpkin caper. So that was October. Since then we've had several more reports of missing produce, primarily root vegetables, many that I've never heard of—things like celeriac, Swedes, and kohlrabi. The interesting thing is that the quantities are small, usually only a few hundred pounds. The thefts are either from unlocked buildings or open storage areas. I've been having Brett follow up on most of these: it's more a show of concern about their loss. They know there's little chance we're going to recover a couple of gunny sacks full of carrots."

"And it's always produce, yes? There have been no reports of livestock being…?

"None. No pigs or steers, not even a chicken or a duck. There's some poaching going on. That's usual. And the road kill, the deer, disappear before they cool off." She looked at Ray and rattled her empty coffee mug. "So what are you thinking?"

"I don't think it is just hungry people helping themselves. And even if it were…. There seems to be a pattern. We just have to figure out who's involved." He looked at his watch. "I've got to get down to the Medical Center. Can we pick this up again in the late afternoon?

"Absolutely."

"Here's some reading for you, Fox's book. Won't take you long. And you'll like the section on where Capone's gold is stashed."

"There's one more thing we need to talk about, Ray. The 911 phantom has struck again. We've had three more incidents in the last week. Same MO. Weekend nights, usually after midnight, always in the central sector. The location is out in some field where the responder has to leave their car and walk around with a flashlight."

"Teenagers," said Ray, "sitting at a safe distance, watching the spectacle, sharing a joint, a few beers, or both. I'm sure it's a good laugh."

"Ray, a lot of downstate departments have stopped responding to these. Should we consider that?"

He pondered the question before answering. "Not yet. I keep worrying about a real emergency situation where we don't respond and should have. Let's look at this on a month-to-month basis. When the summer people come back and we're stretched to our limits, maybe then we will have to stop responding. The kids will have to find another source of amusement."

"How about digging for buried treasure by moonlight?"

"Or maybe we can teach them about snipe hunts."

"What's that?"

"I'll explain when we have some time."

16

~

Ray carried the tray with the two cups of coffee to the far corner of the Medical Center's cafeteria. The room was almost empty; still he wanted a place where they could have a private conversation. Joan Barton, Vincent Fox's daughter, lowered herself in the chair across from him. Ray placed one of the coffees in front of her, took the second, and slid the tray onto a nearby table.

He took a sip of his coffee and looked across the table at Barton. Her eyes were red. She looked older than she had only two days before.

"This part of the process is always difficult," said Ray. "The formal identification by a family member or friend is something that we have to do, and it's painful. Thank you for coming in."

"I wasn't ready for it," Barton responded. "I mean, I thought a lot about his dying in recent years—when someone gets up near 90, well, you know. And I've been afraid for a long time that I would be the one who would go out to his house and find him. I always worried about his safety." She picked up her cup, sipped her coffee, and looked at Ray. "I mean, I thought about him getting ill and needing some help, but nothing like this. I never expected... Who would've thought? And after you called me about his house getting trashed, I didn't know what to... I was trying to prepare myself for the worst..." Her voice trailed off.

Ray held her in his gaze. He considered several possible responses, but each seemed trite. These were always difficult encounters.

"Please," said Barton, "tell me what you know. Where was he found? Had he been harmed?"

"His body was discovered along North Bass Lake Road, just before it intersects with Township Line Road. The medical examiner found no injuries, no wounds, fractures, anything of that nature." Ray chose not to mention the charring on the bottom of Fox's foot.

"How did my father die?" she asked.

"I hope to be able to answer your question when we get the autopsy results."

"Why does the body have to be sent to Grand Rapids? We have pathologists here."

"Your father's body is going to be examined by a forensic pathologist, a person trained to perform postmortems in cases of suspicious death. We need to establish whether or not his death was connected to any criminal behavior."

They were both quiet for several minutes. Then Barton broke the silence with a soft question. "So he was found a long way from his house?" She shook her head. "None of this makes sense. How do you explain what's happened?"

Ray kept his gaze steady. "It's difficult to say for sure. But I think there's a strong possibility that your father was abducted."

"Like kidnapped?"

"Yes."

Barton put down the coffee cup she'd been holding with the fingers of both hands. "And this might be connected with that Capone book?"

Ray pushed his cup away as well. "Perhaps," he said. "Whoever trashed his house was clearly looking for something. They took his computer. It might have been somebody looking to fence it, but more likely he was looking for the Capone treasure. He might have thought there would be additional information on the hard drive."

Once again they sat quietly, Barton staring vaguely towards the bank of windows. Ray waited and watched. Again, Barton broke the silence: "I just can't wrap my brain around this. To think that he might be harmed because of that silly story. I never thought anyone would believe it, those stories." She paused. "They ran the story on Dad being missing on television. Did anything come of that?"

"Yes, we did get some useful information. Your father and two friends went to the casino on Friday."

"Who were they?" Barton asked.

"Mildred Hall and Tommy Fuller."

"Ah, yes. Mildred Hall, Dad mentioned her. Someone he met at the library a few years ago, his only friend still driving." She laughed. "They had a cooperative agreement of sorts. She's got some kind of very old car he likes to work on. In return, she takes him wherever he needs to go around the village. Now, Tommy Fuller is an old friend. I'd sort of forgotten about him. My father hasn't talked about him much lately. So they were at the Casino on Friday?"

Ray nodded. "Joan, you told me the other day that you'd talked to your father on Friday. What time was that?"

"It would have been pretty early, probably around eight. I try to get hold of him in the mornings, find out about his night and catch him before he goes out and about. I'd always ask him what he had planned for the day even though he'd usually just give me the 'same-old, same-old.'" She smiled and wiped away the tears. "He liked his privacy, liked to be on his own; he hardly ever told me what he was really up to."

"That was the only time you talked to him on Friday?"

"Yes."

"Your father had quite a day at the Casino. He won $6,000."

Barton hooted. "That old coot! He won all that money, and he didn't bother to call me! All right, I'm not surprised. What's happened to it? The money, I mean."

"According to Mildred Hall, your father gave Tommy Fuller $4,000 of it for a trip to Florida. Mildred arranged for the flight, and she and your father took Tommy to the airport on Saturday. You weren't aware of any of this?"

Barton's eyes, again filled with tears, spilled over before she answered. "That's like him. He's enormously generous, with his friends, anyway. So what happened then? Was Mildred the last person to see him?"

"Sometime after 3 o'clock she dropped him off at the library. That's the last anyone reported seeing him. Can you tell me how your father carried his money? A wallet? We didn't find anything on his body."

"He wouldn't have lost it. It was this huge leather thing with a chain attached. The kind bikers have."

"How about in the house? Was there a place where he hid his cash?"

Barton shook her head. "I don't know. Like I said, he was very private about most things. But I can't imagine that he ever had much cash around.

He lived on Social Security and a small retirement annuity. This thing with the casino, that's pretty crazy, not at all normal as far as I know." She paused. "But what do I know? Even if he did win all that money, I can't imagine he'd be carrying it around on him. I have no idea where he might have hidden it."

"How about credit cards? Did he have any? Did he carry them?"

"Not in recent years. He liked cash. He didn't trust plastic, had little faith in banks. You know, part of his story. Capone."

"In our last conversation you told me about your father's business."

"Vinnie's Import Auto."

"You told me that he took care of the exotics, often the cars of the summer people."

"Yes, the Jags and Mercedes, some lovely sports cars. I'm not sure what they all were."

"There's a family that has a large piece of property along Lake Michigan; it's the only place that's specifically named in his book as a possible Capone treasure site. Hollingsford is the family name. Do you know anything about them?"

"I don't remember that, but…."

"I was wondering if he might have worked on some of the family's cars."

"Dad was the only game in town if they needed anything more than an oil change. Hollingsford." She repeated the name and looked thoughtful. "I don't remember that name, either from back in the day or from reading his book. If it's there, like you say, I totally missed it."

"Just one more thing," Ray said, "and we've been over this before, but I need to ask again. Did your father have any enemies, or might there have been someone overly interested in any of his possessions or money?"

"I can't think of anyone, Sheriff." Barton smiled weakly. "As you can see, I didn't know much about my father's life."

They sat in an uncomfortable silence, Barton fidgeting with her empty cup.

"I need to do some planning for a memorial service," she said finally. "When do you think his body might be available?"

Ray waited for her to look at him. It didn't happen. "I will get that information for you," he said gently. "I'll call tomorrow and tell you what's happening."

17

"Here are the original photos from the crime scene," Sue said, pushing the stack across the table. "I've looked at each one very carefully. It's pretty much what you saw. Nothing new."

"And you searched the surrounding area?"

"Yes, and found nada. We fished around in the water where the body was recovered. We also checked both sides of the road for a fair distance. Only the usual detritus: beer cans, plastic bags, fast food containers. None of it recent."

"How about the other boot?"

"It wasn't there—not in the water or anywhere else." Sue crossed her arms. "So what do you think?"

"The same thing that you do," Ray answered. "Fox was abducted. They used torture to try to get information out of him, probably a wood stove. How he died is still an open question, but they were putting a lot of stress on a very elderly man."

"Bastards, I'm surprised they didn't want to water board him," said Sue.

"That would take work, assembling a teeter-totter and finding something to hold water. These guys aren't into heavy lifting. They didn't even go to the trouble of burying him. It would have been so easy to put Fox in a shallow grave. His body would have quickly decomposed, leaving almost no chance of ever being found. We would be looking for an old guy who had gone missing under suspicious circumstance rather than a couple of killers. These thugs are lazy and stupid."

She moved on to the next pile. "I have lots of pictures from his home, plus fingerprints and the shoe casting."

"Did you run the fingerprints?"

"Uh huh. No hits." Sue took a moment to look at Ray's notes on the whiteboard. "So what do we know so far?"

"Sterling reviewed the surveillance video of Fox and friends from the time they entered the casino to the time they drove away. He couldn't spot any of the other gamblers paying Fox more than the normal interest that a big winner attracts for a few minutes. That said, given his age and costume, Fox was easy to spot. I'm sure some of the people recognized him as a regular, even knew where he lived. They could have taken their time tracking him down and snatching him."

"And the other scenario, the Capone book?"

"Yes, there's that too: some fool who's been taken in by the book abducts Fox and tries to extract the location of the treasure. I guess I should say the many locations of the treasure. And the person or persons who tore up his house and stole his computer might have thought the info was on the hard drive."

"Or," countered Sue, "maybe they snatched him off the street, found $2,000, and went to his house looking for the rest. They took the computer with them because it's something they could use or sell." She paused and frowned at Ray. "What's going on with you? You can't sit still."

"I'm trying to stay rational and control my anger. We're just spinning our wheels here. We need to do a press release this afternoon and follow up with a news conference early tomorrow. That will get the Fox story on tonight's news and keep it there."

"I'll write the press release," said Sue, opening her laptop. "What do you want in it?"

Ray remained silent for a long moment. Finally he said, "The body of Vincent Fox, 89, first reported missing on Monday afternoon by family members was found late yesterday in northern Cedar County. The cause and circumstances of Fox's death are under investigation.

"Fox was last seen on Saturday afternoon in Cedar Bay. If you saw Mr. Fox on Saturday, or later, or have any information that you believe might help the investigation, please contact the Cedar County Sheriff's Department at …."

"That was easy. Usual distribution list?"

"With the tip line and e-mail address. Attach the photo. And put in a sentence that we will be holding a press conference tomorrow at 9 a.m.."

As Sue continued to work on the e-mail, Ray added more information to the whiteboard. After a few minutes, Sue said, "Proof it."

18

When Ray entered the bookstore, Phillip's head was down. He only looked up after Ray had pushed the door closed.

"Good timing on your part. A signed copy of Harrison's new book of poetry arrived in this morning's post. I thought that I should offer it to you before putting it on the shelf." Phillip slid the thin volume over the counter to Ray.

Ray admired the cover art, and then opened it to the title page to see the signature. "I will treasure this," he said.

"I heard about Vinnie on the news," said Phillip, standing up and resting his elbows on the counter. "Do you know what happened yet? Did he just wander off and die? Pensioners have been known to do that."

"I'm sorry, Phillip, I don't have any answers yet. We're still investigating and waiting for autopsy results."

Phillip wagged his finer. "You're being terribly mysterious."

"Not at all," said Ray. "I'd just rather not say anything until I have all the facts. Which brings me to the reason for my visit—apart from always liking to come in here, of course."

"What do you need?"

"Fox's book. You told me that some copies were stolen. Would you go through the numbers again for me? I'm trying to get a sense of how many are in circulation." Ray watched the reflection on Phillip's glasses as he keyed in the title and looked at the screen.

"Right. I had ten copies from Vinnie: six went through the till, two went missing, and I gave you one of the last two."

"Do you have any idea who purchased the six copies?"

Phillip worked at the keyboard again. "Fortunately not," he said at last. "They were all cash sales. Most unusual. More than 70 percent of our sales are on cards. Furthermore, none of the purchasers is in our Members Club. Statistically improbable."

"And the 'fortunately not' part?" Ray asked.

"Cash purchases provide no data other than title. I am clueless as to who purchased the books. Which is fortunate because I have nothing to tell you about him, or her, and am, therefore, able to avoid any kind of right to privacy mishap. You wouldn't want me telling your opposition during the next election that you're a Robinson Jeffers fan, would you? I can just see one of those adverts on the telly, the shrill-voiced bubblehead going on and on about how Ray Elkins is palling around with pacifist poets. Of course, there will be that little line at the end when the narrator says, 'Call Ray Elkins and tell him not to read pacifist poets.' And then your phone number would be flashed on the screen." Phillip was laughing so hard he could barely get his final sentence out.

Ray sighed. "So tell me this—and I know you can't give me names, I wasn't asking for any—what kind of people bought the book?"

"I would have thought you'd be more interested in what kind of people nicked the book," Phillip responded, still giggling slightly. "Too bad I can't tell you. All the purchases happened during the holiday rush. You know, I'm slow all fall and then we go mad from Thanksgiving to Christmas, especially the last two weeks. And to make things more complicated, I was often gone at the busiest time. My wife's father was in the hospital in Detroit. Some temps, college kids, were running the asylum. When I was here I was focusing on inventory and orders. We don't have much storage space; everything has to be just in time. It's a bit of a dance."

"So nothing really unusual?" probed Ray.

"Well, book buyers are sort of unusual, more all the time, don't you think?" Phillip raised an eyebrow and looked thoughtful. "There was one thing more than a bit unusual. Nothing to do with Vinnie or his book, though, just odd. A couple of men were in here on the day before Christmas: two men, black suits and hats and beards."

"Hasids, or Amish?" asked Ray.

"The second, the ones with the buggies."

"Were they looking at Fox's book?"

"No, I don't know what they were looking at; I don't think it was his book. They did buy something, quite curious at the time, but I can't remember what it was…." Phillip snapped his fingers. "You know, it might have been a map or a calendar. And after they left I went out to see if there was a buggy on the street," he confided. "I was wondering if some of them were moving to the area. Might be good for the tourist trade. They do crafts and furniture."

"And?"

"Nothing. No buggy, they just disappeared into the crowd."

Ray set the volume of poetry on the counter and placed a credit card on top. Phillip picked up the card and ran it through the reader. Handing Ray a slip to be signed, he said, "See, with this sale your name gets recoded twice: once for the charge, and once as a member of our discount club. But I'll never disclose this purchase to anyone, especially potential opponents." He winked. "By the way, whatever happened to that guy that ran against you last time? What was his name?"

"Hammer."

He chuckled. "Yes, Hammer."

"Last I heard he'd moved to the Texas, border country somewhere. Bought a gun shop."

"Ahhh." Phillip picked up the store receipt and shut it in the register. "I must say your elections are, how should I put it, well I hate to see one coming. You just can't watch the telly without one or more bits of outrageous propaganda at every break."

"It does get noisy," said Ray. "In your home country, politics are rough and tumble, too. And nothing more outrageous than British press coverage."

"You're right on about the tabloids, little truth there. At least we don't have the adverts, there just isn't that kind of money. And our politicians, well, our scandals are… But there is one important difference."

"What's that?" asked Ray, enjoying the banter.

"When our politicians are hearing voices and talking to God, they end up in hospital. They don't get to stand for Parliament, let alone become Prime Minister. We don't allow people, even politicians, to embarrass themselves completely."

"How about Thatcher?"

"She wasn't talking to God. She was God."

"This has been fun," said Ray, "but I've got to scoot. I do need a favor, however."

"Anything for a loyal customer."

"If you ever notice that I'm talking to myself or seem to be hearing voices, get me out of public office and into treatment."

"No problem, old friend. I'll just put out the word about the pacifist poets. I'll even organize the recall."

Ray found Penny Storrer, the Cedar Bay District Library head librarian, in her crowded office in the basement of the 60s modern brick building. Her door was open, and she was talking on the phone. Noticing Ray, she pointed to the empty chair in front of her desk. Then she completed her conversation. After returning the phone to its cradle, she crossed her hands on her chest and said, "Horrible news this morning, Ray. Vinnie has been a part of our community here at the library for years. The TV report was rather vague, not that there's ever much content. I don't understand what happened." She looked at him inquiringly.

"I can't tell you much, Penny. I'll know a lot more in the next few days." He smiled. "There is something you could help me with, though."

"What's that?"

"Two things, actually. First, what can you tell me about Fox's book? And secondly, Phillip at Ye Olde says you told him you've had two copies stolen...."

"That's right," Storrer sniffed. "We checked them in, put them in circulation, and they disappeared."

"When did you notice they were missing?"

"Vinnie called my attention to it—he liked showing people his books on the shelves. He was constantly dragging people over to his title. First he noticed one was gone, then the other. He asked me if I wanted additional books because both copies were checked out. He was sitting right where you are sitting, and I checked his title on the computer as we were talking. I remember that one copy had circulated; then it was returned in a few days. The other had never circulated. Logically, that meant both copies should have been on the shelves. Anyway, I told him I'd be happy to have two more, and after he left, I went to see if I could find the originals. They weren't anywhere: not on a return cart, not left on a desk, not shelved incorrectly. Just gone." She turned to a book-covered table by her desk and rummaged through several piles of books, finally extracting two fresh copies of Fox's book. "Here are the new copies he brought me, sometime last week it was. They're still waiting to be cataloged."

Ray looked up from his notebook. "Is it normal to have books stolen from the library?"

Storrer shrugged and brushed back her shoulder length salt and pepper hair with the writing end of a pencil. "Well, yes and no," she said. "It doesn't happen much. Here anyway. Our loss rate is way below the national average. And, as you know, we don't have any of the electronic detection gear at the door. We've never really needed it." She looked to the ceiling, thinking. "There've been a few cases where particular books have disappeared, like new Harry Potter books, the Twilight series too. Our way of dealing with the problem is to put those titles behind the circulation desk. Patrons must ask for the book in person. Anyway, it's not a common event. Not here."

"Any idea who might have walked away with Fox's book?"

Storrer shook her head. "I don't know. I've never thought about things that way."

"But you were familiar with the contents of the book," said Ray.

"Yes, very." She smiled. "In fact, I helped Vincent with his research, the Capone part—Cicero and Chicago. I had to get most of the books he used via interlibrary loan, as there's not much demand for Capone material up here. I also pulled things off the Internet for him. Have you read the book?" she asked.

"Yes."

"Then you know," she said, her smile growing weak. "The first part of the book might be termed historical fiction with emphasis on the fiction, and the rest is just over the top, Vincent having fun. I liked to kid him about his story, but he'd say, 'It's all true!' The couple of times I pushed harder, he'd amend that to, 'Well, it's mostly true.' And he would sit there and sort of laugh with a Cheshire cat grin, like we both knew he was just blowing smoke."

"So you can't remember anyone lurking about, reading Fox's book?"

"No."

"The new patrons at the library, anyone looking out of place?" asked Ray.

"No one comes to mind. We have our regulars; some people come in daily to read the papers and periodicals. Others are here once a week, or every other week, to get a new supply of books. And then there are the walk-ins: summer people, weekenders, or people just passing through town who come in and use a computer or our Wi-Fi to check their e-mail. We try to be helpful without being intrusive."

"Any Amish?"

"Amish?" Penny responded. "Not here. Not in my career. I don't know if they use public libraries. Interesting thought. I'll have to research that." She paused briefly, "I think the nearest Amish community is south of Cadillac."

"Fox was reportedly dropped off near here last Saturday afternoon. We haven't found anyone who saw him after that time. Did you see him? Did he come into the library Saturday?"

"I'm sorry, I didn't work Saturday. I went into Traverse. Joyce Points, one of my assistants, was running the desk."

"Is she here now?"

"No. She's part-time; let me check her schedule." She typed for a few seconds and then looked back at Ray. "She's on again tomorrow. Joyce is a college student. Do you want me to call her right now?"

"That's okay. Could you just send her a note? Ask her if she would respond directly to me." Ray placed a business card on the desk, pointing out his e-mail. He waited silently as Storrer keyed a note.

"So these books," said Storrer, pointing to *Al Capone's Michigan*. "What should I do about them?"

"Just like you said: put them behind the circulation desk and make them available."

19

L ost in thought, Ray climbed the stairs leading from the basement of the library and pushed his way through the aluminum doors into the dull gray afternoon. Outside, he took a few minutes to look around the area adjacent to the library—the parking lot and the sidewalks leading up to the village and the harbor. The village sidewalk was a quick to and fro, but at the harbor he walked slowly past the slips lined up at right angles along their long slender ribbon of land. The marina had stood empty since late October, when the last boat had been moved to winter storage. Today only a few clumps of snow remained in areas protected from the sun and rain.

A gentle rain was falling from low hanging clouds. The large homes on the west arm of the bay, mostly seasonal dwellings, were shrouded in a mist that clung to the shoreline. Standing at the end of the pier, next to a tall navigation light, Ray gazed out at the big lake. Beyond the harbor there was the bay, and, beyond that, open water stretched north to the Straits of Mackinac. Ray stood for a long moment, concentrating on the sound of the wind and the rhythmic splash of the gentle surf against the side of the pier. He closed his eyes. The air, still with a bit of winter's frigid bite, smelled fresh and clean. He opened his eyes slowly retracing his steps back toward to the library.

Against the gloom of the day, Ray found the interior of the Last Chance with its familiar smells of burgers and beer welcoming. Jack

Grochowski, the longtime owner, leaned over the bar and gave Ray a warm greeting.

"The usual," said Ray, settling onto a stool.

""Fraid we're not doing the usual anymore," answered Jack. "I can give you a Columbian supremo, I have a very nice French roast, a Viennese, and my current favorite's a dark roast with hints of mocha and cinnamon."

"What happened to the Eight O'clock from Sam's Club, made with that special water you were always bragging about?"

"Progress," answered Jack, rubbing a wrinkled hand across his grizzled beard. "People don't want that old style anymore. I'm just keeping up with the times. Let me recommend the French roast. I think that's close to what I used to serve you."

"Sure," Ray said. He watched as Jack inserted the coffee pod, his hands unsteady, into the shiny new machine that occupied the same shelf space where generations of Mr. Coffees had lived and died.

"Tell me what you think," said Jack, setting a new, white mug with the steaming brew in front of Ray.

"It's good, Jack," said Ray, after several careful sips. "It'll take some getting used to, but it's good. Never thought you'd be one to buckle under pressure, though."

"Well, you know, it's the girls that work here," Jack said, perching himself on a stool he kept behind the bar. "They keep saying it'll be less fuss, that we wouldn't be throwing so much coffee away. Yeah, I'm not sure of the economics. I think it's mostly that the girls are into all these yuppie flavors." He paused while he sipped from his own mug. "Yeah, well, things are changing. Point in case. I've been stocking these 'craft beers,' whatever that means. They sell like crazy, especially to the summer people. In fact, it's worth having Bell's or Shorts on tap during the season." He took another thoughtful sip of coffee. "But I know you didn't come in to talk about coffee or beer. I saw the news on TV. And I was sorry to see it. Good old Vinnie. I'll miss that old boy." He leaned close to the bar. "What happened Ray?"

"We're still trying to figure that out. We'll know more in a few days."

Jack slouched. "Which usually means you know more than you're telling, but that's all you're letting out."

This time Ray leaned into the bar. "So I heard from several people that Fox was a frequent customer."

"He was," Jack responded, perking up. "Came in three, four, five days a week. Have a shell or two. 'Course when his daughter'd bring him in for a burger, he'd make a big thing of it, like he only came here with her, like it was such a treat. And there's a perfect example of what I was talking about."

"Example?"

"People wanting new things. Vinnie, for years, would only drink Bud or Bud Lite. We've always had some imports in bottles, but I don't think he ever tried one. Now these craft beers, I've got one on tap for the first time last June. In fact, I gave him a glass just for fun, expecting he'd swear it wasn't a Bud. Hah! He loved it. That's all he's had since. And that old tightwad was willing to pay twice as much. And instead of nursing one for hours, he'd drink two.

"This past Saturday, do you remember Vinnie coming in?"

"Ray, that's almost a week ago. I'm struggling with what happened yesterday."

"Well, give it a shot," pressed Ray.

"I can't say for sure. The days sorta blend."

"Was he alone? Did he come with a group? Did he meet people here?"

"Well, there was a group of them over the years, seven or eight of them back in the day. Most are gone now. Last year or two, it's mostly Vinnie, his buddy Tommy, and Mildred Hall."

"Mildred Hall, really?"

"Yea. Now she wasn't as regular as the other two, but she was often with them."

"Was she drinking craft beer with Vinnie?"

Jack laughed and rolled off his stool. "Mildred has her special tea."

"That makes sense," said Ray.

"You don't understand." Jack walked to the end of the bar, brought back a teacup and saucer, and set them in front of Ray. "And here's the special tea," he said, retrieving a bottle from the back row next to the mirror.

"Lagavulin, 12 years old."

"Yup. I stock it for her; never had it in the place before. Two shots in this teacup, she'd have." He pointed. "They liked to sit over in that booth, the two guys on one side, Margaret on the other. She'd always drink one tea and I'd ask her if she wanted another, and she'd always say, 'I can't, I'm driving.' The guys thought it was a good joke, the tea and all. They never caught on."

Anyone new hanging around lately, anything unusual?"

"Nothing I can remember. This is the slowest time of year."

"Do you know about Fox's book?" asked Ray.

"Oh, yeah, that book. It's all he's talked about for a year. Before the book, he mostly talked about World War II and all his bomber adventures. Then that whole Capone thing took over."

"Have you seen the book?"

"I got a copy back at the house. He gave it to me for Christmas. I'm not much of a reader, but I've made my way through most of it."

"And?"

"Well, Vinnie's a good story teller, he is. And there might be some truth in his book. I mean we all know Capone made a lot of money and was doing his best not to give it to the taxman. But, well, I can say there's always lots of fun in the telling, and the listening."

Ray finished his coffee and set the mug back on the counter. "It's pretty good coffee, Jack. I'm not a convert yet, but this could grow on me. Listen, if anything occurs to you about Vinnie, give me a call."

"I'll do that, Ray. I'll miss old Vinnie. There aren't many of us left."

Sue Lawrence scraped back a chair at the conference table. "I thought you were going to be back earlier," she said to Ray.

"Did I say that?"

"No, not exactly, but I thought you were just going to talk to Joan Barton."

"Well, I was going through the village, and I got inspired." Ray told Sue about his several conversations.

"So," said Sue mildly, "what you established is that we're clueless as to who walked out with Fox's book, no one remembers seeing him after Mildred Hall dropped him off in the village on Saturday afternoon, and that he drank craft beer."

"No, there's more. Not that they're relevant to this investigation. But still surprising and interesting."

"Like?"

"Mildred Hall, my old chemistry teacher, Fox's sometime driver. She told me that she only spent time with Fox at the casino and the library. Turns out she also would have drinks with Fox and Tommy Fuller at the Last Chance."

"That's pretty scandalous, Ray."

"It gets better. Jack keeps a special bottle of high-end single malt Scotch for her and serves it up in a proper teacup."

Sue shrugged. "What can I say, or as my Grandmother would say, 'A lady has to protect her reputation.'" She smiled and added, "And what you high school boys didn't know was that Mildred Hall probably had a number of interesting lovers and spent her evenings drinking Scotch and having torrid encounters while you were home memorizing the periodic chart."

Doing her best to control her mirth, Sue unrolled a plastic covered map, turned it 180 degrees for Ray, and pushed it across the table. "I read Fox's book very carefully and highlighted the possible burial sites for the Capone stash."

Ray looked at the large ellipse that encompassed the coastline from Frankfort to Charlevoix and included the Manitou and Fox islands.

"Where do you think we should start hunting for the guys digging in the sand?" she asked, doing her best to control the grin.

Ray just shook his head.

"This weekend…" began Sue.

"Yes?"

"I'm running down to Ann Arbor to spend some time with friends, and I was wondering about Simone. Could she stay with you?"

Ray took a moment to respond. "That should be fine," he drawled. "If something happens that I'm mostly on the job, she can ride with me."

"And I'd like to take a little extra time. I should be back here Monday by 1o'clock. Are you okay with that?"

"No problem," Ray said, looking at the map again. "You've got a mountain of leave time. You should be using it."

"Great. And here's the *quid pro quo*: on my way out of Ann Arbor on Monday morning I'll stop at Zingerman's for you."

"Now you're talking," said Ray. "Give me a few minutes to make a list."

20

After leaving the office, Ray drove to the Lake Michigan shoreline for a long walk with Simone. Ray started their hike at a brisk pace and held it for several miles, but when they turned to retrace their steps, he allowed Simone to dictate the pace. They stopped frequently so Simone could carefully inspect pieces of driftwood, clumps of dune grass, and the assorted detritus that collects on a beach.

It took several trips to carry all of Simone's weekend supplies into the house: her bed, a crate, a bag of food and treats, a doggie raincoat, and a bag of toys. All were neatly packed and organized in Sue's usual fashion.

For dinner, Ray constructed a sandwich with bread sliced from a peasant loaf and some aged Vermont cheddar. After he pressed it into a Panini pan, he opened a can and dished out food for Simone. She approached the bowl warily, smelled the contents, and returned to Ray's side, and looking up at him with large, expectant eyes.

Ray had promised Sue that he would not share his gastronomical creations with Simone and that she would be kept on her usual diet of gourmet canine food. But after a session of sad eyes he retrieved her dish and topped the brackish mixture of congealed gristle and meat with some pieces of cheddar. He watched with delight at how quickly she ate her dinner.

The rest of the evening was spent quietly. He filled several journal pages and then looked at the stack of books that had been collecting on his desk. He passed over several newly released novels. He needed something calming, something that would complement his pensive mood. He settled on Jim Harrison's newest volume of poetry, and, starting at the back, he paged through it in a random manner. This was the first read. He knew that he would return to the book many times over the years, finding favorites among the carefully crafted poems.

Ray woke in the early light to the sound of snoring. He opened one eye and peered across the floor to the empty dog bed. Rolling over, he found Simone stretched out on the pillow next to him.

Ray parked behind Nora Jennings' Ford Explorer, pulled Simone into his arms, and walked to the back door of the cottage. Ray had done odd jobs for Nora and her husband Hugh when he was in high school and college, and had stayed in touch with them through the years. After Hugh's death, he had made a special point of checking on Nora by phone, and occasionally dropping by her isolated home on a bluff above the Lake Michigan shore.

His rapping brought a cacophony of barking as the resident dogs, Falstaff, a Labrador, and Hal, a Welsh terrier, charged the door to welcome the visitor. Nora pushed back the curtains and peered out before sliding back the deadbolt.

"I thought you were coming right over," she said, hustling him into the kitchen. "The coffee's not completely fresh."

"It just takes longer to do things," Ray explained. "I hadn't factored in how long Simone would insist on walking this morning. Is it okay that I bring her in?"

"She's in already. Just set her down. She gets along fine with the boys." Nora started filling the two coffee mugs that were already standing on the table. "I made those cookies, oatmeal with walnuts, just the way you like them."

Ray settled at the table and looked out at Lake Michigan through a wall of glass. There were modest swells in the light wind, the water dull and gray under a thick overcast.

"How was Detroit?" he asked.

"The best part was climbing in my truck and pulling onto I-75. God, was I glad to get out of there. Two weeks in Grosse Pointe was more than I could bear. I know my daughter means well, but that's just not where I want to be." Nora pulled a chair next to him to share the view, "The guys hate it, too." She looked off toward the couch where they were curled up, one at each end, Simone in the center."

"How's your daughter?"

"Same old. She tried to drag me off to a couple of retirement communities. Keeps telling me she'd sleep so much better at night if she knew I was in one of those awful places."

"And you?"

"Are you kidding? Look at the lake. Is that magnificent or what? I don't want the noise of the city. And I don't want to be around all those people, especially in one of those places with a bunch of old crabby geezers."

"And I suppose…."

"Yes, I told her. I'm not much of a diplomat anymore. I say what I think. It's one of the prerogatives of old age. By the end of two weeks, she was happy to see me go. Think I've finally convinced her that she doesn't want me just down the road." She added a spoonful of sugar to her coffee, stirred until it was dissolved. "You said you had some questions, some history questions. What are you going to do when I die, Ray?"

"You don't get to. But," he said, pointing to a desk on the south wall covered with books, binders, loose papers, and an old IBM Selectric, "I'd really like it if you would get this history of Cedar County in print. It's been, what 10 years now?"

"Yeah, just in case, right?"

"Is there some way I could help you?" asked Ray. "I could find someone to get all this on a computer and ready for printing."

Helen was silent for a long time. "I think I'd like that, Ray," she said finally. "My fingers." She held up her hands.

Ray noted the swelling around the joints and the misalignment of the digits.

"It's always worse in the winter. I've talked to the doctor about it. He gave me some medicine for the pain, but said there's not much he can do about it. It's the damn age thing." She paused and looked at her paper-laden desk. "The book, would it cost much to do that?"

"Not so much. It isn't the investment it used to be. There are new technologies called print-on-demand. Basically, you just pay to get the book formatted. And I could probably help you find some underwriters."

"Let me think about it. So what do you need today? You said you had a question."

"The Hollingsford Estate, what can you tell me about it?"

"Hollingsford…my, I haven't thought about that in a long time. Is it still there?" She answered her own question in a few seconds. "Yes, it's down at the end of the National Shoreline. It should have been part of the Park, but talk was they had better lawyers and more political connections than everyone else. When the final boundaries were drawn, it was excluded."

"Did you know the people, the Hollingsfords?"

"No, but my mother did. My mother, she was from Chicago, and I think they were, too. I don't know if she knew them from up here or down there."

"Where you ever there? Did you ever visit the estate?"

"I may have as a child. My mother was a real gadabout. But I have no memory of it."

"Here's another question: When I was growing up, I heard lots of stories of Al Capone coming up here in the '20s. There were rumors that he and his boys may have tried to hide some of his misbegotten wealth up here, bags of gold coins buried on beaches and hidden away in houses like the one on the Hollingsford Estate."

Nora scowled. "I was just a little girl when that could have happened, but let me tell you, Ray, those stories have been around for as long as I can remember. And that's all they've ever been, rumors. Let's see, what do they call them now? Urban legends. I've heard about Capone having a house in Frankfort. He also had a place in Leland, and maybe a place up in that Methodist summer colony in Petoskey." She chuckled at her joke. "And, Ray, how we girls were warned to avoid swarthy city-types, sharpies, men driving big Cadillacs and Buicks, men coming up here to woo young farm girls and take them back to Chicago or Cicero to a fate worse than death."

"Never to be seen or heard from again," added Ray.

"Worse than that, they were seen again. A year or two later they'd be back—dropped off by a Greyhound at the end of the drive with their name and address on a label hanging by a string around their neck. Their bodies would be covered with oozing pustules and their brains rotted by syphilis. The girls would either die quickly, surrounded by distraught relatives, or they would end up at the Traverse City State Hospital for the rest of their miserable days."

"Yes, I see, you were duly warned."

"Never mind that I never saw anyone fitting the description. And actually, I've always really liked dark-haired, olive-skinned men—those brooding Mediterranean types. But," she said wistfully, "in the end it was Hugh that captured my heart. His reddish-blond hair, his light freckled skin, and his Scotch heritage." She paused briefly. "Anyway, by that time I was old enough to be in danger, Capone was either in jail or long dead. And I was a college girl in Ann Arbor."

"I sense you don't put much stock in the Capone story."

"Stock, schlock, it's a bunch of junk. You know, Ray, people are always getting excited about stuff that has little or no truth to it. The important things that they should be concerned about go unnoticed. But why all this talk about Capone?"

"Vincent Fox, he spends a lot of time around the library. He's written a book on Capone."

"Vinnie, the old guy in the buckskin jacket?"

"Yes."

"I know who he is, nothing much more."

"He was found dead Monday, while you were away." Ray gave her the information his department had made public and told her about Fox's book.

"Well, I'm sorry he's dead. Truly, there's too much of that going around. And I missed the fact that he's an author. Probably a good thing. I may have ridiculed the book. I've become such a sarcastic old crone, bit of a book snob, too." She got up to refill their mugs. "I'm afraid I'm not giving you much help. Is there anything else?"

"A drowning on Lake Michigan about twenty years ago, the body ended up on the Hollingsford beach."

"Drownings," she sighed. "There were so many over the years. Was there something special about this one?"

"It was early in the season, late May or early June. The victim was a 15-year-old kid from Sandville."

Nora took a sip of coffee, set her mug back on the table. "The warm air fools the kids. They don't understand the difference between air temperatures and water temperatures." She paused, "But 20 years ago, nothing particular comes to mind. I'm sorry. And now there's something I want to know."

"What's that?"

"A security system, my daughter thinks I should invest in one." She waved her hand. "It's more about getting help if I'm sick or something rather than burglars."

Ray sat for a long moment without responding.

"Well," said Nora. "Cat's got your tongue?"

"They're the bane of my existence. The summer people are always putting them in their cottages, and we respond to lots of false alarms. But, Nora, in your case I think it's a good idea. You'd wear one of the lavaliere call units."

"Who should I call?" she asked.

"Let me get back to you on that. I'll ask around and give you a call or stop by at the beginning of the work week." When he stood, Simone jumped off the couch and raced to his side, ready to get back on the road.

21

At home, Ray found Hannah Jeffers' Subaru parked next to the garage door. Both of their kayaks were again secured to the roof rack of her car. Inside he found Hannah curled up asleep under a fleece throw in the great room. Simone welcomed her by jumping up on the sofa and barking enthusiastically, followed by wet kisses.

"What did I leave open this time? Ray asked.

"The front door. But both the garage and the door from the garage to the house were locked. You're getting more diligent, Elkins. We did talk about kayaking today, didn't we?"

Ray couldn't remember any such conversation. "You look more like you're into napping than kayaking," he said. "Did you work last night?"

"Got off at seven, picked up my boat and kit. Thought I could catch a nap here before we launched."

"And where did I say we should go when we talked about kayaking?"

"I detect a note of incredulity in your tone. In truth, I may have just dreamed that we talked about kayaking today. And it might have been in the same dream where we talked about kayaking out to South Manitou. I've checked the weather…."

"Is this in a dream or…."

"This is the real thing. I checked it this morning, NOAA and the local TV guy. The wind will be from the southeast at five to ten, and the waves one to two. Temps are going to be pushing into the high 40s and low 50s."

"What's the water temperature?"

"30s at the buoy, but that's the middle of the lake."

"Hannah, even if the conditions hold, and NOAA's forecasts are less than perfect, it's a hard paddle. Eight miles out, eight miles back. That's more than two hours each way, hauling ass. There will be wind, waves, and current. How much sleep have you had?"

"Enough."

"How much is that?"

"Three hours, maybe a little more. I can sleep tonight, and I'm off for the next four days. Lots of time to catch up. Let's take advantage of the sunshine."

"I can't believe what you talk me into," said Ray with a sigh. "Take Simone for a walk while I change and gather my gear together."

Thirty minutes later they were at Lake Michigan, carrying boats, one at a time, from the parking lot to the shore. They made a third trip for their gear bags and paddles.

On the beach they packed thermoses of hot coffee, sandwiches, energy bars, and extra clothing and gear into the watertight hatches.

"What are you thinking?" asked Hannah, noting that Ray was standing at the side of his boat looking thoughtful.

"Now that I'm standing in the wind, I'm not sure I'm layered up enough under the dry suit."

"I had the same thought. You packed extra fleece?"

"Yes. You?"

"Ditto. But you don't want to be too hot, either. I think once we get going, we'll be plenty warm enough."

They pulled on their spray skirts and zipped up their PFDs, slid into their kayaks, attached the neoprene skirts to the cockpit coaming, and launched into the gentle chop. The waves picked up once they got beyond the headland and turned toward the island.

"Are you warm enough?" asked Ray.

"Perfect, but my skeg won't deploy. I must have gotten a stone in it when we launched. Would you see if you can set it free?"

Ray brought his bow close to Hannah's cockpit. She reached across and grabbed his deck lines. Pulling off a mitten, Ray unclipped the knife from the front of his PFD and carefully ran the squared-off tip along the groove between the fiberglass hull and the plastic skeg. He found the offending pebble with his knife and pushed it free.

"Try it now."

"Perfect. Thank you. What's our final destination, by the way?" Hannah asked as they drifted.

"Let's head for the lighthouse. Part of that shore is rocky, but there are also some sandy places where we can land."

They paddled for few minutes side by side. Ray looked over and saw Hannah's joyful smile. "What's going on?"

Hannah laughed. "I get on the water and within a few paddle strokes I connect with this world and everything that has me on the edge of blowing up evaporates. The wind, the water, the blade—there's nothing else."

With little more conversation, they held a steady cadence for close to two hours, finally landing on a sandy beach a few hundred yards from the old lighthouse.

"It looks like we're not alone," said Ray pointing toward a Zodiac high on the shore beyond the sand.

They spread their spray skirts and PFDs over their boats and settled into a lunch of sandwiches and steaming coffee on a small promontory at the top of the beach.

"I never thought peanut butter could taste so good."

"It's one of my favorites," said Ray, sounding a bit defensive. "Great bread, organic peanut butter. Of course it's going to be good."

"What do you think that's about?" Hannah asked, pointing toward the Zodiac.

"I don't know. Awfully small boat for this water. Before we leave, we should have a quick look around and make sure no one's stranded here."

Later, as Hannah disappeared into the woods, Ray walked up the beach and inspected the Zodiac. Two nylon-covered orange PFDs and a wooden canoe paddle were on the floor of the seatless craft. A small, worn-looking outboard was secured to the transit.

Ray climbed past the boat and looked up the beach. Two young men were approaching him. The first—portly and carrying a metal detector with a backpack hanging by one strap over his shoulder—wore khaki shorts and an unzipped nylon jacket that covered a grey hoodie. He was moving at a good pace. The second boy—carrying a shovel and trailing behind—was tall and extremely thin. He looked cold and morose in his cut-off jeans and a faded red Henley, which was open at the collar, exposing a cotton undershirt.

"How you guys doing?" asked Ray.

"Great," said the first one, eyeing Ray cautiously.

"Doing some treasure hunting?"

"You a park ranger?" asked the teenager, looking at Ray's dry suit.

"No. I just paddled across with a friend," Ray motioned toward their beached kayaks. "We were just about to start back. You guys park rangers?"

The kid with the metal detector laughed. "Sure."

"So what are you looking for?"

"Asshole thinks he's going to find buried treasure," said the taller of the two.

"Screw you, Ty. If I found anything, you'd be first in line to share it."

"Are you looking for lost items, or are you …."

"It's some wild idea Win got out of a book," sneered Ty.

"Really," said Ray. "You guys hungry? I've got some energy bars in here." Ray pulled two bars from a pocket in his PFD. There was a momentary hesitation from the boys; first Ty and then Win accepted the offer.

Ty grabbed the wrapping with his teeth, peeled it, and bit off a large chunk of the bar. As he chewed he said, "Go ahead and tell him, Win. Like it's no big fucking mystery."

Win fished a smart phone out of his pocket. "It's a book on Kindle," he explained. "It says some of the money was buried on the Manitou Islands, just beyond the shadow of the lighthouse. It didn't say which lighthouse, but that other one is clear out in the water." He pushed the last piece of the bar into his mouth, and then fidgeted with the phone, holding it out so Ray could read the screen.

"Interesting," said Ray. "Too bad the author didn't tell you what time of day or the date. There's a lot of territory just beyond the shadow of the lighthouse."

"Yeah, well, the author says early in the book that most of the money was buried at night, so I don't get how he knew about the shadow anyway. He also says that they buried most of the money during mild weather, but some of the biggest stashes were made during the winter when Capone thought the 'Untouchables'" were about to close him down."

"So we're talking about Al Capone here?"

"Yeah," answered Win.

"If there ever was any treasure, it's long gone," added Ty. "And I'm out here freezing my ass off on a wild goose chase."

"What's the book's title?" asked Ray.

"It's something about Capone's lost treasure in Michigan."

"How did you find out about it?" asked Ray.

"A kid at school. He got a copy for Christmas, a real copy, a book. I got it on Kindle for four bucks. Lots of people downloaded it."

"Win decided he'd be the first one to the island to get the treasure. Like most of it's already been found on the coastline," said Ty, who shivered as he delivered his sarcastic line.

"He's just pissed because he got splashed a little on the way over. He's always bitching about something," retorted Win.

"If I was fat like you, I wouldn't be cold," Ty shot back.

"We have some hot coffee," Ray said. "Would you like some Ty, Win?"

"That'd be great."

"And I've got an extra fleece jacket."

"I'm okay," said Ty.

Ray was pouring coffee when Hannah reappeared. "We've got a couple of boaters here," he said, introducing her and giving his first name. "Ty here seems chilled. I offered him a fleece, but he doesn't think he needs it. We did energy bars and now hot coffee. Hannah's a doctor."

"Can I check your pulse?"

Ty reluctantly held out his left wrist.

"Have you had any alcohol today," she asked.

"No. Nothing."

"Are you sure?" she asked, looking directly into his eyes.

"Nothing," he repeated.

"You need to get warmed up a bit. I want you to put Ray's jacket on, and I'm going to get a space blanket from my boat."

They wrapped the reflective, plastic sheet around Ty and continued to give him hot coffee and another energy bar. The shivering went away, and he began to display more affect and a sense of humor.

"Are you local?" asked Ray.

"We live in T.C."

"And you go to West?"

"No, we're both at Central."

"So how many kids are looking for Capone's treasure?"

"We've been kidding about it at lunch for a while," explained Ty. "Win's the only one who really believes it. And he's the only one with a metal detector. Tell the man what you've found the last several years. Tell him about the beer cans and nails and that piece of chain."

"I did find a watch," said Win.

"Yeah, an old Timex."

Ray looked out at the lake. The waves were beginning to build. "We've got to start back, the wind's come up." Ray stood up and helped Win to his feet. "What're your plans?"

"We're ready to go, too."

Ty started to unwrap the space blanket.

"Keep it on," said Hannah. "You'll need it for the crossing."

"How do I get it back to you?"

"Where did you launch from?"

"The Cannery."

"Same as us," said Ray. "There's a green Subaru in the parking lot. Just leave it on the roof or hood. Do you have enough gas? I noticed that you weren't carrying a fuel can."

Ray watched Win check the tank on the engine after they had dragged the boat down to the water's edge."

"We should have enough," said Win. "And we've got a paddle." They pushed off, Ty sitting on the floor near the bow, Win in the rear, paddling the Zodiac into deeper water. He pulled the starter rope several times before the engine coughed to life, sputtering a cloud of white exhaust, then stalling. He started the engine a second time, and when it was idling smoothly, he engaged it in gear and with a backward wave, headed out into the Manitou Passage.

"Let's get going," said Ray, "we may end up towing them to shore."

"So they were looking for Capone's treasure," said Hannah soon after they launched.

"Yes," said Ray, "they say the book is on Kindle and cheap. We'll have a summer of shore diggers with smart phones. Petoskey stone hunting is a thing of the past, at least for this year."

The wind continued to pick up and they were pushed across the open water, their boats occasionally broaching from the following seas. There was little conversation, just a focus on their final destination. Hannah stopped yards off shore and waited for Ray to paddle near the side of her boat.

"How are you doing?" he asked.

"Hungry, exhausted, but I hate coming off the water. You?"

"Same."

The boats felt heavy as they carried them from the beach, up over the dune, to the parking lot. The space blanket and jacket were wound around one of the kayak racks. A note was tucked under a windshield wiper.

Hey Guys,

Thanks for the help. I'll remember you when I'm rich.

Win

Simone was waiting at the front door, a note of distress in her otherwise ebullient greeting. Hannah walked the dog while Ray changed his clothes and started supper, pulling a container of potato soup from the freezer, setting it into the microwave, and warming a baguette in the oven. By the time Hannah returned with Simone, Ray was putting the finishing touches on a salad of assorted greens with slices of avocado when Hannah walked in.

"Thought you two might have gone missing," he said.

"Quality girl time. We understand one another. When's dinner?"

"Everything's hot. The sooner the better."

"Can I eat in my fleece long johns?"

"This ain't the Ritz. No dress code." He put down Simone's dish of dog food, enhanced with some aged Vermont cheddar. Then he ladled up steaming bowls of soup.

"One question," said Hannah, before taking her first spoonful of soup. "How come you didn't try to get more information on Ty and Win?"

Ray smiled. "Win is Winifred Steward III. His father is a dentist in town, and his grandfather was a dentist in town. I recognized the boat. His father uses it for duck hunting."

22

Mackenzie reached forward and turned the temperature up a bit in the shower. After several minutes of soaking up the warmth, she stepped out of the spray to examine the collection of soaps and shampoos provided by Ken Lee. She started with a shampoo, squeezing a palm full of the greenish liquid, and working it into her hair. There was no scent, just lather. Mackenzie carefully scrubbed her whole body with liquid soap the same bilious color, removing any trace of makeup and residual feminine scent from her usual toiletries. After rinsing away the last traces of soap, she dried herself with freshly laundered towels. She had washed her underwear and linen in detergent also sent by Ken Lee. He had emphasized that she should keep her gender a secret, be more male-like than feminine. He joked that if he could re-teach her how to walk, he could make her gender invisible.

In panties and a flattening bra, Mackenzie settled into a chair in front of the bathroom mirror. She carefully applied greasepaint, again supplied by Ken Lee, to her face, neck, hands, and several inches above her wrists. *This is crazy* she said out loud, watching her mouth open and close in a face she barely recognized.

There were times when Mackenzie thought Ken Lee was utterly wacko—much more than overly cautious, perhaps more than a little bit paranoid. The history he had shared with her passed through her mind like a series of black and white snapshots: growing up in Texas with a black mother and a Korean father, learning to be a scrapper before he even started kindergarten, escaping the poverty of his childhood by joining the military as soon as he was out of high school, eventually becoming a Navy Seal, and picking up a college degree along the way. Ken Lee's military and college training coupled with his extraordinary facility with technology enabled him to get a high-paying job in corporate security.

Combing her hair and securing it tightly in a knot at the back of her head, she thought about the *List of Cautions* Ken Lee had given her. She'd once teased him that they read like quotes from Chairman Mao mixed with Jay Gatsby's plan for self-improvement. Today she was following the first item on his list: *Always be more prepared than your potential adversary.*

Mackenzie went into the bedroom where she'd laid out her clothing, all black and still sealed in plastic bags. She pulled on a long-sleeved, skintight turtleneck shirt and black long underwear of the same material. She followed with loose-fitting outer pants that somewhat disguised her feminine form. She pulled on long, thick wool socks and black duty boots that Ken Lee had forced her to thoroughly break in before the trip to Michigan. Then she shrugged on body armor that ran from her shoulders to her waist. A bear claw knife, a small tactical flashlight, and a GPS-enabled satellite phone were already secured to the armor. Finally, she added a hip holster and a black balaclava, taking care to push back and under any wisps of hair. Before pulling on a black winter jacket, she holstered the two loaded and chambered pistols.

Fully outfitted, she turned slowly in front of the three bathroom mirrors, and for a moment she felt silly. Then she remembered why she was in Michigan: the helplessness when she had been surrounded by the boy, the fear like poison, the knowledge that rape was imminent, and the rescue by her brother.

Every aspect of the mission had been carefully planned. Mackenzie had laid out a detailed scenario, and then e-mailed it to Ken Lee. He had sent back a few suggestions that she had incorporated into her final "operations plan." Ken Lee would monitor her progress back in California.

Tonight was just a rehearsal: checking equipment and getting used to moving around in the dark. She had earlier found a place to park the car where it would go unnoticed. Using Google and geological survey maps, she had calculated the distance from the parking lot to the approximate position where her brother's body had been found. A little more than 4 miles, it was a journey of an hour and 20 minutes in daylight on a solid surface. But she would be walking in darkness, a heavy overcast preventing any moonlight from breaking through. And she would be walking on sand, perhaps sprinting for the shelter of the woods if anyone approached.

Mackenzie pulled into the shadow of a large pickup truck at the far end of the unlit resort parking area. Earlier, she had deactivated the Subaru's interior lights, so opening the door she moved from one area of darkness to another. She stood for several minutes listening carefully and allowing her eyes to adjust. Then she started out along the narrow road that ran down to Lake Michigan. Skirting the steel barrier at the end of the road, she climbed over a small dune and moved toward the shore.

The trek along the beach in heavy boots proved to be more tiring than she had anticipated, but she was relieved that even without maps or GPS, her destination would be easy to find. The creek that emptied from Lost Lake was the only interruption on the shoreline for miles.

Mackenzie looked at her watch when she arrived at the stream. She was running 10 minutes behind schedule. In the dull, watery light, she peered up and down the shore, then sloshed across the shallow stream and climbed the embankment. Catching a boot, she lost her balance, her outstretched hands bracing the fall. She brushed the sand off her hands and paused again to take in her surroundings. The area appeared to be a small burial plot. With increased caution, Mackenzie moved higher on the dune to get a view of the whole area. Used to the steady hum of an urban environment, she had been working on developing her awareness to the sounds and shapes of darkness. She stood for many minutes absorbing the scene. Her thoughts then shifted to her brother, wondering where he had died, and how he had died; wondering how his body had ended up on this strip of sand.

Her attention was suddenly drawn to lights moving rapidly along the beach from the north. Three separate beams were quickly closing in on her position. Sliding back into a tamarack swamp at the edge of the dunes, she found cover behind the roots of several overturned trees.

The drone of small, high-pitched engines increased, then abruptly stopped. She could hear voices. She stayed low and waited. The voices moved closer as flashlight beams swept the area, and then they moved away.

Mackenzie waited for several minutes before slipping out of her hiding place. In a crouch, she climbed up the dune to where she could better see the lights and perhaps catch bits of conversation. Unholstering her Glock, she crept closer, taking cover behind a large cedar. She was sure she could feel Sabotny's presence.

"So where am I supposed to dig?" whined a male voice.

"Right where I told you, asshole. Near the big headstone in the snow."

"Which one?"

"That's the only big marker, fuck-head."

"But there's no snow."

"You were supposed to be here two weeks ago. There was lots of snow then. That was the deal."

Mackenzie could see the shape of a man on his knees, arms flailing. He lifted an arm and held it out to the shape of a standing figure. "It's empty," the kneeling man said.

"I know. Some old broad walked with it. Ended up taking it to the police."

"How do you know that?"

"I've been watching."

"Why didn't you do something then?"

"I didn't want the police involved. Now it looks like they are anyway."

"I was drunk that night," whined the kneeling man again. "I came the next morning. The jar was empty, just like now."

Mackenzie heard a scream as the two shapes collided. Sabotny was kicking a man on the ground. Bluish LED beams washed over the area, and Mackenzie noted a third man on the edge of the shadows. She looked back to see the man on the ground had pulled himself into a ball. The attacker stopped, and there were only the sounds of wind and whimpering. "Get up," Sabotny demanded. When the man pushed himself back to his knees, she saw that his face was covered with blood.

"Why did you drag me out here?" he cried.

"I'm trying to make a point, asshole. I sent you out here to pick up some money. I was testing your honesty. You failed."

"I couldn't come that night. I was drunk. When you called, I told you. I told you I was drunk, and you said, 'Go anyway.'"

"When I give an order, I expect you to follow it. So what if you were drunk? That's never stopped you before. You got to get the drinking under control. I got big plans, and I need people I can trust. I'll give you one more chance. Clean yourself up and let's get out of here."

Mackenzie watched them move away from the cemetery, their lights dancing. They climbed onto their ATVs and drove back north along the shore. She held her position for 10 minutes by her watch to make sure that they were totally away from the scene, that they weren't coming back. Then she secured her pistol and walked south. An hour and a half later, still shaking, she was back in her car.

In the security of her home, the bowl of a wine glass in her hand, its delicate stem threading between her middle and ring finger, she slowly swirled the scarlet liquid as she recounted the events of the evening with Ken Lee.

"I was wondering why you took so long," he said after she had described what happened. "I was beginning to get concerned. I'm glad you were armed."

Mackenzie sat for a long time without responding. "It bothers me that I need a gun."

"After this is all done with, you may never need one again," Ken Lee reassured her. "But right now you've chosen to deal with some killers, people who wouldn't hesitate to take you out. It's the old fight fire with fire. If they had spotted you—and people like that don't go around unarmed—could you have stopped them before they killed you?"

Another long silence followed. Finally Ken Lee asked, "Could you identify them?"

"The one was Sabotny. I think the guy he was beating on was Jim Moarse. The third man was silent. I never really saw him."

"So this deal with the money, what do you think that was about?"

"I have no idea."

"Sabotny, what was it like to see him again?"

"Frightening, almost paralyzing."

"Are you sure that you don't want me to fly out? I could probably be there by dinner time."

"Not now, not yet. This is my problem. I'd like to solve it myself. I did okay tonight. And you're giving me plenty of support as it is." She paused. "What I'd like to do now is get in the shower, go back to my natural color, and then sleep for about 10 hours."

"The face paint is designed to wash off. I've included a special soap. Just follow the instructions."

"You think of everything."

"What can I say?"

"Always be more prepared than your adversary?" she quipped.

23

When Hannah emerged in fleece pants and a jacket many sizes too large for her small frame, she found Ray hunched at the kitchen table, staring at the screen of his iPad.

"I like your costume," he said, sitting up and smiling.

"Best I could find in your closet," she responded, pulling out a chair. As if on cue, Simone appeared from the bedroom, leapt onto Hannah's lap, and started inspecting the contents of the tabletop.

"The women are hungry," said Hannah.

"I can see that," said Ray.

"What's going on?" she asked, noting Ray's attention returning to the screen.

"The downside of technology," he responded. "In the old days when you requested a forensic autopsy, it would take days to get the preliminary results. It went something like this: After the body arrived in Grand Rapids, a pathologist would do the post mortem during normal weekday working hours, then dictate his or her findings. The dictation would go to someone in the secretarial pool, who also worked normal business hours. He, or most likely she, would send a typed copy back to the pathologist for revision and approval. Any changes would be made on a paper copy and returned to the typing pool. The secretary would make a final copy and return it to the pathologist again for review and signature. This alone would take days. A week after this back and forth, we might get a fax with the preliminary findings, followed in another week or so by an official signed copy with photos via snail mail. Then, a week or two later, we'd get the final toxicology."

Ray pushed the iPad across the table. "Now, it's all here in a couple of days: the report, photos, everything but the toxicology. All neatly typed and organized by Samantha Redding, M.D., Fellow, AAFS."

Hannah glanced at the screen. "Rule one in medicine, never read an autopsy before cappuccino."

"I'd be happy to do that," said Ray, putting down the iPad, "but there's a problem. Something isn't right. I'm not going to complain about technology again, so I'll say it's mostly my technique or lack thereof. The shots I make are bitter, and all I do is warm the milk up—big bubbles, no micro foam."

Hannah set Simone on the floor. "Come here," she ordered. "It's time for Barista 101. We start with the grind."

She inspected the grinder. "The first problem is that someone messed with the settings. Or maybe it just got out of kilter in the move." She pointed to a mark she had made with a Sharpie on the adjustment scale. "This is where you want it. It took me several weeks to find the sweet spot and get this dialed in." She poured in some beans, then pushed the "on" button until the change in sound indicated that all the beans in the hopper had been ground. Then she worked through the rest of the process, filling the portafilter and tamping the grounds. She frothed some milk and pulled the shot. Standing at Ray's side, she offered gentle coaching as he repeated the procedure.

Settling again at the table, Hannah moved the iPad close to her. "Have you read this?"

"Just started. I was getting mired in the boilerplate." Ray watched in silence as she carefully studied the report, occasionally moving the text backwards to review a paragraph or two. He got up and gave Simone her breakfast. A few minutes later she was at the door, demanding his attention and a walk with a sharp, command bark.

Hannah was still concentrating on the screen when they returned from their stroll around the neighborhood. Ray made her another cappuccino and then repeated the process for himself.

Finally she looked up, held him in her gaze, and asked him a second time how much of the autopsy he had read.

"Like I said, just the beginning."

"This is all so interesting. For an old guy, Fox was in awfully good shape. He had some plaque buildup in his coronary arteries, but it wasn't too bad for a man of his age who'd been eating the American diet forever. His muscle tone was quite remarkable."

"So how did he die? What killed him?"

"Fox had a pacemaker. Did you know that?"

"No. His daughter never mentioned it."

"Did you see the note on the burn marks on his neck consistent with the kind made by a stun gun?"

Ray stared at her. "Where's that?" he said, pointing at the iPad.

"Several pages into the report." She pushed the tablet in his direction, pointing to the section. She pulled it back, flipped through multiple pages, then slid her chair close to his and pointed at the photograph showing burn marks on the left side of Fox's neck, below the collar line.

"What was he wearing when you saw the body?" she asked.

"His usual costume: jeans, a shirt with a sweater of some sort, and an old buckskin jacket. He had a boot on one foot, it was missing on the other." He zoomed in on the burn marks. "I can see how the medical examiner might have missed the stun burns," he admitted, "given the conditions where he made his preliminary observations." Ray sat for several minutes absorbing the information. "Why would someone do that?"

"The perpetrators were trying to snatch him off the street, right?"

"That's a likely scenario."

"Fox was probably a tough old bird, much stronger than his assailants expected," said Hannah. "He wasn't going to go anywhere without a fight."

"But who carries a stun gun?"

"You tell me. You're the cop."

"Well, under current law only people in law enforcement-related activities can carry Tasers. Of course, the legislature could change that in the next few months."

Hannah was keying on the iPad. Then she was flipping screens. "There are only a few hundred sites selling Tasers and stun guns. Here's one with Christmas specials. I can't tell if the page is left over from last Christmas or out there for people who do their shopping early."

"I can't believe it," Ray said. "I thought Fox had been grabbed by some people thinking that he really knew where the Capone treasure was, and that they could pressure him into leading them to the gold. The use of a stun gun just makes it all seem incredibly sinister."

"What we are capable of almost defies imagination. You should spend some time in a war zone," Hannah answered, her tone dark, tension in her voice.

Ray let her comment hang for a long time. "So what killed him?"

Hannah shrugged. "Here the pathologist equivocates a bit. Because of the absence of bruising, she doesn't think that he was constrained for any period of time. And there's no evidence that he was ever bound at the hands or feet. She speculates that the stun gun was used during the initial assault and wonders what effect that may have had on his pacemaker. She notes the literature on this type of weapon and its potential effects on pacemakers are extremely limited. Three citations to recent articles are appended at the end."

Ray got up and carried his mug to the sink.

"What are you thinking?"

"You see, I've invented two scenarios. The first one involved a couple of our locals: somehow I'm seeing two middle-aged guys, down on their luck, not incredibly bright, who got started into this whole thing by stealing a copy of Fox's book. They quickly figured out that they weren't going to find the money based on the descriptions or maps, so they grabbed Fox off the street, and, based on the burns on his foot, tried to get information out of him by holding his foot against their wood-burning stove. I can see the interior of the house, the stove their only source of heat." Ray returned to the kitchen table, pulled his chair away from Hannah's, and sat down. "Unfortunately, Fox just up and dies on them. The guys panic, load him in their car or truck, head up the road 15 or 20 miles from the scene, and dump the body."

Hannah nodded. "Okay, what was the other scenario?"

"Much simpler. Someone saw him make the big win at the casino and abducted him off the street hoping to get the money."

"And the burns to the foot?"

"Same motive as the first; when he didn't have the cash on him, they tried to use torture to find out where it was."

"How about just modifying your scenarios. They're just crazy, sick, and weird. They use a stun gun to aid in the kidnapping. If you search the APA list of mental disorders, you will probably come up with a multisyllabic, multiword Latinate definition for this type of behavior."

They sat in silence for several minutes. Finally, Hannah asked, "What are you going to do?"

"I'm going to make breakfast."

"And if I weren't here?"

"I might start by splitting wood. Then I'd go to the office and try to make something happen. I'd create diagrams and lists, look through old files, think about our usual cast of characters. There would be no breakthroughs, but somehow just being active makes me feel better. Then I'd go for a long, fast paddle until I was totally exhausted."

"So is that what you want to do?"

"The office part, no. It's a waste of time. It's just me trying to cope." He smiled at her. "And I'm glad that you're here. What would you like to do? It's really blowing outside. I think kayaking is out."

Hannah spooned the last of the foam out of her cappuccino cup. "How about taking Simone for a really long walk on the beach and then going shopping."

"Shopping? I didn't think you...?"

"For food. You know the right places. We could get a duck or a chicken or a pot-roast, something that takes hours to cook. Vegetables or squash, and we'll bake something. We fill the house with lovely aromas, we drink tea or maybe a little wine, and we listen to some quiet music to go with the day, things like the Goldberg Variations. I'm sure you have a good...."

"Yes."

"Do you think we can survive a slow day together, a slow day of doing normal kinds of things?"

Ray smiled, "I'm sure that after a three hour walk on the beach I could settle into this very nicely."

24

It was mid-afternoon, and Mackenzie was sipping her first cup of coffee after an hour of yoga and 40 minutes of meditation. Behind her great room's expanse of titanium-tinted glass, she peered across the bay through her powerful telescope. Heavy rain and mist were being pushed off the big lake into the bay by a strong northeast wind, but she could see the back of a figure moving on a treadmill framed in the center of a large HDTV, the jogger almost in proportion with the soccer players in the background.

Plato's cave, she said, making the figures larger and sharpening the focus as the scope cut through the haze. Her concentration was suddenly shattered by the vibration and techno music beat of the ringtone Ken Lee had installed on her cell phone.

"What are you doing?" he asked.

"Watching Sabotny on his treadmill."

"Is he fit?"

"I've only been watching a few minutes, but he's moving fast. My guess is that he's in good shape."

"File that away. Might be an important bit of info. Listen, I've been thinking about your encounter last night. We need to get some things in place. Also, I've got additional info on Sabotny. You may want to make notes."

"Give me a few. Let me get to a keyboard."

Mackenzie hit a switch on the wall, and the floor-to-ceiling drapes started to close. When the whirling noise of the electric motor stopped, the room was left in almost complete darkness. Mackenzie navigated her way to her desk and touched the space bar on her keyboard, bringing the screen to life.

"Okay," she said, "ready to make notes."

"First," said Ken Lee, "we need to start tracking Sabotny. I'd like to get a GPS transmitter in his car. You said he had a Land Rover. What year?"

"I have no idea; looks new. How do you tell?"

"Get me a photo. I'll e-mail you a diagram of where to place the unit. It's held by strong magnets, and it just takes a few moments to get it in place. I'll send you two in case he has a second vehicle. They should be in your box at the UPS Store by Tuesday. Also, I want you to have a personal locator beacon with you before you go on any more jaunts. I'm researching what's out there. I should have that unit in your hands before the end of the week."

"Ken Lee…I don't want to be weighted down with extra gear."

"These things are tiny, about the size of a small cell phone. And I need to know where you are. If things go south, just pull the tab, and I'll direct law enforcement to you. Now, let's move on to Sabotny," he said, cutting off any further protest on the PLB. "I talked to two people—an ex-marine friend, and a foreign service officer—who were in Baghdad early on after the invasion."

"And?"

"Sabotny was career military, a high-ranking noncom. But something happened during the run-up to the Iraq war. My friend doesn't know what. There's no record of a court martial, but Sabotny was separated from the Corp. It was all hush-hush."

"Your friend, does he have a name?"

"Yes, 'X,'" came the response. "The next time X saw Sabotny was in Baghdad right after the liberation. Sabotny was in command of a group of contractors. X said they looked like they came from central casting. Everything new and clean: clothes, weapons, and vehicles. He said they were all in black, not desert camo. Scuttlebutt was these guys were getting $1,000, $1,500 a day. That's about what the troops at the bottom get a month. X said what really pissed him off was the contractors hadn't done any of the fighting, but there they were collecting the big bucks escorting diplomats and civilian employees through corridors that regular troops had secured and were defending. X said he quickly learned to hate them for other reasons."

"Like what?"

"First, he said it was their swagger and their high living, the single malt Scotch and young Eastern European whores that were smuggled in on private jets. And they were answerable to no one. And they used the anarchy of a war zone to enrich themselves. Most were ex-military: Russian, South African, Israeli, French, and American. But here's the big thing: that first year after the invasion, $12 billion in C-notes were shipped from the U.S. to start the rebuilding effort. Most went missing. That and billions of dollars worth of oil, loaded on tankers and shipped who knows where. X says he doesn't know what scams Sabotny was running, but he does know that Sabotny soon parted company with the original contracting group and started his own operation. X says Sabotny came into a lot of money, big money, fast, and set up a shipping business. He says he heard Sabotny laundered the profits through an offshore corporation."

"And that's a lot of hearsay," observed Mackenzie.

"Yeah, well, I next called this woman who was there the first year. State Department. She's in Thailand now, still has a 202 area code. She confirmed most of the story. Said the loss of the money and Bremer's total incompetence was reported long after the fact and never seemed to get any traction in the press. She said she heard that in addition to the no-bid contracts and lack of oversight, some contractors and/or their employees just helped themselves to pickups filled with boxes and bags of bills. And they did it with impunity because there could never be any prosecution. There was no accounting, no tracking of serial numbers. No doubt some of the money was used to pay for legitimate expenses, but most was stolen, and there is no way to trace any of it."

"Is this for real?"

"It is." Lee paused briefly and Mackenzie could hear him tapping keys on his keyboard. "So I call a friend at the Bureau. This guy owes me, and I know that he was involved in an investigation of a number of things that happened that first year in Baghdad—the theft of antiquities, the missing billions, contractor fraud, you name it. I asked him about Sabotny. He says they gave him a good look, they knew he was a key player, but they didn't have enough evidence. Then he tells me they just ended up letting it go, the whole thing. The Pentagon and the administration, right from the top, were leaning on them to cease and desist. Too many people in powerful positions had either been in on the take or were complicit with what went down. He said that it could have been a scandal that rivaled Watergate. They wanted to make sure it got buried. Sure enough, in the end, it attracted little attention."

"Okay, interesting, but all old news," said Mackenzie. "What's Sabotny up to now, and why is he here?"

"Your guess is as good as mine," answered Lee. "But I have a bit more, and some of it I don't quite understand—offshore corporations, wire transfers, that sort of thing. Sabotny is believed to have several offshore corporations in the Caribbean and Seychelles where he laundered his millions in 2003 and 2004. Since then he's been living as an expat, mostly in Eastern Europe, seldom coming to the States. He pays for his day-to-day expenses using credit and debit cards issued by offshore banks. Both the Bureau and the IRS have noted his return and are looking into his activities. And the laws are changing for people like Sabotny. They're not going to be able to live like this much longer. The loopholes are being closed."

Mackenzie, lost in thought, didn't immediately respond.

"What's going on?" Ken Lee finally asked.

"I'm just trying to absorb all of this. I thought Sabotny would be an ordinary up-north guy."

"Hardly. He's a trained killer with anything he needs at his disposal. Sure you don't want me on location?"

The offer was tempting. Mackenzie was feeling lonely and vulnerable. "This is my war," she answered. "You're giving me plenty of help."

"Get me those pics," said Lee. "And we'll see if we can find out what he's up to. In the mean time, I'll send you everything I've gotten so far, including some info on his woman friend, Elena Rustova. Give it a good look."

25

Ray had rehearsed what he was going to say to Joan Barton, Vincent Fox's daughter, as he drove south on M22 early Monday morning., But once they had settled over coffee in her kitchen, the windows looking out on a small yard busy with birds visiting a collection of seed-filled feeders, he still felt anxious. Joan read his tension. "You don't have good news, do you?"

"I know a bit more about your father's death," Ray admitted, "and I want you to have that information before we release it to the press." He briefly explained the autopsy findings, the fact that Fox had two small burns on his upper torso suggesting that the assailants had used a stun gun, probably to control him.

"Just like him," she said, giving Ray a weak smile. "When you're a kid you think your father is the strongest man in the world. My father really was strong, even as an old man. Anyone who tried to force him to do anything was going to have a fight on their hands."

"I'm sorry that I...."

"Don't be. In fact, this has really helped. I like the idea of my dad going out fighting. That's what he was, a fighter. He said he did Golden Gloves as a kid. I don't know, probably just another of his stories. But he fought his way out of a tough Chicago neighborhood, made it through the war, created a successful business, provided a nice home for my mom and us, and put my sister and me through college. He gave us a good life. He was a tough, determined character." She paused for a long moment.

"There was a poem we studied in high school. What was it? The teacher made a big joke about not confusing the poet with the folk singer.

"Probably Dylan Thomas. *Do not go gentle into the good night.*"

"That's it," she said, "Do you know any more of it?

"*Do not go gentle into the good night,*
Old age should burn and rage at close of day;
Rage, rage against the dying of the light.

I think that's about all I can do with any accuracy," Ray said.

"That's enough, thank you. He went out fighting. I'm sure he would have picked that over dying in bed. I'm sorry you never knew my father. He was a wonderful character."

"I'm sorry, too," said Ray.

By 10 a.m. Ray was back in his office writing a press release on the Vincent Fox investigation while Simone nested in the overstuffed chair. He worked through the draft of the release several times, adding a comma, changing a word, putting a sentence into a new paragraph, then changing his mind. Finally, he sent the draft to Jan, asking her to proof it once more before forwarding it to their media distribution list.

Ray sat for several minutes, running the details of the Fox murder in his head before pulling down the large whiteboard and adding details to the branching case diagram. Slouching into a chair at the conference table, he studied the drawing. All the events and facts were there, but he could not see how they connected to any tangible motive. For the moment, the investigation into Fox's death seemed stalled.

Going back to his computer, he reread the notes from his conversation with Ma French. Although logic dictated that these were unrelated events, there was something alluring about the timing, the man on the personal watercraft, the cash. He thumbed through Fox's book, finding a section that referred to an old estate on the shore of Lake Michigan, many miles below the Sleeping Bear Dunes. Fox wrote that that location once had been a major drop-off point for liquor by the Capone Gang, a possible burial place for part of the treasure, since it was terrain with which the mobsters were familiar. Like the rest of the book, Fox could have been referring to any number of places along the coastline. Not that that would stop the true believers from spending months looking.

But could it be that the cash Ma French found was connected to the Fox hoax? Ray returned to his desk and pulled up the notes from his conversation with Ma French. He needed to know more about the Hollingsford Estate. French had identified Perry Ashton as the caretaker of the property. He looked for his number in the regional phone directory. Finding none, he looked back at his notes. Ma had mentioned a Carol Truno in Traverse, and Ray found her number. A sleepy and somewhat irritated sounding woman came on the line. Ray identified himself and explained that he was trying to reach Perry Ashton. His said his call was related to a matter at the Hollingsford estate. Truno gave him Perry's cell number and added that she knew he was planning to go out to the place in the afternoon.

A few minutes later Ray was explaining to Ashton that they were looking into a cold case—not mentioning Ma's recent find—and was wondering if he could show him where he found the body of Terry Hallen. Ashton agreed to meet Ray at 2 p.m. in the driveway of a house just off the highway near the entrance road to the estate. He said he would bring a boat so they could get across the lake.

Ray wrote a short e-mail to Sue, inviting her along if she was back in the area. Then he and Simone headed out to find some lunch. They shared a lavish sandwich filled with organic chicken, greens, red peppers and a tangy mayonnaise in the parking lot of the Bay Side Family Market, then headed across the county toward the big lake.

Reaching the designated meeting place almost an hour early, Ray continued to drive south, eventually turning onto a two-track that led to a small parking lot near the shore. Simone followed him out of the car, and they climbed over a small dune to get to the beach. He undid her leash and they walked north near the water's edge, Simone running ahead, stopping, looking back over her shoulder until he approached, then sprinting forward again ebulliently, repeating the process over and over.

The wind was blowing out of the northwest, creating a modest chop. The sun in a cloudless sky warmed his back. The last vestiges of winter, the remains of once-deep snowdrifts, were decaying into slush and gradually slipping away into the sand.

After 15 or 20 minutes, Ray settled onto a large, bleached tree trunk that had been pushed far up the beach by the storms of fall and winter.

Simone approached and tried to crawl into his lap, her paws and belly wet and sandy. They reached a compromise: Simone perched beside him on the log, her head on his leg as she accepted head scratches.

Ray peered out at the lake and concentrated on the scene: the sounds, smells, rhythms, and colors of early spring. He tried to let everything else go and just enjoy the moment. On the periphery of his consciousness were visions of Fox and the disturbing autopsy report. When these thoughts intruded, he would push them back and refocus on the scene. This was one of the times he needed the wild places—empty of people— to refresh and refocus.

Eventually he looked at his watch, surprised that so much time had slipped by. He reached for his phone to see if Sue had responded to his e-mail. His pocket was empty; the phone was in the car.

When they arrived at the access road to the Hollingsford estate, Sue was already there, talking with a tall, lean, graying man next to a rusted Ford pickup with oversized tires and a raised suspension. A battered aluminum boat hung out of the truck's bed, its pram bow extending far beyond the lowered tailgate.

"Have you met Perry Ashton?" Sue asked as Ray approached, holding Simone in his arms.

Ray passed the wiggly dog to her mistress and shook hands with Ashton.

"Was she a good girl?" asked Sue.

"Couldn't have been better," said Ray. Looking over at Ashton, he explained, "The dog was orphaned, and we co-parent her."

"Cool," responded Ashton in a low, raspy voice. "She coming along, too?"

"If it's okay with you."

"No prob, man," he said, fishing for a cigarette.

"Mr. Ashton…"

"Perry, please."

"Perry," continued Sue, "was just telling me that this property was sold and he's been terminated as of, what did you say, April first?"

"That's right," Aston agreed. "Got a certified letter last week. Been here 40-some years. All I get is a short letter saying that my services would no longer be needed, and would I please remove my personal things and vacate the property before April 1. My last paycheck was there, too.

No thank you, no separation, no nothing other than a FedEx overnight envelope for the keys."

Ray could tell by his tone and body language that he was angry and hurt.

"So, Sheriff, what do you and the deputy here want to know?"

"As I mentioned on the phone, we're looking at a few cold cases. One of them involves the death of Terry Hallen. Our records from that time are less than complete, and it's unclear if any final conclusions were ever reached in that investigation."

"How is it that after all these years you're finally looking at this? At the time, no one seemed to give a damn. As I remember it, they ruled it an accidental drowning." He paused for a long moment, dragging on his cigarette. "I had to deal with that asshole deputy. I know you ain't supposed to speak evil of the dead, but…." Ashford stopped and looked embarrassed. "Sorry, Sheriff."

"It's okay. And to answer your question, in the course of another investigation, this case came up, and we decided to take another look."

"It's about time. Poor kid." He let his last comment hang for a moment, then said, "Let's get going." Ashton took a final drag on his cigarette and flipped it into a water-filled ditch. "We should just go in my truck. The frost is coming out of the ground and there're some big muck holes along the way. Those things won't make it," he said pointing at their vehicles.

Sue climbed in the passenger side of the truck and Ray passed Simone to her before pulling himself up, aided by a step and a handle—both coarsely fabricated from rebar and crudely welded to the side of the vehicle. The interior—old and battered—smelled of tobacco and gasoline. A faded car deodorizer hung from the mirror. Ashton turned the key and the engine sputtered to life. He revved the engine several times, let it drop back to idle, engaged the four-wheel drive, shifted into gear, and started up the access drive, bouncing through low spots, throwing water and mud. Ray, now holding onto Simone, smiled. He hadn't been in a truck like this since high school.

Eventually, Ashton made a sharp right turn and reversed toward an opening in the trees that ended at the shoreline of Lost Lake. Ray helped drag the boat off the truck to the water's edge and stood by as Ashton attached a small outboard.

They crossed the lake, Simone standing at the bow, Ashton at the stern, Ray and Sue in the middle. Running the front of the boat onto the beach, Ashton raised the outboard, and he and Ray pulled the boat halfway onto the beach. They followed a wide trail, marked on each side by a line of half-buried fieldstones.

"I used to put fresh woodchips on all these walkways every spring. Haven't done it in years. No one has used the place in years except me and Carol," said Ashton.

"How long has it been exactly since anyone from the family has been here?" Sue asked.

"A long time, years. Back before my time they'd come up every summer season. That lasted 'til the 1970s, almost 100 years. Then the kids and grandkids started to build vacation homes in other places: Maine, the Outer Banks, California. Over the years they just seemed to get richer, don't ask me how. Sometimes other folks, the extended family, would use the place, but the last few years, no one. I suppose it's old, doesn't have the stuff people expect these days. Plus it's all going to hell. Back in the day, I'd submit a list of things that needed to done, give an estimated cost, and the money would come. I still send the lists, but nothing's been funded for five years or more." Their march along the path suddenly opened to the view of an imposing log structure. Ashton led them to the enormous front door that was standing slightly ajar.

"Someone's kicked in the door again," Ashton mumbled. "When I checked the place two weeks ago, everything was okay."

"This has happened before?" asked Ray.

"Not in the old days. But seems like every other winter the last years. ATVs and snowmobiles make it easy to get in here."

"Have you been reporting the break-ins?" asked Ray.

"I did the first few times, that's before you were sheriff." Ashton shrugged. "They weren't much interested. I took out most everything worth stealing, got it in storage in Traverse." They followed Ashton into the gloomy interior—the small, widely spaced windows were partially covered by thick maroon curtains. "Just hope I don't have a big mess to clean up."

"Would you switch on the lights?" asked Ray.

Ashton chuckled, pulled a small flashlight from his pocket, and turned it on. "This is it, Sheriff. If you want the overheads, I'll have to start the generator. Since it hasn't been run since last fall, it'll take a little doing."

Ray and Sue followed Ashton on a walkthrough of the main lodge, Sue carrying Simone. There was little evidence that anything had changed over many generations—chintz-covered furniture, worn oriental rugs, shelves lined with faded books. Two snowshoes, bent ash with leather decks, hung above a large stone fireplace. A half-dozen antique duck decoys sat on the dark mantle. The air was damp and heavy and smelled of mildew.

"Usually I find the remains of a party, probably teenagers," Ashton remarked as they moved from room to room. "You know, beer cans and cigarette butts, things tumbled over. I don't know, though. Nothing out of place this time. Maybe they were just looking the property over. A prospective buyer." Ashton laughed at his own joke. "Hell, it's not my problem anymore."

"So what else is here?" asked Ray as they exited the lodge through a back door.

"There are four extra cabins left over from the days the Hollingsfords had lots of company. Over there is the staff quarters. In the early days, they used to bring some of their maids and cooks from Chicago, and they also hired lots of locals. That's before my time; my father told me about it." Ashton lit a cigarette and surveyed the property slowly, like for the last time. "Just behind the lodge is the main kitchen," he said pointing. "There's a bathhouse on the hill below the water tank. The main house wasn't plumbed at the time it was built. They added two bathrooms later. You can see them," he said, turning back toward the lodge. "That addition with the shed roof. Everything is gravity feed. And there's a big old wood-fired water heater up there, too."

"They never ran electricity in?"

"Nope. The older folks wanted to keep things the way they remembered them."

"So where did you find Terry Hallen's body?"

"Along the Lake Michigan beach."

"Could you show us the exact place?" asked Ray. "I checked a map for this area, and it looks like more than a mile of shoreline is part of this parcel."

"Yes, I think it's like a mile and change. Let's go out to the beach, and I'll show you the exact spot."

They followed Ashton up a winding trail through a rolling hardwood forest, a low swampy area, and finally over the top of a series of dunes to the shore. Simone tugged on her lead when the water came in sight.

They all stood for a long moment in silence, enjoying the warmth of the afternoon sun and looking out at the lake.

"We need to head south a bit," Ashton said, trudging forward. Ray and Sue followed until he stopped on a promontory of dune grass. "It would be somewhere near here. It happened during that period when the lake was real high for four or five years." He waved his arm along the coast, then he pointed with a long, bony finger at a stand of small, wind-bent trees. "Most of the beach was gone here. The water had eaten away the sand right up to the roots of those cedars."

"And the body?" asked Ray.

"It was along here. Not at the water's edge, more thrown up on the top. We had some big storms and the waves did break up on the shore. I guess it's possible, but it seemed a little unnatural."

"I know it was a long while ago, but can you talk about finding the body? What do you remember?"

Ashton scanned the area, his deep-set eyes slowly moving from right to left, then back again. "It was a day like today, much later in the spring, but about the same temperature. I had worked all morning and came over here with a sandwich and beer about noon. It was one of those spring days where you're just filled with joy. You know, sunshine and warm air. The lake was like glass, not a ripple.

"I sat for a while and ate, then I thought I'd walk down the beach a bit. I could see something white from a long way off. I didn't think anything much about it till I got close. Just sort of curious. At first I thought it was the body of an animal, being partially covered with sand and all. It took me a while to be sure what I was seeing. He was a skinny kid, a boy, maybe 120 pounds.

"I went back as fast as I could. I had one of the pontoon boats by that time, and I crossed Lost Lake and went to that house on the road where you parked. I called the sheriff. He sent a deputy, that Lowther guy, and an ambulance showed up, too. Lowther acted like he was really pissed about having to get in a boat and then walk out here. Maybe he was worried about his spit-polished boots.

"So he looked around, made a few notes, had the guys bag the body. Later on, on the news, I saw that they'd called it an accidental drowning. I don't know how they came up with that. Didn't get the sense that there was ever an investigation or anything."

"What's wrong with an accidental drowning?"

"Something wasn't right about it. I mean, the lake was still real cold. They said he must have been skinny-dipping and drowned, then the body drifted up here. But I don't think so. I don't know about these things, but I don't think he'd been in the water long enough to be a floater. And I never heard that they found his clothes, not here or wherever he was from."

"What was the condition of the body? Do you remember?"

"Sure. It was white, sorta waxy looking. It wasn't really rotting or anything. And the animals hadn't gotten to it yet, not the crows or the gulls. I think it was pretty fresh."

The three of them stood for a long time in silence.

"Anything else?" Ashton asked finally.

"Not for me," said Ray. "Sue?"

"No. Thank you, Perry. That was helpful."

"Good. I better get you back to your cars. I've got to start collecting my tools and stuff and packing out."

"Before we leave," said Ray, "I've heard the Hollingsfords had a family burial plot."

"Yes, it's just over that dune. Do you want to have a look?"

"Yes, if you have time."

"Yep, I'll make it, follow me."

"I've got your order from Zingerman's in a cooler," said Sue after Perry Ashton dropped them off. "I'm surprised you didn't ask about it immediately."

"I didn't have to. I have great confidence in your successful completion of every mission."

"And you owe me about a gazillion dollars," she said, fishing a receipt from an interior pocket.

"Not so bad," he said, scanning it. "Life's pleasures come with a cost."

"So what did we learn?" she asked.

Ray looked at his watch. "I need to think about it. Let's get together tomorrow morning around 10," he said, passing Simone into Sue's arms. "We'll see if we can make any connections."

26

Just before the economic collapse, a downstate developer purchased a large track of cherry and apple orchards on the ridgeline north of Cedar Bay and spent a few million dollars reshaping the landscape to develop 15 luxury home sites. At the entrance road stood two large fieldstone columns and a faux gatehouse. A large billboard announced, "Build your dream house in Bay Ridge Estates, a detached luxury condominium community with views of your personal piece of paradise." A crisp, white sticker reading "Now Bank Owned" in bold red letters had been added across the bottom of the sign.

Mackenzie drove slowly up the hill and inspected the vacant building sites. There were five cul-de-sacs in the subdivision, each connected by an access road that ran at the top of the development. Mackenzie passed the first four roads, turning into the fifth, and pulled onto a short paved spur intended to be the beginning of a drive.

She had been up here once before, briefly, and knew where she could get the best view of Richard Sabotny's house. This time she came with a camera, one equipped with a telephoto lens. Peering through the viewfinder, she first located Sabotny's house, then focused on the vehicle sitting beyond the open garage door. She took several shots of the rear of a Range Rover, then turned her attention to the second car, a Lexus.

After checking the quality of the photos, she returned the camera to the bag. Just as she switched her car back into drive, she noticed the brake lights and then the backup lights of the Range Rover. The vehicle reversed into a turnaround, then headed out the long drive to the highway, pausing briefly as the steel gates at the end slowly swung open. Mackenzie grabbed her camera a second time, but it was too late; the vehicle was almost out of view, heading south.

Mackenzie accelerated onto the access road as she drove toward the highway. Her pursuit of the Range Rover momentarily stalled as she waited to turn right. Two slow-moving gravel trucks, followed by a school bus, crept by.

After the bus turned onto a side road, Mackenzie continued through the village behind the gravel trucks. The reduced speed allowed her to survey the sides of the highway and the adjoining village streets for the large, pearl-white English SUV.

She spotted it a quarter of a mile south, just as the trucks ahead of her started to accelerate. It was parked under the canopy of a local bank, next to the drive-in window at the near end of the parking lot that served the Bay Side Family Market, a small number of shops, and a medical clinic. Mackenzie parked near the market where she had a clear view of the bank. She was tempted to reach for her camera, but hesitated, unsure that the smoked glass of her Subaru would totally conceal her in the brilliant sunlight.

After a few minutes, Sabotny drove away from the bank and pulled into a space near The Espresso Shot. As Mackenzie watched, the doors on each side of the vehicle swung open. A short, petite woman with dark red hair—a color Mackenzie remembered noticing on so many women in Paris—stepped lightly from the vehicle, then turned and waited, one hand on her hip, for Sabotny to join her. Together, they walked into the coffee shop.

Elena Rustova thought Mackenzie. She pulled her laptop from under the camera bag, opened it, and punched in the security code. A search for *Rustova* brought her to an open document, her name highlighted in green.

Elena Rustova, b. 1980 Chisinau, Moldova. Ethnically Russian. Educated in public schools, undergraduate degree State University of Moldova. Religion unknown. Linguist and translator. Believed fluent in English, Romanian, Russian, French, Arabic, and Urdu. Ranked martial artist in college. Employment history: assignments with European and American companies in Africa, Asia, the former Soviet Republics, Iraq, and Pakistan. No known criminal activity.

Mackenzie suddenly felt a need to see Sabotny up close. She was sure he wouldn't be able to ID her, dressed as she was in baggy faded jeans, a worn pair of L.L. Bean duck shoes, a shapeless jacket, a floppy knit hat that hid her hair, and large, dark sunglasses. Ken Lee had suggested the outfit would give her a local look without attracting attention.

Backing up and driving around to the side of a dental office, she found a location out of sight of the coffee house. Just in case, she wanted no connection between her person and her vehicle. Then she walked back on a route parallel to the front of the building so her approach couldn't be seen from the interior of the shop.

A brass bell at the top of the door announced her entrance. Mackenzie marched toward the counter and scanned the interior without removing her sunglasses. Sabotny and Rustova were at a small table in a corner at the back. Sabotny was positioned in a way that provided a clear view of the entire interior.

She studied the overhead menu as the barista prepared a latté for a large man in Carhartts. When he picked up his drink and moved away from the counter, she ordered a medium cappuccino. She fidgeted as the barista left her alone to prepare the drink. It felt like Sabotny was focused on her, his eyes burning into her back. Coffee in hand, she headed quickly for the door, not looking in Sabotny's direction. Outside, she wanted to run to the safety of her car, but did her best to maintain a normal gait, looking back only once to ensure that she wasn't being followed.

Back in her car, doors locked, the engine at idle, Mackenzie was surprised at the alarm she felt from the encounter. She put down her coffee and went through a series of breathing exercises trying to calm down. *There is no way he could have recognized me,* Mackenzie said out loud, trying to put her rational side back in control. *He's just one of those men who scopes out every woman he encounters.*

Determined not to be beaten, she drove once again through the parking lot and pulled into a position where she could view the Range Rover from a distance. A few minutes later Sabotny and Elena emerged and walked hand in hand toward the Bayside Family Market. Again, Mackenzie was tempted to follow, but talked herself out of it. What could be the value trailing them through a grocery store? Instead, she took a couple of photos of the front of the Range Rover.

Eventually the couple reappeared, each carrying a brown paper bag. As soon as the doors of their vehicle closed, she put her engine in gear and was soon one car behind them at a stop sign. Sabotny turned north. Mackenzie fell in behind him, now separated by two cars. She followed him back through the village, three cars between them, and eventually passed him as he pulled into his driveway. Mackenzie continued on for a mile, then turned around in a motel parking lot. The steel gates at the entrance to Sabotny's compound were closed when she passed.

At home, Mackenzie moved the photos to her computer and e-mailed them to Ken Lee Park. A few minutes later, Ken Lee was on the phone. He told her that he could identify both vehicles, and in the next day or two he would send her information on where to place the GPS transmitters.

"How did you get the photos?" he asked.

"There's an empty sub on a ridgeline north of his property. I had an excellent view of his compound, and fortunately his garage door was open."

"That wide-angle shot of the whole area, it looks as if he's taken some serious security measures."

"I'll say—tall fence, gated entrance. I'm sure he's got cameras and motion detectors everywhere. You don't see that up here. This isn't Brentwood, it's northern Michigan. And he's not in some remote spot. His place is on the highway, just a mile or so from the village. I'm sure he's attracting lots of unwanted attention by his over-the-top security setup. It just leaps out at you when you drive by."

"Good. Being noticed probably doesn't help his cause, whatever that is."

"How do I install the tracking device?"

"It's easily done. That vehicle has lots of plastic on both ends. You just need to slide it in behind some plastic. The magnets on the unit will hold it securely to any metal surface. I'll try it out on similar models and send you diagrams of good places."

"And how am I suppose to do this undetected?"

"You'll have to find a time when the vehicles are parked and unattended. Probably takes less than 10 seconds to get a device in place. Wasn't your last picture from a parking lot?"

"Yes, I followed him this morning. He went to a local coffee shop with Rustova, then did some shopping." Mackenzie didn't mention following Sabotny into the coffee shop or the panic she'd felt.

"You're going to have to keep him under surveillance, see if there is a pattern to his activities. The last picture—is that a strip mall?"

"More than a strip mall. There's a grocery, a bank, some offices, and the coffee shop."

"That's a good place to start. How often do they go for coffee? Is there a movie theater in town? Do they market every day? You just need a chance to get next to his vehicle for a few seconds." He paused. "Are you okay with this?"

Mackenzie's answer was slow in coming. "I think so."

"Here's something, then: I'm curious about the fact that you've put all your attention on Richard Sabotny. You told me there were three or four others involved."

"He was always the biggest bully in the group. I think the other guys were just following along. Plus, from what we've learned, their lives are unremarkable, where Sabotny's activities seem quite nefarious."

There was a long silence at the other end of the line. Then Ken Lee said, "Mackenzie, you're working with a memory of something that happened more than 20 years ago. What if you're wrong about Sabotny?"

After a long silence, she responded, "Okay, I'll give the others a look. But it means I'll have to shift my focus. It will take more time, and it's probably wasted time."

"This is your thing. I'm just trying to help. Listen, I'll send you the diagram later today. And I'm going to FedEx you a unit for your own vehicle, so I can keep tabs on you, too. Oh, and one more thing, what's the name of the bank, the one Sabotny stopped at?"

"Northwoods Bank and Trust, why?"

"I might want to look at Sabotny's accounts."

"Don't do anything that you can get caught at."

She could hear Ken Lee chuckling as he rang off.

27

Sue released Simone from her grip and set a large insulated cup on the conference table. "Did you eat your way through the Zingerman's box last night?" she asked.

Ray looked up from his computer and smiled. "That wonderful bread and perfect piece of Stilton got me through a no-cook dinner. The rest went in the fridge or freezer. I'll have to organize a dinner party to share the bounty with friends. Thank you for going through the hassle of working through my rather extensive list." Simone begged to be picked up, and Ray pulled her into his lap briefly before returning her to the floor and getting up himself to move to the conference table. Simone, used to the routine, headed for the overstuffed chair in the far corner of the office and her morning nap.

"Glad I could do it. Where should we start?" Sue asked.

"Vincent Fox. Let's go back over what we have so far."

"I read the preliminary autopsy report last night."

"I thought we were going to try to have a life away from the office?"

"I was going through my e-mail. There it was. How could I not read it? Thank you for the summary and for disambiguating the medical jargon. The whole thing sort of creeped me out—the stun gun, the burning of his foot. What's going on here? Who are these people? What's this about?"

"We're back to motive," said Ray, pointing at his diagram. "We've been working with two possibilities. First, someone was after the money that Fox won at the casino—getting it from an old man would look like easy pickings. Second, a true believer in the Capone treasure story grabbed Fox with the idea of getting more exact information from him on the actual location of the stash."

"How about this just being a random…."

"There's always that possibility, but I don't think so." Ray pointed to his diagram. "We assume that Vincent Fox had $2,000 on his person or at his home. You didn't find any cash there or on his body, right?"

"Correct. The money might have been taken at the time of his abduction or stolen from his house."

"There are other possibilities. He might have hidden it so well that no one has found it, or he might have given it away the same way he did with the $4,000 to Tommy Fuller."

"Those two are a long reach," countered Sue.

"Yes, they are."

Sue scanned Ray's graphic. "You don't have Fox's computer listed."

Ray got up and added *computer* below the $2,000 cash. "Okay, so here's a possible scenario. A couple of the Capone true believers have been keeping track of Fox's movements. They grab him off the street or at his house. When he struggles, they use a stun gun. When they apply some torture, he dies. Later they grab the computer because it might contain information that would lead them to the treasure. The money was just an unexpected bonus."

"Our perps are on a continuum from being sadistic bastards to totally weird psychopaths."

"But is what we're seeing all there is? Could something else be going on here?" asked Ray.

"What are you suggesting?"

"We're running old scripts, things that have come up before. We're pushing the Fox murder into a familiar paradigm. It's not working. And then we have the Terry Hallen case. It's unlikely that we'll ever figure out what happened to him. Finally, perhaps coincidently, there's the ten grand that Ma French found in the cemetery." Ray sipped his coffee and asked, "So what did you think of the Hollingsford Estate and Perry Ashton?"

"I'm always surprised," she responded. "Like I think I know this area well, and then there's something like that place. Mind blowing. How many times have I rolled past that muddy road with no idea of what was hidden in those woods."

"I'd heard about it some over the years," said Ray. "It always seemed more mythical than real, but, yes, I was amazed, too."

"What do we know about Perry Ashton? Has he ever been on our radar?" asked Sue.

"I checked this morning. Nothing recent. There are two DUIs and speeding tickets. All years ago."

"So what we learned," said Sue, "expands and confirms what we already knew. Terry Hallen's naked body was found on the beach of the Hollingsford Estate. If he had indeed gone skinny dipping, the logical place for him to enter the water would have been closer to his home, 10 miles below where the body was found. As far as we know, his clothing was never recovered. Perry Ashton says the water was still very cold, and the victim appeared to be terribly thin. Those two things would delay the number of days it would take for him to become a floater. We're probably looking at 10 days to two weeks. Mrs. Schaffer's memory is that he was found a few days after he disappeared. We have no record of when he was reported missing or who identified the body. There's no way to date anything. There was no autopsy, just a certificate of death. No evidence of any investigation. The mother is deceased, as is the grandmother, and his siblings disappeared shortly after his death. To top it off, there's Perry Ashton's memory that the body was high up the beach, higher than it might have been carried by waves. Lots of unanswered questions. Lots. And I wonder what was going through Dirk Lowther's head."

"Dirk wasn't into heavy lifting," said Ray. "If Terry's people weren't moxie enough to challenge the finding, nothing more would have been done. So it was open and shut, accidental drowning. Case closed. Dirk had better things to spend his time on." Ray paused again and sipped his coffee, then pointed to the right side of the whiteboard. "What about Ma French and the $10,000."

"I need to tell you about that, the money. I e-mailed the serial numbers from those bills to an agent at the FBI—I met her at that financial fraud workshop I went to last year. She forwarded my inquiry to another agent who works on cases involving currency, you know, things like money laundering. The guy's name is Braeton Jackson. He could tell from the serial numbers that the bills were part of 12 billion in cash sent to Iraq right after the invasion to keep the provisional government running. He went on to explain that approximately eight billion of the 12 went missing. There was no chain of custody after the money was offloaded in Baghdad."

Ray's coffee mug had been hovering between the table and his mouth. He put it down as Sue continued. "Jackson says these bills have turned up all over the globe. He was curious how 100 crisp new C-notes suddenly turned up on a beach in northern Michigan after all the years they were out of circulation."

They sat in silence for a long moment, then Ray asked, "What do we know for sure?"

"We have two tire castings that might be from the perp's car."

"And they might be from the meter reader. Iraq. Eight billion. Who knew?"

"Even more amazing than a lost estate, huh. So what do we do now?"

"You know the answer as well as me. We sit tight, turn our attention to our usual duties, and wait until something else happens. Or we have a sudden flash of brilliance."

"Well, did you note that more root vegetables were reported stolen yesterday?" said Sue, smiling.

"Yes, carrots and potatoes," agreed Ray, sighing. "Same M.O. Theft from an unlocked building. The farmers are unsure of when the robbery took place. They don't go into the storage area more than once or twice a week during the winter, and they're unsure of the quantity. They don't keep a tight inventory. Assign this to Brett. He can work these into his road patrol duties. At some point, we should be able to figure this one out."

"Brett is just back from his first major crime workshop, and what do we drop in his lap? The case of missing celeriac."

"It's all the same kind of leg work, and it gets him out of his car and meeting people. How was Ann Arbor, by the way?"

"Ann Arbor is Ann Arbor. Saw a good movie, had some fantastic food, went to a jazz club." She smiled, thinking that the real answer was she ate too much, drank too much champagne, and spent most of the weekend in bed making love.

28

Mackenzie had followed Ken Lee's instructions carefully, and yes, there was a regular pattern. Mornings about 9 a.m., Sabotny and Rustova would leave their compound. After half an hour or so at The Espresso Shot, they would head for the Bayside Family Market, sometimes hand in hand like a loving couple, other times exhibiting some tension and distance. They would return about 20 minutes later with two or three paper bags, never plastic. Mackenzie speculated that they did European-style shopping, picking up what they needed for the day and not stocking a larder.

After several days of this, Mackenzie was ready to make her move. She positioned her car in an area of the parking lot used by the employees of the market, a far corner that afforded her a clear view of the entire area. From the moment they drove into the shopping area, she would have them in sight. Sipping on her own tall cappuccino, she watched them first enter the coffee shop and later head for the grocery store. She waited five minutes, then pulled into a parking place next to their vehicle. She'd rehearsed the placement of the GPS the evening before following Ken Lee's step-by-step diagrams.

Taking several long, deep breaths, she glanced around to ensure that no one was in a position to observe her actions. Then, with the engine still running, she pushed her door open. After a quick second scan of the area, she moved to the rear of the SUV, dropped her purse, then quickly knelt to pick it up. In the process she slid the transmitter into position at the rear of Sabotny's vehicle. Mackenzie slipped back inside her car, closed the door, and took one last look around before driving away.

That evening she and Ken Lee—2,500 miles apart—watched Sabotny's movements from their separate locations, using Google Earth to get street-level views of his travels. Sabotny stopped at three spots: an Outback Steakhouse, a multiplex cinema, and a bar just south of Cedar Bay.

In the course of their conversation, Ken Lee reminded her that she needed to look again at the other guys who were in Sabotny's company on the day of the attack. Her rational self knew that he was right, but her emotional self pushed back on the idea. The character she always saw in her nightmares was Richard Sabotny.

Before the conversation ended, Ken Lee mentioned that a friend in Florida had run the plates on the Range Rover and the Lexus. Both vehicles belonged to RS Investments, LTD, a company registered in Belize. "I had my friend do a little a more checking. RS Investments also has a couple of Visa debit cards and a merchant account at Belize Caribbean International Bank. That's probably how Sabotny is getting around U.S. currency and tax laws. He has total access to his fortune because these transactions are currently almost untraceable."

"How much is all this research costing me?" asked Mackenzie.

"Nothing. This was a *quid pro quo*. I'll let you know if and when the meter is running. By the way, did you put the GPS transmitter in your Subaru?"

"Yes, and if you stay up a few more hours, you can watch me go to a 7 a.m. yoga class in Traverse," she answered. "I'm taking a vacation day tomorrow. Living like a real person."

"Good idea. Have fun," he said. "I'll watch your travels with my morning tea."

Mackenzie woke at five, made coffee, and searched her almost barren cupboards and refrigerator for something appealing to eat. Her choices were one large brown egg, a navel orange, assorted energy bars, and some wilted celery. She opted for the egg and orange, tossing the celery in the garbage.

Lingering over her coffee, she used her iPad to check the web for times and locations and quickly came up with a schedule: yoga at 7 a.m., and a massage at nine to be confirmed by e-mail. She thought about having her nails done, maybe some shopping. She would ask the women in her yoga class to recommend places. She'd find a bookstore, too, and take time to browse—sheer luxury.

Several hours later, Mackenzie drove back north with new books on the passenger seat and bags of food and wine from the organic co-op filling the back hatch. The tension building for weeks had finally dissolved. Just doing a few routine things had pulled her away from the cloak and dagger world in which she had immersed herself.

A late season storm had rolled in the day before from the southwest, bringing a mixture of heavy rain, sleet, and snow, but this afternoon the drapes of her great room opened to a brilliant, sunlit landscape. The bay had only a modest chop and yesterday's snow had all but disappeared while she'd been in Traverse. Even the grass on the hillside above the shoreline was starting to show the first signs of green.

Mackenzie pivoted back and forth in her desk chair as she studied at the names on her computer screen. Ken Lee was right. She had focused on Richard Sabotny as the main perpetrator and let the other boys who were present that day slide into the background.

Restless, she pushed back from the desk and walked to the wall of glass. There was his house across the bay. She looked through her telescope, zooming in on the windows. In the bright daylight, her scope couldn't probe the interior, but she took some satisfaction in knowing that the mirrored glass on her windows provided a similar barrier to prying eyes.

Mackenzie returned to her computer and looked again at the file that contained the names and rather limited information she had been able to collect on the four boys, now grown men. Each entry included her personal memories of them.

Richard Sabotny, aka Rich. Leader of the group on the day of the assault. Known as the toughest kid in the school, even some of the teachers seemed to be afraid of him. Often involved in fistfights in the parking lot after school hours. Known for bullying people. According to Classmates bio, he was career military. Recently resettled in Cedar County. No hits on Google other than the Classmates piece. See more extensive note on Sabotny in Ken Lee file.

Zed Piontowski, aka Smokey, followed Richard Sabotny around, probably enjoying the status of being a buddy of the toughest kid in the school and also enjoying the protection that friendship probably afforded him.

Zed got on the bus several miles north of Sandville. He lived in an old trailer with a multitude of brothers and sisters from various fathers. His siblings had different last names.

At 15 or 16, he was short and rail thin. Like a small dog, Zed didn't have a sense of his size. He was ready to throw a punch at the least provocation. What he lacked in stature, he made up for with his loud, obscenity-filled speech. He always smelled foul—lack of bathing, soiled clothes redolent with the smell of wood heat, tobacco, and greasy food. His jeans and tattered shirts were soiled, the holes genuine, not fashion statements. Away from school, he always had a cigarette in his mouth.

Listed in online yearbook at Classmates, but *no photo available.* No current phone listing in Cedar County or the surrounding area for anyone with the last name of Piontowski. Ditto for Facebook and Twitter. One hit on Google from the Galveston Daily News for a Zed Piontowski: homeless man identified by a former girlfriend, her name not given. No age given. Death caused by drug overdose. Deceased found with needle stuck in his arm.

Zed was with the other boys the day of the attack. He was hanging back, watching. In a strange kind of way he was a friend of Terry's. Maybe it was a bond of poverty.

Jim Moarse, medium height, lanky, sandy hair, uneven home-cut look, bad teeth, empty gray eyes. He was in the special ed. class with the kids who had emotional problems. Known for uncontrolled rage, getting suspended from school, and problems with the sheriff.

Liked breaking windows. I remember him dancing on the glass that had been popped out of a classroom door, grinding the shattered pieces into finer shards with his heavy black construction boots, the steel heel-plates pounding the bits against the terrazzo surface.

Major player in the assault, roughly grabbing my breasts after Sabotny tore my shirt open. Moarse said something about my having a tight ass. Sabotny said it wouldn't be tight when he got through with me. Everyone else would have to settle for seconds.

Local address available online. No phone listing. Arrests for domestic violence, DUI, and assault listed in local paper archives.

Chris Brewler, medium height and stocky. Brown hair, chipped teeth in lower jaw, scar across his forehead that separated his right eyebrow. His nose was off center, pushed over to the left at midpoint. The facial injuries sustained in a motorcycle accident. Chris also sported several tattoos—crudely done artwork and lettering. He bragged that his uncle had learned to do tats while in Jackson.

Chris was in Terry's graduation class, but he was older, held back once or twice. He had been in several of my classes, usually a disruptive element on the infrequent occasions he showed up for school. He was on our bus route. Always talking about sex, hitting on girls in the crudest terms. More than once he said to me, "My uncle says your mother is the best piece of ass in the county. Bet you're a chip off the old block."

The day of the assault he was cheering Sabotny on. Made an attempt to pull off my jeans before Terry fought them off, giving me a chance to escape.

No local or regional phone number. No listing in Classmates, Facebook, Twitter. No hits on Google. No listing for anyone in the region with the last name of Brewler.

Mackenzie opened a new file and keyed a title at the top of the document: **What Happened at the River:**

It was a spring day, one of the first warm days. Terry and I had ridden our bikes down to the river a few miles east of Sandville. We had taken some lines and hooks. Terry collected some crawlers and crickets near the river, and was showing me how to hand cast, how to toss the lead weight and baited hook into the stream without getting entangled with the hook.

She stopped suddenly, pulled her hands from the keyboard. *I need to see the place again,* she thought. *I need to go there, shoot pictures, and record everything that I remember, then come back and write it down.*

29

Mackenzie dressed in her bird-watching costume: baggy jeans, hiking boots, a flannel shirt, and Carhartt vest. She strapped a holster to her left ankle, slipped the Rohrbaugh R9 in place, pulled her hair under a stocking cap, and slipped a pair of compact binoculars into her vest pocket—something she would later drape around her neck as part of the costume. She also packed a notepad and a small camera, nothing expensive looking, nothing that would attract attention.

Reviewing the area on Google Earth, Mackenzie considered the probable route from Sandville to the part of the river where she and Terry had confronted Sabotny and the other boys. Her memory was that just north of the village they had biked down two-tracks and the bed of a deserted railroad. Then they got back on a two-track again. She scanned the area on her computer display, trying to determine the possible site.

There was an old bridge built from timbers just wide enough for a car that she remembered too—no side rails, just a deck. Upstream from the bridge was a low dam with a spillway in the middle and a pool behind it.

Twenty years before, she and Terry had been fishing below the dam, letting their bait swirl in the eddies at the side of the stream. But looking at the map, she couldn't see a widening in the stream or anything that looked like a dam. She found what she thought was the bridge and the road that ran across it. It now appeared to be more than the trail of her memory, still dirt, but wider. The bridge also looked more substantial.

She scaled back the map until Sandville was in the lower right corner and plotted distances and directions in her head. When she got to Sandville, she would use the map function on her iPhone if she needed any assistance finding the location.

She was surprised by how quickly she found the place, even though her estimates of distance and time were way off. The big curve on the river was only about two miles north of the village. She remembered it as being much farther—a long slog or a hot dusty bike ride. Parking in a small lot at the side of the dirt road, she walked out onto the bridge. It was a new structure two lanes wide with steel rails bolted to concrete pillars. Looking upriver, Mackenzie searched in vain for the dam, but nothing remained of the structure or the wide pond. Crossing to the south side of the bridge, she peered down at the stream, much narrower and shallower than she remembered it. The only sound was the wind and the gurgling of the river as it snaked around and disappeared in the low shrubs on the flood plain. There were no humans or their machines. She snapped several pictures.

Returning to her car, Mackenzie noticed a trail running from the parking lot toward the stream. She followed it, concrete at the beginning, turning to sand as it wound through the brush and small trees near the water's edge. Small patches of grass bordering the track were beginning to shed winter's hues, green replacing brown. The willow buds, turgid with new growth, were on the edge of opening and the reeds in the wetlands approaching the water were taking on a summer's green.

A small wooden dock was secured at the trail's end, a launching point for canoes and kayaks. She stood on the platform and slowly surveyed the scene, looking upstream first, and then following the flow of rushing water to the south. She focused on sound—the gentle gurgle of the water dominating the wind moving through leafless trees. The air was heavy with decay. The leaves and dead plants emerging from winter's cover were beginning to degrade under the hot sun, making way for a new season's growth.

She gazed at the pallet of hues of the early spring landscape, earth tones mostly, a range of browns and dull greens. The water, lit at an acute angle by the early spring sun, was stained by the decaying oak leaves to the shade of weak coffee. Scanning the trees and bushes, Mackenzie could find no birds flittering about, no chirping, no cries of alarm or passion.

She thought briefly about how silly her bird watching costume would look in this location to anyone who knew about such things. *So much for disguises.*

She scanned the air and water. Insect life seemed to be limited to a few water striders, their long legs floating on the smooth surface of the slow-moving eddies at the edge of the stream. In her memory the air was always filled with mosquitoes. She knew they would quickly emerge in the sudden surge of warm air. She took several more stills, and then switched to movie mode, sweeping from right to left.

Mackenzie slowly swept the scene a final time, her eyes taking it all in, recording the images, meshing this moment with the old memory, resizing and revising her knowledge of the area. Then she retreated up the path, awash with emotions, lost in the past. She was standing next to her car, still deep in thought, keys in her hand, when she was startled by the roar of an engine. A rusty Jeep came rolling down the sandy road, slowing and turning in to park. Four boys climbed out, dressed in cutoffs and t-shirts, one in flip-flops, the others sockless in battered running shoes. Each boy held a blue and red beer can. They all seemed focused on her, not in a menacing way, just as something out of place in an environment with which they were familiar.

"Hi, guys," she said. "How about this weather?"

"Amazing," said the tallest of the group. "Should still be winter."

"Well, enjoy," she laughed, sliding into her car, hitting the door lock as she engaged the starter. But she didn't leave. She sat for a while after the boys had disappeared down the path. Then, on her way back toward Sandville, it hit her. It all came rushing back. The sound of the engine, the smell of cigarettes and beer. She pulled to the side of the road, shaken. A Jeep, rusty, with oversized tires. She and Terry had seen it cross the bridge. And a few minutes later, Sabotny and the others were upon them, surrounding her. Terry had grabbed a piece of wood and used it as a club, allowing her to break free and run.

Yes, the Jeep explained so many things. Terry's body didn't get dumped. He was hauled up to where his body was found. A Jeep with big tires could have gone miles on the beach early in the season with little or no notice, especially back then. The question was, did they kill Terry, or just leave him on the beach to die of injuries and exposure?

30

Ray's brain was somewhere else when his iPhone emitted a text message tone.

Ray—need to kayak. H.

He looked out the window at the brilliant sunlight, noting the trees swaying in the wind. He went to the NOAA website to check conditions. Record high temperature for the date, 81 degrees, winds 15 to 25, gusts to 35. Waves 4 to 7 feet. Water temp. 40 degrees.

Conditions on big lake marginal. Suggest quiet water or a walk on beach. R.

Want to do big lake. Can we meet at ur place in 45? H.

Will do my best. R.

Ray's rough water kayak, a boat with lots of rocker built into the hull, was already strapped to the roof of Hannah's car beside her own boat. Dressed in a fleece jumpsuit, she was leaning against her car talking on her cell. Ray thought she looked tense, perhaps even angry. He heard her finish the conversation as he approached.

"How are you?"

"I'll be better when we are on the water. Get changed," she demanded, her manner not lightening.

A few minutes later they were rolling toward the big lake. Ray glanced over at the speedometer. "I can't get you off if you're pulled over."

She looked over at him briefly, then back at the road. Ray felt the car decelerate.

"Worried about your boat or your reputation?" she growled.

"The kayak," he responded. "That was a special order. It would take months to get a replacement."

She smiled weakly. "You're one of the few people I know with their priorities straight."

"What's going on?" he asked, sensing the softening.

"Paddle first," she said. "Talk later."

"Are you sure you want to go out in this?" Ray asked as they stood and looked at the tempest—foam and spray blowing off the crests of the breaking waves.

"Yes," she yelled back, protecting her eyes with her left hand from the blast of sand being carried along the shore from the southwesterly winds.

At the car they pulled on dry suits and spray skirts. Then they belted on towropes, and clipped and tightened their PFDs. Finally, they strapped on helmets and returned to their boats, securing back-up paddles under the bungee straps on the front decks.

"Do you want me to help you launch?" he asked.

"I can do it myself."

They stood for another few minutes and observed the wave sets, before dragging their kayaks forward. Then they waited for a lull before quickly dropping in their boats and attaching the spray skirts. Ray was looking at Hannah when a massive wave pushed up on the beach, broaching and flipping her boat. He could see that she had been knocked onto her back deck, the boat now on top of her in the water and sand. He pulled the release strap on his skirt, but before he could get out, her boat was over and she was positioning it again to launch into the surf.

Ray reattached his spray skirt, waited for the next large wave to float his hull, and fought his way into the surf zone, positioning his bow perpendicular to the breakers. At times, he had to separate the surges crashing over his boat with his broad paddle to keep from getting hammered in the chest.

Using almost vertical paddle strokes, he slogged forward, trying to get to the deeper water beyond the breaking waves, the boat rising up and crashing through the marching walls of water. As he neared the top of a large swell, it began to break, standing his boat vertically, then toppling it as the stern slipped violently backward, the end catching on the bottom as the full weight and force of the wave crashed into him.

Upside down in the swirling water, he attempted to roll, only to get hit halfway up by the next breaker. Submerged again in the sudden darkness and quiet, he reached for the release strap on his spray skirt and tumbled out. Catching the bow toggle with his left hand, he allowed the waves to carry him toward shallow water. When his feet touched the bottom, he walked toward shore, keeping the lake at his back and the boat to his front. He emptied the boat—now filled with water and weighing hundreds of pounds—on shore.

Then it was back out into the torrent, joining Hannah beyond the surf zone. Bracing on breaking waves, surfing toward shore, turning and paddling out into the safety zone for a respite, then searching for the next ride. Ray got capsized again, rolling up successfully. He saw Hannah get trashed two or three times, her finessed rolls bringing her back into paddling position within seconds.

Eventually, as they bobbed out beyond the surf, Hannah pointed toward the beach and paddled forward to catch a wave. Ray watched her progress and successful landing, and then followed her. He scrambled out of his kayak before he was broached and dragged it out of the water, falling to the sand next to Hannah.

"It's starting to drop," he said, after several minutes.

"I know. We got the best of it. You got tumbled."

"Too shallow. Face in the sand. Couldn't roll."

After a while, Ray stood, grasped Hannah's outstretched hand and pulled her to her feet.

They returned to Ray's house in silence, both physically exhausted and Hannah not ready to talk. When Hannah emerged from the bedroom, dressed in fleece pants and top, her hair still wet from the shower, Ray was standing in the kitchen, opening and laying out his stash from Zingerman's—farmhouse cheeses, bread, olive oil for dipping, and some Italian salami. She slipped into his arms, and he pulled her tight. After a long embrace, he could feel her begin to sob, gently at first, then violently for many minutes before beginning to regain control. Reaching past Ray, she grabbed a piece of paper towel, drying her eyes and blowing her nose, then slipped back into his arms.

"What's going on?"

"Everything," said Hannah. "This morning I was seeing patients when I was paged to the ER. Gunshot victim, a young woman six or seven months pregnant. She was flat-lining. Rolled her to surgery, opened her chest." She pulled back from Ray and held out her hands. "Look at these: small, delicate, and very skilled. How many miracles they've given me." She paused and inhaled deeply. "No miracle today. Too much damage to repair. I went to find the husband. He was in the ER too, a young deputy in the room guarding him, a nurse monitoring his vitals. The guy was comatose, drugs and alcohol. The deputy gave me the scenario. They were staying with the shooter's mother. The husband had just been released from a downstate hospital, PTSD, two tours in Iraq, one in Afghanistan. Suicidal. He had OD'd on his meds, drunk a bottle of bourbon, and was trying to kill himself with a pistol his mother kept around for self-defense. He and his wife struggled for the weapon. She caught the bullet.

"I left the ER, walked outside. People were on lunch or breaks, celebrating the sunshine and the warm weather. Then a helicopter landed. It all came rushing back. The slap of the blades, the screaming jet engine, the blood, the carnage. I fell to my knees, people rushing to help me. Walking me back inside.

"All I wanted to do was get a bottle of Scotch and obliterate everything. That's what I did in Baghdad; that's what I did here." She paused briefly. "I called my therapist in Boston. Probably talked to her for an hour. She walked me back. But Ray, I'm like that guy in the ER. I'm damaged goods. I'll always be an outsider. I don't think I can find a normal life. I listen to my colleagues talk about new houses, or daycare, or vacations. Just the usual, nothing wrong with it, but it's not my world. I wanted to yell and scream about a world I couldn't change. Then I texted you."

"And now?"

"Better, at least for the moment. I'm like an epileptic after a seizure. Exhausted. Can I have a glass of wine?"

"You're asking for alcohol."

"A glass of wine, maybe two. Nothing more. Just some wine, food, music. Being here with you. Being quiet, maybe a walk later. Can I spend the night? I don't mean to make you my minder, but this is what I need. I trust you. I think you are a survivor, too."

"Let's have some food," said Ray. "Then a walk before it gets too dark."

31

Mackenzie boiled some water and poured it over a tea bag in a large earthenware mug. She leaned against the counter, allowing the tea to steep, then added some honey, stirring, tasting, and adding more honey. Setting the mug in easy reach, she settled at her keyboard, sliding the memory card from the camera into a port on the computer. One by one, she looked at the still images on the large display, at times her fingers sliding across the track pad to manipulate and enlarge parts of an image for closer inspection. She moved to the video, turning up the volume to get the sound of the wind and water. She replayed the video several times, switching to full-screen, then returned to still images, slowly scrutinizing each one a final time, the tea growing tepid as she absorbed every detail.

This was the place, she said in a soft voice. She sat for a while considering her next move. Putting the images into a string of e-mails with short descriptions, she sent them to Ken Lee. On the subject lines she keyed, "Where it happened."

"I thought you were on vacation yesterday," were Ken Lee's first words when he called Mackenzie a minute or two later.

"I was, but once I got home and put the food away...." She stopped and reflected on what had happened to her planned holiday.

"Are you still there?" he asked after an unusually long silence.

"Sorry."

"That's okay. I'm growing used to your considered responses."

"What was your question again?" Mackenzie asked,

"The vacation day, the holiday…?"

"Yes. I did all the things I told you I was going to do. Went to yoga. Nice studio. Good instructor. All women in the class, not one guy, not even a geezer. Not like California. And the women were exceedingly helpful. If I lived up here, these are people I'd like to know. I got a massage, strong woman, good hands. I went shopping. And I found a terrific local bookstore with an espresso bar. The day was so ordinary, I was filled with joy. When I got home I thought I'd eat some good food, drink some wine. But…."

"What?"

"I was right back in it, trying to figure this thing out. What was I thinking when I came here with no real plan? You're right, what you said the other day. I was totally fixated on Sabotny. He was the ringleader. It wouldn't have happened if he hadn't been there. None of it."

"Slow down, slow down. You've lost me. You've just given me two things. One has to do with a plan, the other with Sabotny."

"There is no plan. I mean, somehow I thought I could just come out here…."

"You did have a plan of sorts. You established that Sabotny was back in Cedar County. You found a house that would give you a view of his. You have been collecting data on his habits. You even had a chance to see him in operation, albeit accidentally. What you are trying to accomplish takes time."

"But what am I trying to accomplish? I started this thinking that Sabotny was Terry's killer, but how can I prove that, and what I would do with the information if I could find some truth…."

"Okay, let's slow down. I've watched you in action professionally over several years. You are an enormously effective leader. Why? Because you think strategically. You find the right people, you tap into all the necessary resources, and you plan for every possible contingency. I won't tell you that you are a risk taker. You're not. You minimize your risks so you can maximize your chances for success. And it has worked out for you.

"But this current pursuit of yours, it doesn't fit the paradigm. There is so much unknown and mostly unknowable. You think this Sabotny character was responsible for your brother's death, but you don't know that for sure. Sabotny, with or without the help of the other boys, might have killed your brother. But Terry's death might also have been an accident."

"Like how?"

"I don't know. Maybe in the course of the fight that allowed you to escape, he fell and hit his head. Another possibility—you said he had something like a branch or board that he was swinging—is that he lost control of it and it was used against him. Maybe someone hit him, not intending to kill him, but did. It happens a lot, especially with teenagers. They don't anticipate the possible consequences of their actions. Or what if he had something like a congenital heart…."

"So where are you going with this?" pressed Mackenzie.

"Stay with me for a few minutes. Let's say Terry died, either as the result of something he did or something that was done to him. They've got to get rid of the body. Easiest thing is to make it look like a drowning."

"If it was an accident, why wouldn't you go to the police?" she protested.

"Look, what you told me about these guys suggests they weren't members of the honor society. They were drinking beer, smoking dope, and looking to gang rape the victim's little sister. They're not going to go the police. They're going to stage a drowning, an accident, something that doesn't involve them."

"But any kind of investigation would have disproved…."

"Was there an investigation? Did you hear of any inquiries?"

Mackenzie was silent, trying to remember what her mother told her. "He was gone more than a day before my mother called the sheriff. Later a deputy came around to see her, someone she knew from the tavern. He said Terry's body had been found on a Lake Michigan beach. Terry had apparently drowned while skinny-dipping. Probably became hypothermic."

"And you told your mother what had happened, the fight, that you were almost gang raped?"

"I told her everything. I was hysterical. I never knew if she was listening. She was usually stoned or drunk or both. She said that Terry was dead. Nothing would change that. So there was no use making trouble. She said if the police got too interested in us, most likely they'd come and take us away from her and put us in foster homes. I didn't understand the police or social services. And, of course, they should have taken us away from her. But, again, what does this have to do with anything? What's your point?"

"Simply that you don't know how Terry died. You don't know who, if anyone, is responsible. And even if you could establish guilt, what could you do about it? Could you go to the law? Would there be enough information for a prosecution? Or would you simply blow him away?"

For a long time, Mackenzie looked at an image of the Sandville Creek, winding out of sight on the screen. Ken Lee let her think. "So what do I do next?" she said finally.

"First, a reality check. You don't know where this is all going to lead. You can't develop a Gantt chart, or create timelines, or do any of the other things you're used to doing to move a project. Face it. It's highly unlikely that you will ever find the circumstances leading to Terry's death."

"What are you saying?"

"I'm saying that given the time that has passed, it's almost impossible for you or anyone else to determine what happened to your brother. Maybe it's time to cut your losses and move on. Continuing to pursue this is probably a waste of time, energy, your emotional resources, and could possibly put you in harm's way."

"So what about seeing Sabotny on the beach. Something is going on. I don't want to cut and run too soon."

This time Ken Lee was slow in responding. "Yes, if we only knew. Sabotny has moved back to the area in a very public way. He's gone to a class reunion, posted on a social network, purchased an expensive place in a very visible location. He's not in hiding. And he's flashing a lot of money. He could afford to live anywhere in the world, but it appears that he's planning to settle in Cedar County. The old story: local boy makes good, then returns home."

"I'm not ready to fold," Mackenzie reiterated. "I need a few more weeks, maybe a month."

"You know, you can afford to hire some very competent private detectives to take this over. You could even put them up in that lovely house of yours. You could be back here living your life, and they could carry on the investigation."

"I need to do this. I thought I had your backing."

"You do, you do. I just think given what you've learned, it would be better to recruit people with the appropriate skill-set to continue with this task."

"Ken Lee, I'm not going to take any chances. Like you said, I'm not a risk taker. I just need to do this a bit longer." She took a deep breath. "What do you suggest I should focus on next?"

Ken Lee took a deep breath of his own. "How about Jim Moarse? Why don't you focus on him for a while, like you did with Sabotny. Get a sense of his patterns, what he does, who he hangs with. And do this from afar. You've got the optics and cameras. I can send you more GPS units if we decide to track his activities. I'd like his address, see if Sabotny ever visits." He paused. "And there are two more things," said Ken Lee.

"Yes?"

"I've sent you some phantom phones."

"What's that?"

"Phones, cell phones. They're set to make 911 calls. If you see something going down and you want to involve law enforcement, you can toss one of these phones near the action. You'll be long gone by the time the police arrive, and your identity is protected. They'll be at FedEx in the morning."

"And the other thing?"

"I've decided to do some headhunting of my own. I'm going to get you the names of people who could take this over. You've got to start thinking of an exit strategy. Start organizing what you've collected so far and think about how you can best facilitate their success."

"Ken Lee, you can go ahead with your recruiting, but I need a few more weeks. I appreciate what you're doing. But please don't bug me too much."

"Hey, you know me. And you, go to yoga in the morning. Pick up those phones on your way out of town."

32

"How was your meeting with the county Board of Supervisors?" asked Sue as she entered Ray's office, holding a coffee mug and her laptop. Simone followed her, dragging her lead.

"As enervating as always," he paused. "Let me take that back; this one was worse than the norm."

"What happened?" asked Sue, setting the coffee on the conference table and opening her laptop.

"It was all about 'over.'"

"Say what?"

"This morning's theme was that under my leadership, this department has grown fat. We are overstaffed, over-benefited, overeducated, etc. That we are living in hard times, and everyone has to sacrifice, and this department hasn't done its share."

"Where does this stuff come from?" asked Sue.

"I don't know. There's a kind of mythology that's not attached to any reality or data. I put up a spreadsheet that showed the department's budget has been flat for several years, and when inflation is factored in, we've been doing more with less year after year. And this isn't new information. I've done a similar presentation the last several years. I've pointed out that while the county's population continues to grow, our staffing has remained the same. And some of them just don't hear this.

"During my presentation, Elmer Lentro kept interrupting me, saying that several of his constituents had told him that they had seen deputies parked at the side of the road playing video games on those expensive, fancy computers we'd put in the cars.

"I told him that was impossible and explained again the use of the computers in the patrol cars, and as they remember, we did a presentation for the supervisors when we first installed them. I reminded them that we were able to purchase the systems with money from a federal grant, and it was an example of how we were using technology to improve our productivity and cut costs."

"Did that shut him up?"

"No. I don't think he hears too well. And I know he doesn't listen. He believes what he wants to believe, and he's playing to an audience that keeps electing him. That was just the beginning of his rant. He wanted to know why I keep hiring college kids; they're overqualified and overeducated. He reminded me that Orville just hired locals, he trained them on the job, and they did just fine. He also said Orville had lots of citizen deputies, so if he needed help in an emergency, all he had to do was make a few phone calls."

"I don't understand," said Sue.

"Back in the day, 30 or 40 years ago, especially before elections, Orville would pass out cards that said something to the effect that so-and-so was a Cedar County deputy sheriff. I don't think Orville was the only sheriff who did it, but he was probably the last. It's a remnant of the distant past when the sheriff would form a posse."

"So what was the reaction?"

"He went too far this time. Everyone was embarrassed. The chair had to be absolutely obnoxious to shut him up. If fact, I think it helped move things forward. The board approved our budget with fewer questions than I expected."

"And how did Elmer vote?"

Ray chuckled, "He abstained, like he was making some kind of point. I think the poor guy is losing it."

"Ray, he's never going to forgive you for that DUI."

"True, that and not hiring his grandson. Like he once told me, 'Orville knew how to make things work for friends, and you don't, Ray Elkins.' I guess I am guilty as charged."

Ray joined Sue at the conference table, Simone in his lap. "So what have you been up to?"

"You left early yesterday. There were some things I want to go over. In fact your early departure…."

"Go ahead."

"Well, we had a 911 call for the marine patrol to provide assistance. I ended up taking the call after dispatch explained that our equipment was in dry dock and water emergencies were handled by the Coast Guard."

"So what was the emergency?"

"One of our elderly citizens was concerned about two kayakers who seemed to be out of control on Lake Michigan. I asked if they were out of their boats. He said sometimes they were and sometimes they weren't, but that conditions were far too rough for anyone to be kayaking. I told him I'd investigate. I was on my way to talk to Mrs. Schaffer again with some more questions about Terry, so I drove over and took a look. Once I established who the kayakers were, I dropped in on our concerned citizen, Curmudgeonly Charlie, and explained that the boaters in question were known to the department, and while we didn't approve of their choice of paddling conditions, they were within their rights. Then I thanked him for his vigilance and concern. I didn't mention that one of kayakers was the sheriff. Given that Elmer Lentro is the county supervisor in that area, I did my best not to throw gasoline on the fire. I mean, weren't you on the water during normal working hours? You never would have caught old Sheriff Orville out kayaking in a storm."

"True," said Ray. "During a howling storm, he would have been standing at the bar in the Last Chance doing right by the voters. So why were you going to visit Mrs. Schaffer? Speaking of efficiency, what's wrong with the phone?"

"You usually get more face-to-face, especially her type. She's spent too many years brushing people off."

"And why are you back to Terry Hallen?"

"Get control of your ADD and listen for a bit." Sue delivered her line with a smile.

"Okay."

"I've been pouring through Vincent Fox's stuff and am totally frustrated. So as a diversion I started through the Terry Hallen material again. I was looking at his death certificate, and I couldn't find anything that stated who identified the body. I started with Julie Sutton in the county clerk's office. She pointed out that they were still using the old death certificates then, something homegrown that only required the most basic information. She went on to say that eventually the county adopted the U.S. Standard Certificate of Death. So my question to her was how do we know that the boy found on the beach was Terry Hallen?"

"And?"

"Easy. You have a missing kid. Two days later one turns up on a beach. Case solved. And since he has no obvious wounds—his skull hasn't been crushed, and none of his limbs appear to be broken—he must have drowned. She reminded me that the coroner used to be the local funeral director, and if the deceased was indigent, the county provided for burial, a very cozy little business arrangement."

"So we don't know if his mother or anyone else ever identified the body?"

"You got it. Not that it really matters, but it's interesting."

"So how does Mrs. Schaffer fit into this?" Ray asked.

"On my first visit, she couldn't find Terry's school records, which she said was very unusual. I was wondering if they ever turned up. I was also trying to jog her memory. Did she remember a funeral, did she know anyone who might have seen Terry's body?"

"And?"

"Terry's folder, his cumulative record, still hasn't been found. She said that in her long history with the district, one has never gone missing before. She's at a loss to explain how it could have disappeared."

"Does she have any theories?"

"None."

"Do you?"

"I looked through a couple she had sitting on her desk. It's just ID stuff—name, address, parent/guardian names, date of birth—and year-by-year grade and attendance data. In the folders I looked at there were also some photos, you know, the kind they take every year. Even if we had it, I don't think we'd learn anything from the kind of data it contains."

"What else?"

"I asked her if she remembers anything about a funeral. She said that there probably wasn't one. And then she carefully explained that there are cases where a family is too poor or too dysfunctional to organize something like that. And if they weren't part of a church community, it probably didn't happen. She said she remembers Terry's family were transients, they weren't really connected to the area. People like that come and go. They enroll, then they sometimes suddenly disappear. Families fall apart, kids go off to live with relatives, kids run away or drop out. She was doing her best to be politically correct, but there was an undercurrent of…I don't know…trying not to be judgmental but…I think she has great sympathy for the kids and a lot of anger about how their lives are totally screwed up."

"I understand," said Ray. After a long pause he asked, "Anything else?"

"I think that's about it. So I'm back to the same frustrating conclusion. Unless someone credible walks through the door and gives us information on Terry Hallen, this is about all we will ever know. And I hope the same isn't true of Vincent Fox."

"It's not," said Ray. "Twenty years haven't passed. There's something going on here. We just have to be patient and vigilant."

33

S ue turned the Jeep onto the sand and gravel road leading to the New Harmony Organic Farm.

"I've always like this part of the county," said Ray as they snaked through the rolling terrain. "It's just this little area, maybe 10 square miles that's hilly and rolling. I think it's one of the most beautiful parts."

"I thought we'd turned the veggie thefts over to Brett," Sue said, nudging Simone away from the clutch.

"We did, but I wanted to handle this one personally. It's my CSA."

"New Harmony?" asked Sue.

"Yes, Jon Merryweather. He's been developing this farm over the last few years. He moved his family from Chicago after working as a commodities trader. He and his wife wanted to give their kids a different kind of life. I've been getting vegetables from them the last two summers, splitting a box with Marc and Lisa. You may not remember, but you've been a consumer of some of the produce."

"Like those ugly tomatoes."

"Heirloom tomatoes, Sue, just like your great-grandmother used to grow. It's about taste rather than appearance."

"I don't remember what they tasted like; I just remember that they were ugly. I probably skipped them." She slowed, approaching a fork in the road. "Is he our contact?" she asking, pointing at a tall, patrician-faced man standing at the side of the road, a cell phone pressed to his ear.

"That's Jon."

"Hey, Ray," said Jon as they climbed out of the jeep, "didn't know you were bringing the K-9 unit."

After introductions, they began walking toward the farm. Ray unleashed Simone who immediately made a happy circle. "Tell me what's been going on, Jon."

"We've heard from other farmers about thefts," Jon explained as they climbed the gentle slope. "I didn't think anything about it. Our root cellars are over here, away from the house, close to the fields. I supposed someone could roll in here at night, and we'd never see or hear him. But I wasn't concerned." He swung his arm toward a low hillside bordering a field still flattened from winter. "These two cellars—we call them the caves, the kids like that—were here when we bought the property. The doors had almost rotted away, but the fieldstone walls were in good shape. I've actually used these as the model for the three additional ones I built." He stopped and chuckled, "Even after a hundred years of farming on this land, there are still lots of fieldstones around to build with."

He pulled a hasp from a loop securing two wooden doors and pulled them open, exposing a cave that had been dug in the side of the hill. Ray and Sue followed a few feet into the interior, their eyes adjusting to the dull light. The air was cool and moist, with an earthly aroma. A pile of potatoes filled the back third of the cavern.

"We store potatoes, onions, carrots, and other root vegetables in these. Most go to our winter shareholders, the rest are sold to organic groceries or contributed to food banks. This cellar is a little bigger than the others, and I reserve it for potatoes. We had a good crop last year, and this one was pretty full, more than I needed, actually. I came down here last week to check on the condition of the potatoes; planting season isn't too far away."

"You don't lock these buildings?" asked Sue.

"Never been a need to. Anyway, as soon I got in here I knew that a whole lot of spuds had gone missing. To make a long story short, we got my daughter one of those infrared cameras for Christmas. We know a lot of animals move through the farm at night, and she was thinking about a science fair project dealing with nocturnal animals. I borrowed her camera and sure enough, captured the images of some two-legged nocturnal animals."

He pulled his cell phone out and started a video.

"Do you know these two individuals?" asked Ray, squinting at the screen.

"That's the hard part. I do. They're neighbors, they're friends. The first few years they were coming around to help, sharing their knowledge. The kids really liked them. I was going to go over and talk with them, but my wife thought you should be involved."

"Would you make me a copy of that?"

Jon reached into a pocket and handed Ray a square envelope containing a DVD.

"Things are not right with them, Ray. Their mother passed a few years ago, she was way up in her 90s, and since that time things have been falling apart over at their farm. Tucker stops by to chat from time to time, says Sam is getting forgetful. And I guess Tucker's had health problems of his own, heart trouble. I dropped off some cookies at the house last Christmas, and I couldn't believe it. When their mother was alive, things were in pretty good order. Now there's so much rubbish in the house, they had to make a path through it. . Tucker and Sam have always been self-sufficient, but now they seem to be struggling financially."

"Will you press charges?" asked Sue.

"No, and I don't think anyone will when they know who's behind these thefts, but it has to stop. The guys need help. What happens now?"

"We'll have to go over there, find out what's going on."

"I didn't want to…."

"You did the right thing," said Ray. "We'll get this sorted out."

Jon led them out into the spring sunshine. "I hope so," he said, shaking Sue's hand, then Ray's.

"Say," asked Ray, "did you ever see either of them dressed as Amish farmers?"

"Yes, funny you know about that. We have an annual Halloween barn party for the neighborhood, all ages, cider, doughnuts, hay rides in the dark. Tucker and Sam always attend; it might be their one social outing of the year. Tucker plays a concertina, and Sam sort of follows along on a fiddle. They're an essential part of the evening."

"By the way," said Sue, "how's the science project coming?"

"Oh, Emma, she got interested in owl pellets," said Jon, rolling his eyes upward and slowly exhaling. "I would have preferred helping her edit video."

34

"Since you didn't ask, you obviously know where we can find the potato perps," said Sue, stopping at the end of the drive and looking over at Ray, waiting for directions.

"Left here, left on the first paved road, and about a half mile down turn right on Veelander. It's gravel and usually in bad shape this time of year."

"Their family name?"

"Yes."

Their progress was interrupted by a call on the police radio asking for a unit to respond to a domestic disturbance. Sue picked up the microphone, "Central. Near that location. Will respond." She looked over at Ray. "The Veelanders will have to wait."

Ray turned the laptop mounted between them in his direction and read the information on the screen to Sue. *Meet woman in drive in a red Mazda.* He moved Simone around on his lap, retrieved his phone, and called the dispatcher.

"Central, this is Ray. I'm riding with Sue. Do you have anything more?"

"Hi, Ray, I'll put it on screen. 911 call is from a Sally Rood who went to this address to reclaim some personal property from an ex-boyfriend. Apparently there was an argument, and he pushed her out of the house. Rood says she just wants her things back, and she's afraid if she tries to go back in, he will hurt her. I instructed her to leave the scene, but she's determined to get her belongings, so I told her to stay in her car, lock the doors, and wait for a deputy."

"Do you have a name for the man involved?"

"I'm sending the info. It should be on your screen."

"How about the caller?"

"Nothing. I've tentatively confirmed her I.D."

"Thanks," said Ray looking at the computer display. "The resident at that address is James Moarse, age 44," he read to Sue. "Suspended license, series of DUIs, and three domestics, years ago."

"I've never heard of him," commented Sue, her eyes on the road. "The guy's not on our top 40. There's the Mazda." She pulled behind the vehicle. "Kentucky tags." They sat for a minute as Sue keyed in the plate numbers. After reading the response, she pushed the screen over.

Sally Rood was leaning against the driver's side door, a cigarette in one hand, a cell phone in the other. "Okay, they're here. I gotta go," she said with a Dolly Parton twang, folding her phone.

Sue stood directly in front of Rood. Ray hung back by the front of the Jeep.

"Look," said Rood, "all I want is my stuff. And that bastard won't let me take it. If you just walk in and give me a little protection, I'll be out of here."

"Slow down. Tell us what's happening."

"Like I said…."

Sue cut her off, "What's in the house, and how did it end up there?"

"Just some clothes. I moved out a while ago, but I left a few things behind. I called him earlier this morning, and he said he was okay with me coming by. But when I got here he was drunk. Big effing surprise. He started yelling at me. Said he was going to bash in my head with a ball bat. Then he pushed me out the door."

"Did you see a ball bat or any other weapon?"

"No, but I wasn't going to stand around while he went to look for one, not that he could find anything in that god damn pig pen."

"The man inside, the person who threatened you, what's his name?"

"Jimmy, Jimmy Moarse."

"Is he alone?

"Yes."

"How long did you live there."

"Four or five months. I came up here to waitress last summer, moved in with him in…maybe…October. I went back south in the late winter. Couldn't stand him or the cold."

"And what are we talking about; what are you trying to retrieve?"

"A couple of suitcases. They're packed already. I couldn't fit them in my car when I went south. He said it was okay if I left them. Now he's just being a prick about it. Saying I deserted him."

"Let's see if we can work this out," said Sue.

The front door of the house flew open as they approached, and a large man, disheveled and unsteady, smelling of booze and cigarettes, charged out. Ray moved quickly to the man's side.

"Sally, you didn't have to go calling fucking Johnny Law. We could have worked this out."

"Asshole. You said you were going to beat in my brains. What was I…?"

"I was just messing with you. Try to tell these cops you didn't screw me over good on your way out." He focused on Ray. "Bitch left in the middle of the night. Woke up, house empty, wallet too."

"Your name please?" asked Sue.

"James Moarse."

"Do you have a picture ID?"

The man pulled out a wallet. He retrieved a card and passed it to Sue. She peered at it for a long moment, briefly looked up at him, then returned the ID.

"Does she have some possessions in your house?" asked Sue.

"Yeah, a couple of bags. Should have thrown them out."

"Where are they?"

"Right where she left them."

"May we enter your house and get them?"

"Just don't let her steal anything else."

Moarse lit a cigarette, offering one to Ray as an afterthought. He shook his head. "She was nothing but trouble."

Ray didn't respond. The two women quickly returned, Rood carrying two red plastic suitcases, one in each hand.

"Mr. Moarse, are these the suitcases in question?"

"Yeah."

"Ms. Rood, is that it? You have no other possessions in Moarse's house?"

"No."

"You are sure?"

"Absolutely."

"And what are you going to do now?" Sue pursued.

"I'm getting in my car and getting outta Dodge. I want some serious distance between me and that asshole before I lay my head down again."

"Fuck you, bitch."

Ray stepped away from Moarse, and he and Sue walked behind Rood as she made her way back to her car, suitcases banging against her knees. They stood and waited as she loaded her car, pulled forward, turned around, and headed south on Town Line Road. Then they got into the Jeep and followed her at a distance.

"What did he give you as an ID?"

"An operator's permit, expired."

"What was the house like?"

"He's sitting on a fortune in returnables."

"Think she'll be back?" asked Ray.

"Hard to tell. Do you think he'd take her back?"

"In a heartbeat."

"Should we head to Veelanders?" Sue asked.

"Let's do lunch first," Ray responded. "I don't think they're going anywhere."

"Our job," said Sue, exasperated. "Sometimes I think most of what we do is social work."

"Yes, social work," Ray repeated, "with a Glock just in case things go south—or in Ms. Rood's case, they don't go south as planned."

35

Mackenzie felt like she was babbling. She took a deep breath in an attempt to slow down and focus. She sat back and looked hard at the Skype box showing Ken Lee's face. It appeared that he was giving her his full attention. His gaze didn't seem to wander off to one of the other screens she knew surrounded his workstation. Ken Lee always seemed available to talk, and she knew that he was spending countless hours researching for her or coming up with and shipping devices to aid her probe. She worried that she had become his full-time project, and, worse, that his emotional tie to her might exceed what she felt for him. *Someday soon this will all be over. What are his expectations about the future, our future?*

She sat up and stretched her neck. "Okay, so I rolled by a second time to get a better look, slowing, but trying not to make it too obvious," she continued. "There was a red Mazda in the drive, and the Sheriff was standing outside with Jim Moarse. It didn't look like they were talking: strange body language, just standing there. Then I did the absolute unthinkable."

"You didn't."

"Yup. I went down the road, turned around in a drive, and came back a third time. I'm sure no one noticed. They were heavily into something. It was the sheriff, Moarse, a female deputy, and some woman with red hair, the Scottish red. Something heavy was going down. No one was looking at the traffic on the road. They were all focused on what was happening right there in the yard."

"What was happening?"

"I don't know. The woman had a couple of bags, suitcases. Maybe she was moving out."

"So?"

"I did the double unthinkable, I drove down the road a couple of miles and came back again. By then the Mazda and the sheriff's Jeep were on the road ahead of me. I followed at a polite distance. They eventually ended up on 22. The cops in the Jeep turned around near the county line, and I followed the Mazda into Traverse City."

"And?"

"Ms. Redhead pulled into a parking lot. I circled the block and found her car, Kentucky plates."

"Did you get the number?"

"Absolutely, I'll send it to you."

"Then what?"

"I parked and found the woman window shopping on Front Street. Then this man came along, and they embraced passionately, a bone crusher. I followed them to a restaurant a block down, quasi-French, almost good, but not quite, like the chef doesn't make sure the greens are perfect and doesn't check each entrée before it goes to the table."

"I sense that…well, never mind. You're sure they didn't see you?"

"They only had eyes for each other. They had a couple of glasses of wine and a lunch that they gobbled down. I'm sure they were screwing their brains out 15 minutes later."

"How do you know?"

"You could tell. They were both in heat."

"So what does that have to do with Moarse?" asked Ken Lee.

"I don't know. The redhead is younger than Moarse, maybe 10 years, more or less. And she looks good; she still has youth on her side. Not real classy, but cute and sexy with a killer body. Maybe she hooked up with Moarse for a while. She's definitely moved on. It's amazing how easily men can be manipulated for a little sex." *Is that what I'm doing?* Mackenzie wondered.

"So what now?" asked Ken Lee.

"I'm going to focus on Moarse. See what I can find out. Maybe pull a stakeout, see if there are any comings and goings."

"You should probably get a GPS on his car."

"I have to figure out what he's driving. There was an old garage there, but the door wasn't open."

"If you're going to pull a stakeout, you need to be very careful."

"His place would be easy. It's real open with woods on three sides. I can also get on some high ground on the other side of the road."

"Dog? Neighbors?"

"No, he's pretty isolated."

"You shouldn't be out there alone. You need to have backup. These guys are killers."

"Come on Ken Lee. Back off. I have a phone, multiple weapons, and like you've said many times, some of the fastest hands you've ever seen. I'm just going to go and look at the dude in the dark with binoculars, a hundred or more yards out. Safer than a walk in the park, a lot safer."

"Okay, I'll see what I can find out about the owner of the Mazda, if she's indeed the owner. Please be careful. Send me a note when you're back."

"You always know where my car is. You've got to give me some space, Ken Lee. This is all stuff I can do safely. Don't smother me."

"I just don't want you to get over your head. Even the best sometimes…. Be careful. And one more thing."

"What's that?"

"The other two characters. I covered the same ground on Zed Piontowski. Not much there, and it's hard to tell if the stiff in Galveston is one and the same. As for Chris Brewler, nothing comes up. Are you sure of the spelling?"

"It's my best guess. So, how do you just disappear?"

"You tell me," said Ken Lee.

"I had a great aunt who needed to protect me from an alcoholic mother. Not that Mom would have wanted us kids back, but she would have used us to try to extract money for the honor of taking care of us."

"Maybe Chris Brewler needed to disappear, too. New name, social security number…."

"But he'd need to be out of here, people would recognize him."

"Are you sure? You're living 30 miles north of Sandville, right?"

"True."

"So a new name, a heavy beard, and change in hair color—you probably don't have to go very far to get a new identity to work. And that night at the beach—was there a third person?"

"Yes, there was. But I couldn't see him from where I was hiding. So I'm going to focus on Moarse and see if I can start filling in the blanks."

36

A rutted two-track led to the old farmhouse, its siding and trim cracked and weathered to gray tones after standing more than a century against the harsh northern Michigan climate. A sagging black Ford panel truck, one of the two rear doors standing wide open, was parked just beyond the house on the path toward a decrepit barn. *Organic Vegetables* had been spray painted in alert orange on the side of the truck in unsteady letters.

Sue followed Ray up the stairs to the front door, avoiding a missing board on the third step. They stood for a long moment outside the door listening, and then Ray rapped on the window with his knuckles. There was no response. He knocked a second time and waited. He tried the handle on the door. It didn't move. "Let's check around back."

Sue chose to jump off the porch, landing on her feet on the weed-covered lawn. She tried to peek in the side windows, but they were too high off the foundation. She detoured to look in the back of the panel truck.

"Should I call for a search warrant?" asked Sue, sizing up the stack of bulging gunnysacks.

Ray joined her. "Go ahead," he said, heading off. "I'll check the back door."

Standing on a moss-covered slab made of split rock and cement, Ray looked through the yellowed remnants of a lace curtain dangling to one side of the smudged window. Inside it was chaos. Every horizontal surface—the kitchen table, counters, sink, sideboards, even the seats of the chairs, save two—was covered with papers, dishes, cans, and bottles. He banged on the door.

"No answer there," he said rejoining Sue. "Let's check the other buildings."

Smoke was rising faintly from the tin chimney that ran through the roof of the larger of the two outbuildings. Ray knocked on the door. Hearing a response from the inside, he pushed it open. The Veelander brothers, Tucker and Sam, were sitting near a potbellied stove, each holding a mug. A large porcelain coffee pot sat on top of the stove and the remains of lunch—a slab of cheese, some apples, and a partial loaf of bread in a plastic bag—were scattered on top of a workbench surrounded by well-worn hand tools.

"Well, Sheriff," said Sam, "must be nearing an election. We hardly see you between times."

"We hear about you, though. You being chauffeured around the county by some pretty lady so you can play games on a computer," added Tucker.

"While us hard working tax payers can't afford those kinda toys," said Sam.

"And our poor friend, Vincent Fox, is dead. Why aren't you chasing his killers instead of bothering with a couple of poor farmers?"

"What's with the costumes?" asked Ray, pointing to their black pants and jackets over white shirts. "You fellows going through some kind of religious conversion?"

"We're trying to seek a simpler life," said Sam.

"How about the beards?" asked Ray.

"In the truck," said Tucker. "We don't put those on...."

"Till when?" asked Ray. He pulled the DVD from his jacket. "Seems you fellows are starting to make it in the movies. I've got some great video of you two from a security camera. You appear to be helping yourself to a few hundred pounds of potatoes. Only I noticed you were wearing your usual clothes. Do you want to tell me what's going on?"

"Why aren't you looking for the killers instead of bothering with us?" Tucker asked again.

"We've heard that two elderly Amish men were seen in the bookstore looking at Vincent Fox's book," said Ray. "We were also told that several copies of the book were stolen from that bookstore and the library."

"We didn't steal no books. We were just looking at the part that interested us," said Tucker."

"And what part was that?" asked Ray.

"Vincent said there was some treasure down in Missionary Cove. That's just down the road, you know," he said, pointing with a finger over his back. "Said we should buy the book and get some of that gangster gold."

"So you knew Fox?"

"We knew him a little. Used to run into him at the casino on Senior's Day."

"Ever see him anywhere else?" asked Ray.

"No, never," said Sam.

"How about the Last Chance?" asked Tucker, looking at his brother.

"Oh, yeah, the Last Chance. Had a beer with him there a few times. We asked him for a copy of his book, borrowed like. But he wouldn't give us one. He was so tight, he squeaked when he walked."

"Yes," agreed Tucker, "he squeaked when he walked."

"Did you ever go to his house?" Ray asked.

"Never," said Sam.

Ray looked at Tucker, "Never."

"And what about this?" asked Ray, holding up the DVD again. "Looks like the stolen goods might be in the back of your truck."

"You can't do that. You gotta have a search warrant. We know our rights."

"The door was open; we just looked. And we've requested a search warrant."

A long silence followed. "Tucker's got a girlfriend downstate in Royal Oak. Hooked up with her again at their 60th high school reunion. She's just crazy about the Amish. So when we go to visit, we sorta dress up. Makes her happy."

"The potatoes, Sam?"

"I'm getting to it, Ray. The farm hasn't been doing too good; the land's played out. And the price of gasoline for that old truck, maybe 12, 14 miles a gallon. So we were selling potatoes at the farmers market down there, you know gourmet, organic. City people have no sense of money. Five dollars a pound. Couldn't bring enough. They'd be gone in an hour or two. Even chefs from fancy restaurants buying 'em. So after a few months we ran through all of the ones we'd stored up, so we've been borrowing a few. I mean, I'm surprised anyone missed them. And we plan to return them next growing season."

"Why didn't you just buy them?"

"Well, like I said, things are tough. The casino and gasoline…."

"So you're stealing from your friends, and you're also cheating your customers."

"That's not true. We just borrowed them. As for those people in the city, a potato is a potato. No one was cheated."

"Should I get a search warrant for your house and look for the book?"

Tucker laughed, "I'd like to see you find it. It's been missing for weeks."

"What happens now?" asked Sam.

"We give you a ride to town in our fancy police car. Sergeant Lawrence here will tape a statement from each of you, separately. We will compare the two interviews to see if either one of you can tell the truth about anything. Then we'll turn the case over to the prosecutor's office and let them sort it out."

"Are we going to jail?" asked Tucker. "We were planning to vote for you. Guess we can't do it if we're behind bars."

"There's no justice in this country anymore," said Sam. "If you're not part of the one percent, you just get screwed."

37

It was almost dark when Mackenzie lay down behind a berm at the edge of a wooded area overlooking Jim Moarse's house. In the fading light, she glassed the area, adjusting the focus on her small, powerful binoculars. There were no signs of a dog or any other animals on the property. The door on the garage, a separate building at the side of the lot some distance from the back door, was closed.

After a few minutes, she moved along the ridgeline, looking for an angle that would allow her to see into the interior of the house. A long set of windows ran along the south-facing wall of the structure. She found a spot near a clump of cedars, halfway down the hill, and slid between the branches. Moarse appeared to be working at the stove, then he moved to a table, carrying a plate. He pushed stacks of newspaper aside before sitting down, his back to the window.

Mackenzie checked her watch. It was after 10 o'clock. When she next looked at the luminous dial again, only five minutes had passed. She was wondering if she could make an hour.

Moarse went back to the sink, plate in hand. He opened the refrigerator, took something out, then walked toward another part of the room. A large flat screen filled a wall with motion and color.

Mackenzie rotated her body, searching for branches that she could lean into. She was becoming stiff and uncomfortable in the cool night air. Her elbows resting on a branch, she kept her focus on the windows. Other than the flicker from the TV, nothing seemed to be happening.

Three vehicles passed during the first hour. First, a pick-up with one taillight going north. Then the same truck in the other direction 18 minutes later. Next, a small, dark sedan with a noisy muffler wheezed up the hill and off into the dark countryside. Then nothing. Mackenzie was lost in thought, going over the same things she had been struggling with for days. She was bored and frustrated and ready to throw in the towel.

A few minutes after 11, a large SUV came up the road, slowed, and turned into Moarse's drive. Her quick scan of the license number before the lights were switched off confirmed her suspicions. As the door opened and the dome light came on, she got a quick look at Richard Sabotny. He reached back into the Land Rover and pulled out a large brown paper bag. He walked up to the front door and entered, not pausing to knock.

Mackenzie could see the men moving around the room, but her vantage point felt suddenly limited. Slipping out of the cedars, she crouched, and then scrambled down the hill into the ditch. She waited, listening and looking, before darting across the road into the brush. Slowly she crept forward until she had a clear view of the interior.

Sabotny and Moarse, both holding glasses, were engaged in an intense conversation. She saw Sabotny reach out and take Moarse's glass, move toward the sink, and hand it back a few minutes later as he continued talking. When the two disappeared from view, Mackenzie assumed that they had settled in front of the TV. She was startled a few minutes later when an exterior light switched on and Sabotny came out into the yard, followed by Moarse. They headed toward a small block building at the rear of the property. As she watched, the two men stacked kindling in the external firebox, squirted on some kind of liquid, and put a match to the pile. Then, they stood around talking, each with a drink in hand, adding wood until the fire began to roar. They shut the door on the firebox and returned to the house, turning off the yard light.

The initial activity had given Mackenzie a burst of adrenalin, yet now she was struggling again with the tedium and discomfort of waiting. It turned out to be a long wait. For the next hour, Sabotny would periodically return to what she'd decided was a sauna to add more wood to the fire. She also observed him inside, making drinks and carrying them out of her view.

Finally the door opened again, and Sabotny appeared with Moarse. With difficulty, Sabotny guided the staggering figure toward the sauna. A small door opened and Sabotny hauled Moarse up the couple of steps.

The door closed for just a moment, then Sabotny was back out. He switched on a flashlight and appeared to be looking through a heap of building materials at the side of the garage, eventually moving behind the building and out of view. She could hear things being tossed about. When he returned, he was dragging a large, heavy piece of metal, which he jammed it into the ground, wedging it against the outside of the door. He loaded the firebox again, then went back to the house.

Mackenzie watched him repeat this process of walking to the house, presumably to watch TV, and emerging to reload the stove with dread. After an hour, he lifted away the metal jam from the sauna. He lugged it back behind the garage where she heard it clang against other metal. When he opened the sauna door, he stood for a long moment, moving his flashlight beam around the interior. Then he kicked the door shut and went back in the house.

For another agonizing 10 minutes, she waited while he paced back and forth between the kitchen and the living area. Finally, the door opened and he backed out, dragging a large garbage bag. Leaving it on the stoop, he opened the hatch on the Range Rover, and then went back for the bag. He lifted it in both arms, threw it into the SUV, got in the driver's seat, backed out onto the road, and drove slowly away.

Mackenzie held her position until the sound of his V8 stopped echoing across the countryside. She crept forward, moving along the perimeter of the yard, trying to stay hidden in the brush. She crawled near the rear of the sauna, then moved along the side, stopping and listening, every few steps. Finally, she reached the door and she pulled it open. A wave of searing heat exploded out, but she entered and pulled the door closed behind her. She switched on her light. Moarse was sprawled, naked, on the floor.

Pulling off a glove, she felt for a pulse in his neck, his skin hot and dry. Then she killed the light and fled the building, retreating across the yard, the road, back up the hill and into the woods, where she stood, heart pounding, inhaling the cold night air. Her first impulse was to keep going, run, but she straightened up, working to control her breathing and quiet her emotions.

She walked back, slowly but openly, and headed to the garage. A quick flash of her light revealed an old Jeep CJ parked in the center of several piles of debris. She slipped back outside, pulled the door shut, and reaching into an inner pocket, removed a phantom cell phone. She tore open its plastic bag as she returned to the sauna. With gloved hands she switched it on and activated the 911 calling program. Then she dropped the phone behind a stack of split logs at the side of the building. Thirty minutes later, she rolled past the scene, driving at a moderate speed, observing the emergency vehicles clustered in the drive.

38

Ray was revisiting a nightmare, a recurring dream he'd had since college. He was in a large lecture hall, the air close and heavy. A stack of blue books occupied the upper right-hand corner of his desk. A Xerox copy of the exam questions was directly in front of him. He slowly scanned the items, searching for one that he could answer. How did he get into this situation? He couldn't remember signing up for the course. It was his roommate who'd dragged him off to the exam, and now he was struggling to find a topic that he could write on that would save him from certain failure.

He integrated the sound of his cell phone into the dream, wondering why anyone would bring a phone with them to an exam. Eventually, the metallic chirp pulled him toward consciousness. He fumbled with the device, finally pulling the screen into focus, the smiling face of Sue Lawrence looking at him. He moved his finger along the bar at the bottom of the screen to take the call.

"Ray, sorry to wake you, but you'll want to know about this."

"What's happening?" he asked, struggling to come to consciousness.

"Jim Moarse, the man we saw this afternoon, the one having a dispute with the former girlfriend."

"What about him?"

"He's dead."

"Dead...what happened? Did the redhead come back and blow him away?"

"Are you awake?"

"Why do you ask?"

"Your response, it seems a bit unusual."

"So what happened?"

"A phantom 911 cell call, a GPS enabled phone. It came in after 1 a.m. Brett responded. No one answered the door. He checked the house and then went out into the yard. He noticed smoke coming from the sauna, looked into that building, found a body, and determined that the man was dead. Central called me. I'm now at the scene, and the deceased is Jim Moarse. The medical examiner is on his way, and I thought you'd want to be here as well. That said, there is no reason why you need to come. It could all wait till morning."

"I'm on my way. Do you need anything? How about coffee?"

"Coffee would be great. See you when you get here."

Dr. Dyskin's sagging Lincoln Town Car, one of the last survivors of Detroit's nouveau-Jurassic period, blocked the end of the driveway. Ray pulled onto the shoulder and walked past Dyskin's car and the three vehicles in front of it, an EMT unit and two patrol cars. He joined the group standing near the open door of the sauna, the area lit by the headlights of the police cars and several flashlights. He handed Sue an insulated coffee mug and looked in. Dr. Dyskin was on the floor examining the body. The figure sprawled on the floor, face down and naked. Brett and Sue were illuminating the scene for Dyskin with their flashlights.

"He looked better with clothes on," said Sue.

"Don't we all," said Dyskin, glancing up. Then he pulled himself to his feet and crawled out of the sauna, wiping sweat from his brow with the sleeve of his fleece jacket. "Wow! Still hot enough to take a sauna in there, even with the door open. And the place smells like a brewery. What was he thinking?"

"Cause of death?" asked Ray.

"A fatal case of roasting," said Dyskin. "The guy had way too much to drink, then he goes into a blazing sauna. Hyperthermia for sure with alcohol as a contributing factor, maybe drugs. He's fat, out of shape. There are probably other health issues, too. We'll know after the autopsy. Let's say an accidental death with extenuating circumstances."

"How long has he been dead?" asked Ray.

"A couple of hours at the most."

"Any sign of….?"

"No fractures, lacerations, contusions, etc. Give me your light," Dyskin said, pulling it from Sue's hand. He moved the beam back and forth in the interior, along the two benches and the floor below. He reentered the building briefly, partially closing the door, then quickly exited.

"What are you looking for?" asked Sue as he handed the light back to her.

"Just curious. I wanted to see if he had a robe somewhere, perhaps behind the door. Nothing. No clothes or towel or shoes. And no water bottle, just an empty beer can." He paused briefly. "Of course, living out here, I guess you could walk to the sauna naked without anyone seeing or caring. And he might have been so intoxicated in the first place that he didn't think to bother with those kind of things."

"We had a 911 call from here. Someone wanted us to find the body," said Ray.

Dyskin held Ray in his gaze for a moment. "But the caller wasn't here when…."

"No. And it was a phantom cell phone; we can't identify the caller."

"Curious, curious indeed, said Dyskin, clucking. "I think we should ship the body to Grand Rapids for a forensic autopsy."

"Yes," agreed Ray. "Sue, how do you plan to proceed?"

"I want to shoot the interior while the body is in place, and then we'll get him bagged and out of here. Then I think we should secure the area and go get some breakfast. We can go back to the office and see what we can find out about Jim Moarse. Get the paperwork done for search warrants. We should probably put out an APB on Sally Rood. She's a person of interest. Once the sun is up, I'll come back and work the scene."

"The phantom cell call?" asked Ray.

"That's a puzzler, isn't it? Let's think about that one."

Mackenzie washed off the last traces of the black greasepaint, then shampooed her hair and applied her favorite conditioner. She lingered in the warm shower, washing a second time with a sponge and a large block of olive oil and lavender soap. The grime of the evening's escapade was washed off, but she felt less than clean. *Should I have done more? Why didn't I see what was happening?* She was startled by the sound of her voice echoing off the tile. These were the questions she asked hours later when she described the events to Ken Lee.

"I don't think you could've done anything differently," Ken Lee responded. "By the time you figured out what was going down, the dude was already dead. Putting the phantom cell out there was as much you could do. It brought the cops running."

"I know, but...."

"Don't dwell on this, baby. You did as much as you could. The thing we need to start thinking about is why Sabotny wanted Moarse dead. Are the chickens coming home to roost? Maybe Sabotny decided that his own safety depends on getting rid of anyone who knows about your brother Terry's death. So there were four guys, right?"

"Yes."

"And one of them might be dead already, the one in Galveston?"

"But we don't...."

"No, but if he was one of the four, he's gone. He might've died on his own, but what if Sabotny knew where he was. Pretty easy to knock off a junkie with a big syringe, and without drawing any suspicion. And now Moarse is gone. So that just leaves?"

"Chris Brewler."

"And he may or may not be in the area. You haven't ID'd him yet. And there's one more person."

"Who's that?"

"You. You are a threat, and you are out there. He just doesn't know where." Ken Lee let his statement hang. Then he said, "I'll get back to you later. There's stuff I want to look at."

39

Ray propped the sauna door open with a board he pulled from a pile of old lumber haphazardly stacked at the side of the building. They peered into the gloomy interior at the chalk outline Sue had made around the body before the EMTs had bagged it and carried it away.

"So he was sprawled toward the door?" said Ray.

Sue switched on a large LED lantern and placed it inside the doorframe. "Yes," she responded. "Maybe he realized that he was in trouble and had to get out of here?"

"I don't think so. Drunk, hyperthermic. But who knows?" said Ray.

"So what if his lady love came back last night with the intent to do him in. She brings a gift of booze, gets him totally smashed, maybe puts something extra in his drinks, lures him to the sauna with, well, you know, an array of enticements, and bakes him for a couple of hours. It's not quite the Hansel and Gretel scenario, but it would work."

"What's her motive? She had her stuff back. And she would have to know she'd be the first person we'd want to talk to."

"How many times have you told me that most of our bad guys and gals don't hang out at Mensa brunches?" quipped Sue. "Give me a few minutes to shoot the interior."

Ray stood outside, watching Sue. Then the door caught his attention. He inspected the lower half first, searching the soft, rough sawn cedar for marks left by the nails of a desperate man. "Is it okay if I close this for a minute?" he asked.

"Go ahead," came the response.

He pulled away the prop and swung the door shut. It was casually constructed of six wide vertical boards held together by two horizontals, one at the top and one at the bottom. Ray ran his hand below the uppermost board where he found an indentation on the surface of the door. Propping the door open again, he looked at the path of widely placed pieces of cracked stone that ran from the house to the sauna. About three feet from the door there was a deep indentation in the earth to the side of a large stone. He began to search the exterior of the sauna. Along the back wall was a jumble of scrap materials—metal and wood. Ray took particular interest in a rusty steel rod—three inches in diameter and six feet in length—on top of the pile.

"I've got something to show you," he said as Sue emerged from the interior. After showing her the mark in the door and the indentation in the ground, he walked her behind the sauna. "Can you pull any prints off that?"

Sue inspected the rod carefully. "Pitted, rusty surface like this, I don't think so."

"Okay, then help me. Let's see if this fits."

They carried the heavy rod to the front of the sauna, sliding the shaft under the crosspiece on the door and bracing it against the boulder in the ground. "Perfect fit. Now let's see if it would have prevented Moarse from pushing his way out." Ray pulled the brace away from the door. "Go in and see if you can move the door. I'll tell you when to start pushing."

"No way," said Sue, a minute later, emerging from the building. "I couldn't budge it."

"This sort of changes things," observed Ray. He kicked at the rod. "Do you think that little redhead could carry this?"

"What does it weigh?"

"Rough guess, 120, 130 pounds. Could you carry it? I suspect you're much more fit than…."

Sue squatted, wrapped her hands around the metal, and lifted it a foot. "With difficulty," she admitted. "It would have been hard for me to move it here and get it in place. Getting it back would have been even harder. We're looking at a homicide rather than an accidental death, aren't we? And that 911 call suggests…."

"I'm not ready to even speculate on that yet," said Ray. He turned around and glanced around at the house, the garage, their own two vehicles. "So now this whole place is a crime scene. Do you want to start in the house or the garage?"

"The house," answered Sue quickly. "I'll be able to see what's changed since the last time I was in there."

An hour later they emerged, Sue holding the door as Ray gingerly carried a Macintosh computer in gloved hands. Sue, holding the keyboard and mouse in a clear plastic bag, opened the back of her Jeep and made room for the machine and its appliances between the cases containing her investigative equipment.

"That's an unexpected find," said Ray.

"He didn't have the computer more than a few weeks, but it was already starting to disappear in the clutter. Any open space in that dump of a house would be like a vacuum. Looks like he made room on that table to look at the contents of the hard drive, then didn't use it again. I shudder to think how long a thorough search of that place will take."

"Let's look in the garage. Then we'll go back to the office and develop a plan for the next steps."

Sue followed him along the gravel drive, weeds encroaching on the uneven surface. Struggling a bit with the heavy garage door on an overhead track, Ray pushed it open.

"Plates are three years out of date," said Sue, slipping sideways through the debris.

"Why bother keeping up to date if you don't have an operator's permit?"

"There's that. Too bad the people who write the laws are clueless about the folks that break them." She bent and looked at the right rear tire. "I bet these bald Eagles match my plaster casts." She paused for a moment. "One more thing to process. We've got the computer and the probable vehicle. Too bad we're a day late and a perp short."

"Great wit for someone who's sleep deprived. Now if you could only tell me about the phantom cell?"

"I think we're just looking at the top of the proverbial iceberg. This case gets more and more complicated."

"I wonder if you can find any residue of burned skin on that sauna stove?"

"I don't know how to do that," Sue said thoughtfully. "I'll need to make some phone calls and send some emails."

40

Ray read Sally Rood the boilerplate from a laminated card. Then he identified himself and Rood, and gave the date, time, and location of the interview. He glanced up at one of the two ceiling cameras as he finished, then settled his gaze on Rood.

"Thank you for coming in," he said.

"Like I had a choice," she responded. "So there's this cop at my hotel room at seven in the morning. I'm sure my new boyfriend is sitting there now, wondering what kind of woman he got mixed up with."

Rood's face was flushed, her body tense. To Ray, she smelled of soap and shampoo, cigarettes and coffee.

"The SOB wasn't even going to give me a chance to shower." She crossed her arms fiercely over her chest. "What's this all about anyway? Is Jim claiming I stole something on my way out? Your deputy was with me the whole time." She made a face. "That asshole doesn't have anything worth taking, and if he did, fat chance you could find it in that dump."

"Jim Moarse was found dead in his sauna this morning." Ray let the words sink in.

Rood stared blankly, her defensive stance drooping. She clenched her arms again. "Jim and that damn sauna," she sneered. "When he was really drunk, he liked to climb in there, said the heat was 'purifying,' that he never had a hangover the next day." She laughed, but her fingers were making white marks on her arms. "He liked to drag me in there with him, but he couldn't keep his hands off me. I don't like being pawed. It was one of the things we argued about, one of the many things." She relaxed slightly and lifted her chin. "So I'm sorry he's dead, but what does it have to do with me?"

Ray slid his notebook into a more central position. "I need some general information," he said. "Where were you last night?"

"I sure as hell wasn't with him, if that's what you're asking. You followed me down 22 almost to town yesterday. And that's where I was. I didn't come back up here to God's country."

"What were you doing?"

"I was hanging out with a friend."

"Where?"

"In town."

"Doing what?"

"What people do when they hang out." She lifted her hair off her neck with one manicured hand and laughed at him.

Ray kept his gaze steady. "Can you be a bit more specific?"

"Like are you trying to establish if I have an alibi? Is that it? Okay, I'll play the game. I met someone in town. We had lunch, walked around. We got a room at the Park Place, had dinner there, and late in the evening we had drinks in the bar up at the top. Get a copy of my hotel bill; it's all there. And the city cop that was pounding on the door of our room before dawn will tell you…I guess he figured out that I was there because my car was in the parking lot."

"The room was registered in your name?"

"Yeah, my name, credit card, my plate number."

"Does your friend have a name?"

"I don't want him involved. Like, he's getting a divorce, and him being with me would just make things worse."

"That shouldn't happen. His name is?"

Rood narrowed her eyes, staring him down. "Okay, it's Dan Ellis. He's a lawyer from downstate. Wyandotte."

"After you left Moarse, did you go back there again?"

"No."

"Did you contact him again by phone, text, e-mail?"

"No."

"Tell me more about your relationship with Moarse?"

Rood crossed her legs, opened her purse, and closed it again. "God, I wish you could smoke in here. Anyway, there's not much to tell. I met

Jim the summer I was waitressing. He was sort of a fun guy and a big tipper. In the fall I was looking for a new place to stay. I'd been sharing an apartment with three other girls, and that wasn't going so well. Jim offered me a room, no strings attached." She uncrossed her legs, re-crossed them. "I know what you're thinking," she said, looking directly at Ray. "At first things were okay, fun, but that didn't last too long. I figured out pretty quick that he had money trouble and was going down fast. Of course, the worse things got, the more he drank."

"What was his occupation?"

Rood snorted. "Like half the men I've met up here, he said he was a builder." She shrugged. "And I guess that was true, or at least it had been once. Jim talked about this formula he had. He'd buy lots cheap at tax sales and build inexpensive homes—bi-levels, half story down and a half story up. He told me that he and his crew, a couple of guys, could throw one of those together in a few weeks, and he cleared about 20 grand on each building. Then, boo hoo, the housing market fell apart, and his bank cut off his credit line. By the time I moved in, he was running out of money. And all the so-called friends he'd screwed along the way wanted their money. They were pissed. People were always coming by, calling, sending letters."

"Did he ever mention Al Capone or buried treasure?"

"Are you kidding?" She laughed. "Pretty funny. He could have used a little buried treasure. He was desperate."

"Can you give me any names of friends?"

"Who knows? Like I said, what friends he might of had were super pissed. The two of us ended up completely isolated out there. He didn't have money to take me anyplace, and he refused to drive that stupid old Jeep of his anywhere—except in the middle of the night. That's a lot of fun. He acted like I was his chauffeur or something."

"So there were no other friends?"

"Not really. Well, there was one guy that came on the scene about the time I was thinking of leaving, a Ricky something, an old friend from somewhere. Jim was pretty excited to hook up with him again, said the guy was rich and knew all the angles."

"Can you tell me about this man?"

"Not really. I only saw him, let me think, twice. The first time he arrived with a lot of food and booze. The food came from some good place in TC, not your usual carryout. The two of them got pretty smashed, and then went off to take a sauna. Jim wanted me to join them, but I wasn't going to have any of that."

"And the second time?"

"Pretty much like the first, but at some point, Jim told me to get lost for a while. They had to talk business. I did, I went to the movies. The guy was gone when I got back. Jim said they were working on some big deal, that things were going to get better."

"Did he give you any details?"

"No, and by that time I just couldn't stand him anymore. I didn't care. He might have been up that minute, but he'd be down the next. Since I'd moved in, he was more and more depressed. I've heard stories, but I've never seen someone so determined to drink themselves to death before."

"So you lived with him from…?"

"Sometime in October till the second or third week of February."

"Can you describe this Ricky fellow?"

"About your height and size, early 40s. He seemed pretty fit, especially compared to Jim. Wore those nylon running suits like ghetto kids. Used too much perfume. Something sort of foreign about him. But it wasn't how he talked. You know, just something different. Not from here. He gave me the creeps." She crossed her arms again over her chest and took a deep breath. "A woman knows a lot about a man by the way he looks at her," she said. "That's one of the first things you learn waitressing. Ricky looked me over like a piece of meat, something he'd use and toss away like an empty cigarette pack. I'm sure if we had ever been alone together, he would of hit on me instantly."

"What kind of vehicle did Ricky drive?"

"Something big, expensive."

"Color, make, model?"

"I don't know. I only saw it at night and not even close. I think it was light colored, maybe gray or silver, a Mercedes or Cadillac, an SUV."

"Do you remember anything about a plate number or state?"

"Are you kidding?"

"And you're sure you don't have a last name?"

"I'm pretty sure he never used it."

Ray took some time scanning the notes he'd made. Rood sat perfectly still for the first time during the interview. "I think that's it for now," he said, finally. "But I want your cell number in case I need to talk with you again. And here's my card. Please call if you remember anything that you think might be helpful. Are you planning to stay in the area?"

"Yeah, I am as a matter of fact. I've got a job lined up at the casino. Start next weekend." Her tone softened, "I'm sorry for Jim," she said. "Really. As men go, he wasn't a bad sort. I just caught him crashing and burning. And I needed to get away. I didn't sign on to be part of the wreckage."

41

Mackenzie ran her hands back, fingers spread, through her hair. She was Skyping with Ken Lee again, but she'd just woken up and the home video feed was a useful mirror.

"I've got your tracks on screen," Ken Lee was saying, "and I've just imposed Sabotny's over yours."

"Anything interesting?" she yawned, stretching her arms and slowly rolling her head from side to side.

"You okay? I thought you were up and at it hours ago."

"I fell back to sleep. Now I feel worse for the wear. What do you have?"

"Lots of stuff. First Sabotny. He was in town earlier in the evening. Looks like he had dinner at Outback, yet again. I've noticed that ex-military types think that's the epitome of...."

"You're ex-military. You wouldn't go near any chain restaurant, especially that one," she chided.

"Got close to dying too many times. Now I make sure every meal is worth eating just in case it's my last. As I was saying, his vehicle was there for about an hour and a half, and then he stopped at that grocery complex on U.S. 31 for 20 minutes before heading back up 22. He was home for 15 minutes before going out to Moarse's place. Looking at your track and timeline, you'd been in place quite awhile by then."

"Yep, I was starting to go crazy. I'm not designed for surveillance work."

"Your track is more interesting than Sabotny's. All I can see is his vehicle's movements. Your movements I can tie to Google Earth and know your exact location, even when you're walking."

"What's so interesting about it?"

"I'm just getting to that. Eventually Sabotny leaves the Moarse place, and you plant the phantom cell. Then you hustle out of there, return to your car, drive around for a bit, then roll by again. Sabotny did sort of the same thing, only he headed south, then came back north. Then he does this really curious thing. He heads west and drives all over hell's half acre before finally going back down to Traverse and home. You two probably passed in the process."

"I did see a car or two. Not much moving up here at that time of night. What do you think he was up to?"

"Here's me speculating. Sabotny does the deed on Moarse, goes off, then comes back to check on something, like to make sure the dude is stone dead. But surprise, the cops are there. Quick switch to panic mode. He's wondering how the heat got there so fast. So he does a run, paranoid as hell, thinking maybe he's being followed."

"Yeah, okay, that's good," said Mackenzie. "I'd like the SOB to feel some of the terror he inflicted on my brother."

"The downside is I don't have his GPS signal anymore. The unit failed or he found it. My bet is that he found it. He doesn't just 'think,' he 'knows' he's being watched. I've told you before, baby, this guy is bad. He's a killer, a psychopath. And now he's feeling like a trapped animal. He isn't going to feel safe until he finds and eliminates whoever's after him. He's going to take out anyone that looks like a threat."

"I hear you Ken Lee. But what can he know? He doesn't know anything about me," asked Mackenzie.

"And that's where we should leave things. It's time to pull the plug, time to get out, time to find an exit strategy, and get your pretty ass out before things go totally to shit."

"I don't agree. He can't possibly know I'm after him."

"Do you know that for sure? One hundred percent for sure? No. And the other thing you don't know is crazy. I mean, really crazy, smart crazy. You don't know these people. That dude is totally wired and he's going to use all his resources to eliminate the threat. If you found him, he can find you."

"All right. I'll think about it. So why did he kill Moarse?" she asked, trying to change the direction.

"Moarse was a liability. Whatever Sabotny needed from him was over. And it would have been a perfect murder. Drunk dies in sauna, someone finds the putrid body days later. Just another dumbshit, accidental death. But things don't go down like planned. And now he's on the hunt. Mackenzie, we need to get you out of there. Let's bring in some pros, see if we can get enough on the dude to take to the police."

"I want that SOB to rot in jail for the rest of his life, Ken Lee. I want him to be caged up with the other human garbage, wherever they put them in this state, Jackson, Marquette...."

"Good. Go to the cops. Tell them what you know. There might be enough to nail him."

"Would they believe me? Do they have enough evidence to build a case, or did they screw up the scene? What if the sheriff is an old friend of Sabotny's—and I've blown my cover?"

"Yeah, yeah. Lots of problems" Ken Lee admitted. "And the prosecutor might have gotten his degree online. Sabotny is going to have the best lawyers money can buy. But still...."

"You know what, Ken Lee, I like the fact that he's crazy. I want to turn up the heat."

"No, Mackenzie. We need to get you out of there."

"I'll say it again: how's he going to find me?"

"Okay, okay. Give me a minute. I got it. When he looked up his old buddies, he was wondering about you. What happened to that skinny little girl, he says to himself? You've made yourself hard to trace, but he's been trying. And don't think you haven't been noticed around there. That's too small of a place. It's not like Manhattan or L.A. You've got to come home, baby. We'll come up with another strategy."

"What's all this 'baby' crap?" asked Mackenzie. "You've never used that term before, but it's been creeping into our conversations lately. I'm not your baby. I'm not anyone's baby. I'm a woman. And I'm not leaving until this is over."

"I should come out then."

"No. Listen. I appreciate all you've done, but this is mine. You can visit after everything is over. We'll walk the beaches, drink wine, watch the sunset, the things couples do. But right now, just keep giving me the support. No more lectures. I'm going to figure this out and nail him myself one way or another."

42

"How did your interview with Ms. Rood go?"

"Just give me a few more minutes," Ray said, his eyes not moving off the screen. "Where is Simone?"

"She's at home."

"All this time?"

"I have a guest; flew in last night. He's looking after her."

"Sorry," said Ray.

"It's okay," said Sue. "He needs to know what I do and the hours I work."

"Sure that's a good thing?"

"I was asking about your conversation with Sally Rood."

"I just posted my notes. You can look at the video when you have time. In short, she's not a morning person, and she has a certain ambivalence about law enforcement, especially when she's pulled from the arms of her lover at an early hour."

"I can relate to that," said Sue, giving Ray a wry smile.

"I may be wrong, but I don't think she's involved in Moarse's death. I believe her when she says that she didn't come north again after we stopped following her. And we can easily check on her alibi if need be.

"Did you learn anything about Moarse that we don't already know?"

"He didn't like driving his Jeep during daylight hours."

"Imagine that," Sue laughed. "Hasn't had an operator's permit in years. Didn't bother to update the tags on his Jeep, either."

"Why should he?" said Ray. "Just a waste of good money."

"I wonder how common that is?"

"More common than either one of us would want to admit. If you took a reasonable amount of care—not that most of these characters are particularly skilled at taking care of anything—I'm sure you could get away with it for years. But back to your initial question. Moarse, according to Rood, was some kind of builder who was crashing financially and had a major drinking problem. The one thing she told me that might prove to be of interest is an old friend Moarse reconnected with by the name of Ricky."

"Last name?"

"She doesn't think she ever heard it. But Moarse told her they were working a big deal."

"Capone?"

"No, no Capone. Never heard of it."

"So that's it?"

"Well, almost. This Ricky has a large, light-colored car, perhaps an SUV that might be a Cadillac or Mercedes. No hint as to plate number or state."

"Can we have the road patrol guys pull over every large SUV and ask the driver if his friends call him Ricky?" asked Sue.

"Only in Arizona," said Ray. He sighed, stood up, and stretched. "I can tell we're both way too tired given the direction of the humor. Let's do some planning." He lowered the whiteboard and retrieved the container with the markers.

"First, I'd like to see if we could establish the fact that Moarse was the killer of Vincent Fox. I'll contact Fox's daughter and see if she's ever heard of him. We can also look through the surveillance tapes from the casino to see if he was lurking around the day Fox made the big hit. And, of course, did he act alone or did he have accomplices?

"Second, we need to know why he was murdered. Is it connected with the Fox crime or something else? We're going to have to find out a lot more about Jim Moarse.

"And third, the phantom 911 call. Someone was watching this crime go down. They wanted to make sure we were directed to the murder scene. So why aren't they coming in to tell us about it?"

"Okay," said Sue. "This is how I would like to go forward. For the first item on your list, proving Moarse killed Fox: I'll need to establish that the computer we found in Fox's house actually belonged to Fox. That's the easy part. Then I'll search Fox's house for evidence that placed Fox there or connects Moarse to his abduction. That's the hard part."

"Approach it like an archeologist, try to stay with the upper layers."

"Ha ha. We also have to bring his Jeep in and go through the interior. I think we'll get a match on the tires with the casts I made at Fox's house. Just with that, there's a lot of work to be done before we move onto the second part: why. I don't even know what to say about your number 3."

"Give me some time lines," said Ray.

"The day's going away, and I'm very tired. I'd like to start on the house tomorrow."

"Are you sure?" said Ray. "It can wait till Monday."

"Tomorrow, not early, by about noon. The area's got to stay secured until I'm done. Let's run one road patrol at night and two during the day. That will give us someone every shift to protect the scene."

"Okay."

"If I could have some help…. Brett, he should be learning this stuff. We'll need at least two days, maybe more for the house, barn, sauna, a good look around the property, and to process the Jeep. We'll have to cover his shifts with people working overtime."

Ray nodded in agreement. "Until Monday afternoon?"

"No, there's too much to do. How about Tuesday afternoon?"

"Tuesday morning is better. How about your weekend guest?"

"I'll see how he and Simone get on. She has a really good sense of character. In fact, she might save me a lot of trouble."

43

Mackenzie was back in front of the screen, caught in another unrecoverable yawn.

"You still tired from the weekend?" Ken Lee asked.

"No, I'm okay. I slept about 12 hours last night and then got up early and went to TC for yoga. Good instructor. I hope I'm in that good of shape when I get to be 60-something. Ken Lee, I apologize about getting pissy yesterday."

"No problem, I understand. Things have been…."

"Here's what's going on," Mackenzie cut him off, "I don't know what to do now. I'm back to not having a plan. I've made a couple of passes of the Moarse property. Looks like the local sheriff's department is securing the scene night and day. On my last drive by, there were three vehicles, probably the crime scene team. The garage door was open with no Jeep in sight. They must have moved it to another location. I wonder what that's all about?"

"Who knows what kind of stuff Moarse might have been into. I imagine the cops are trying as hard to figure this out as we are. And by now they've found the phantom phone. Bet that's a real puzzler. What did you tell me the last major caper was up there—someone chopping down cherry trees? Lots of them?"

"Yeah, during the late winter. Made both the paper and TV. Some kind of revenge thing."

"How's the media covering this one?"

"Nothing yet. Not a peep. Local news seems to shut down during the weekend. Actually, I didn't turn the TV on this morning, and there's nothing in the paper. I imagine the sheriff's department does a regular press briefing. I'll watch the local news tonight."

"I'm going to say it again. This would be a good time to say sayonara to all those pines and lakes you've been telling me about and get back to civilization. Let the local heat figure it out. Look at the facts. First, you're breaking the law. You've observed a murder and not brought that information to the police. Second, Sabotny now knows that someone is watching him."

"And I'll say it again, too. He doesn't know who I am. I'm invisible."

"Are you? How invisible? You live in a little village. You're new. In spite of all your precautions, people notice."

"Like who?"

"There's the mailman."

"I get my mail in Traverse City or electronically," she answered.

"Yeah, but the mailman drives by. He needs something for his brain to chew on as he covers his route. He notices the house is occupied. He sees you getting in the car. He wonders why you don't get mail. He mentions it to his favorite waitress in town. She works at that cafe you go to; she recognizes you, and that night she tells her boyfriend.... Want me to go on? How about the UPS and Fedex drivers, the garbage man, the cop on the road patrol? How about the bag boy at the grocery who also sees what kind of car you climb into when he's out collecting carts? How about the guys who upgraded your security system?"

"We hired a downstate company," she countered.

"What if they farmed out some of the work to a local contractor?"

"Well, I don't think so," Mackenzie replied.

"Yeah, but you don't know for sure. You don't know anything for sure. I'm saying, you may not be seeing any of these folks, but some of them are seeing you. And now that Sabotny is tipped off, he's trying to figure out who is watching him. Is it one of his neighbors? Someone with a view of his house?"

"Dozens of people have the same view I do."

"And are all those houses occupied?"

"Well, no. Not during the winter."

"So, he scans the environment and says to his old friend, the mailman, 'Hey Herb, anyone new living along the shore on West Bay or up there on the hill?' And Herb says something like, 'No one permanent I'm delivering to.' So Sabotny asks, 'You haven't heard about anyone new, maybe a woman in one of those expensive lakefront properties?' And Herb thinks for a moment or two and says, 'Well my brother-in-law put a dish on one of those trophy houses for some single woman. Says she must have big bucks.'"

"Ken Lee, that's all just fantasy. You have a great imagination."

"Yeah, that's fantasy, but that's the way things go down. Sabotny's probably got a network of friends among the locals. Right now he's looking in every direction. For Sabotny, this is a life-or-death situation. He's on full alert. You've been so totally fixated on him, you haven't seen anyone else, but lots of people have seen you."

"So what do you think I should do?"

"You know what I think. You reject that straight up. So I want you to go on full alert. Make sure your security system is working and always turned on. Keep weapons within easy reach when you're at home. Any time you leave the house, go fully armed. Don't be surprised if someone tries to run you off the road. Watch out for a car jacking. Carry that satellite uplink on you at all times so I know where you are. Hit the panic button if you're in trouble."

"How can I go to yoga?"

"You know the answer."

"So now I'm a captive?"

"The game totally changed Saturday night. Maybe it isn't a checkmate, but it's close. You're going to have to figure out how to escape."

"What would you do?"

"Exactly what I've been saying over and over. Pull you, and put three big, ugly ex-Seals in your place. Figure out a way to put some heat on Sabotny. Get him to do something desperate and stupid, then figure out how to get justice for your brother."

44

Simone walked into Ray's office, the end of her leash in her mouth, the remainder dragging behind. Sue followed, armed with a folder and her ubiquitous coffee mug. Ray spent several moments attending to Simone, collecting enthusiastic kisses as he scratched the ears of the wiggling terrier.

"How did your weekend work out?"

"We sort of had dates around the edges of my work. He took me out for dinner Saturday, then we went to a movie. I don't think I made it past the opening credits. Sunday morning I took him for a forced walk across the top of Sleeping Bear before I went back to the Moarse place."

"It was raining cats and dogs all morning," said Ray.

"Yup, but he didn't complain too much. And I made him a special dinner Sunday night."

"Yes?"

"Stuff you taught me. Salmon with a caper sauce. I cooked the fish on the grill just like you do. And I served salad with a baguette that I resuscitated with a few minutes in the oven. I had a good bottle of Vouvray chilled, and topped the meal off with thimbleberry jam on Ben & Jerry's vanilla, sort of an up-north touch."

"The jam or the Ben...."

"Here, check this out," said Sue, sliding a plastic bag containing a rectangular object the size of a cigarette pack in his direction.

"What is it?" He held the bag up to his face and inspected the device, olive drab in color with a hard plastic exterior.

"It's the phantom phone," said Sue.

"Really? I've never seen anything like this before."

"Neither have I. But I verified that it's the source of the 911 signal." She put her finger on the bag. "Notice there are two buttons on the front. You have to push them in sequence to turn the thing on, the small one first and the large one next. It looks as if it was designed so it couldn't be accidentally activated."

"Where did you find it?"

"Behind a pile of firewood next to the sauna."

"Why would anyone go to all that trouble to have a device like this fabricated when old cell phones are a dime a dozen?"

"My question, exactly," said Sue. "I sent photos to a guy I've taken workshops from at the Bureau. I asked the same question."

"Any response?"

"Well, yes, I also phoned. I wanted to make sure he still remembered me. So, Nigel, that's the guy, English sounding name, but I don't think he is, or at least he doesn't sound like it, said that's a new one on him, and he's a specialist in this kind of exotic stuff. He wants me to send it on to him when we're done so he can have a look. His speculation is that someone built a super 911 phone with quality components to make sure it did what was needed. He said it probably has an excellent GPS function and a high output cell signal. He really liked the two button arrangement."

"Any prints?"

"No, and I didn't expect any, either."

"We've talked about this already, but what's going on here?" asked Ray.

"Seems pretty clear that the person who put the phone in place was either watching Moarse or the perp who did him."

"Or perhaps, both," said Ray.

"There's that."

"Did this Nigel have any idea about the source? Maybe we could trace it to the person that way."

"He said this kind of device comes out of boutique shops, ones that build specialty equipment for corporate security. They do one-offs and small production runs. He said you won't find this on the Internet. Someone probably dropped a few K or more to get a product with this kind of functionality." Sue looked across at Ray. "And I take it no one has come forward looking for their non-phone?"

"No."

"How about the press?"

"I did a briefing this morning. No one showed. Here's the release I put out," he passed her a single piece of paper.

"So Moarse died under suspicious circumstances, and his name is being withheld pending notification of kin. How are you doing on that?"

"Everything I've done is in the file," Ray tapped the aluminum cover of his laptop. "I have yet to find any relatives. Moarse has no outstanding warrants. We've talked about his priors—nothing recent. He's got a number of civil actions pending against him. Property tax is a year in arrears. We need to do a lot more digging."

"Maybe you just need to get the name out there. Make an appeal to the community for help. We might get lucky."

"Yes," agreed Ray. "Will you have the scene processed by tomorrow? The two of us need to…"

"No way, it will take a month of Sundays to sort through that mess. But your first charge to me was to definitely connect Moarse to Vincent Fox's death. I've got that. The tires on the Jeep match the casts I made at Fox's house. More importantly," she said, pushing a photo across to Ray, "look what I found in the back of the Jeep under the passenger seat."

"The boot, the missing right boot. Did it look like it had been hidden?"

"No, it was just lying there. My guess is Fox's body was thrown in and his boot caught and was left behind when the body was tossed in the ditch. Moarse didn't seem to be too good with the details, even something that could send him to prison for the rest of his life."

"How about the burned skin on the sauna stove?"

"I'm still trying to figure out how to do that. The guys at the State Police lab are helping me."

"What did you find in the house?" asked Ray.

"A couple of things. First, I found a copy of Fox's book."

"Where?"

"It was in the bathroom under a copy of the *Northern Express*. You're smiling."

"Yes, but I won't comment. Prints?"

"Not yet, Ray. I haven't processed them. Tomorrow."

"What else?"

"This is even more interesting than the phantom cell." She set a plastic bag containing a worn leather wallet in front of Ray, then two additional plastic bags, one containing a few small denomination bills, the other containing several $100 bills.

"How many?" asked Ray, looking at the $100s.

"Five, they were folded and concealed in a separate compartment."

They sat in silence for a moment. "And?" said Ray.

"Same series as Ma French found. Crumpled, but they appear to be uncirculated 100s. So new question, how did that Iraq money end up in Moarse's wallet? Did you find any service record for him?" asked Sue.

"No, none."

"There have got to be a ton of Iraq war veterans living in this area. How do we get a list?"

"And even if we could, how do we get enough legs to run this one down?" said Ray.

45

Mackenzie sat at her desk, staring at the screen. With her index and middle finger moving slowly across the surface of the Trackpad, she scrolled up the page. Then she dropped her hands in her lap, folded them left over right, and gently swiveled in her chair from side to side, her eyes still fixed on the screen.

She thought about the mystery she had been reading the evening before, how the gutsy P.I. took on the bad guys with her fists, her gun, and her guile. Mackenzie liked that image, but she had to admit that she wasn't that character. *I've never been in a real fight,* she thought. Yes, she had taken martial arts classes and proven herself in countless competitions, but everything had taken place in a controlled environment. They weren't real world battles. She reached up to feel the budge of the gun holstered under her left breast. Again, she had proven to be an apt student and an expert shot, but how would she react in a firefight. *Could I really pull the trigger?*

Her mind wondered back to the tough Chicago P.I. If she emulated that character, what would she do? Directly confront Sabotny with gun in hand? *No, that's fiction,* she thought. If there was only some way she could force a confession from him. But what was the likelihood that he would tell the truth?

Mackenzie opened the first page on the original planning document. At the top in bold letters was the overarching goal:

Conviction and imprisonment of everyone involved with Terry's death.

She copied the goal statement and pasted it into a graphic outlining program. Then, she laid out her options with **direct confrontation** on the far left and **going to the police** at the far right. Mackenzie tried to make other possibilities fit between the two polar positions, but nothing seemed to work. She was just spinning her wheels. At this point those other possibilities were just modest variations on the extremes.

Ken Lee's nagging thought that it was time to go put this investigation in other peoples' hands continued to push into her consciousness. Maybe he was right. Maybe it was time to bring in the cavalry. That's what she would have done in the corporate world. As a manager faced with overwhelming problems, she'd contract with the best people in the business to generate and implement solutions.

Mackenzie keyed *Vision of the Future* at the top of a new document. As she wrote, she could see how elements could be put into place to keep a close watch on Sabotny and further explore his background. Maybe they could find incriminating evidence to tie him to other crimes. Even if she couldn't get him for Terry's death, she hoped that she could bring havoc to Sabotny's life, strip him of his fortune, and send him to prison.

Rereading her words, the dreariness that had enshrouded her for weeks started to lift. She could get away from the cold, damp Michigan spring and go back to California. From a safe distance, both physically and psychologically, she could monitor the progress of a group working on this project.

Mackenzie picked up her phone. She texted Ken Lee a four-word message. *Put a team together.*

Four minutes later he was on screen, "Why the sudden change?" he asked.

"Okay, so it took me awhile to figure out I wasn't Wonder Woman. I apologize again for being less than nice to you. I just thought I could do this, find these people, and I don't know...."

"You had to do what you had to do. And all the information we've gathered thus far will be a good starting point for the team. I've already started putting together a list of people, specialists, to pull together for this."

"Am I going to end up broke?"

"I don't think so. No. We should be able to move fairly quickly. If nothing else we can tip the IRS to the stolen cash. There's enough there to put him in the slammer for decades. And his sweetie, Elena Rustova, may be implicated too. Once we feed them the info, I'm sure the I.N.S. will be happy to ship her back to Moldova."

"But Sabotny, I don't want that SOB to go to one of those federal country clubs for tax dodgers. I want him rotting in a dingy state prison for life."

"I hear you. Maybe we can find a way for him to go down for Moarse. Your brother, that's almost an impossible case. But I'll do my best to get him one way or another."

Mackenzie was playing with airline schedules as she listened. "I'm coming back to California."

"When?"

"How about tomorrow. There's nothing direct. I'll have to go through either Chicago or Minneapolis. I could be there by late afternoon."

"Dinner someplace on the ocean?" asked Ken Lee.

"Sounds like a date. Then I've got some other plans for you."

"I've missed you, baby," he said.

"Ditto, baby.

"I'll get things in place. Leave your car in long-term parking. I think I can have people on the ground in a few days. Okay if they use your house?"

"Absolutely. And when this is all over, I want to bring you back here. It's beautiful, especially in the summer, and I want to share it with you."

"You're on. Now get back here. I'll need your brain and your skills in getting this thing organized."

Mackenzie was feeling ebullient as she drove down M22. The lake glistened under the brilliant sunlight. The overture to "A Midsummer Night's Dream" was playing on the radio. She cranked up the volume.

Once at the yoga studio, she slid into the first of two unisex restrooms, carefully locked the door, and removed her weaponry and extra clothing. Clad in black Lycra, feet bare, and her tactical boots stowed with her other gear in her Patagonia backpack, Mackenzie rolled out her mat in a far corner of the studio and tried to quiet her thoughts.

An hour and a half later she was back outside in the warm spring air and sunshine, her spirits soaring. Stopping for dinner at a small French restaurant, she savored every bit of the exquisitely prepared meal and two glasses of Quintessa. The only thing missing was companionship, and tomorrow night she would have that.

Mackenzie noticed the white van with two orange cones behind it on the road just beyond her drive. She focused on them briefly, then reached up and pushed the garage door opener. She was looking down, collecting her things, when the side window of her car came crashing in. There was a violent jolt just before the world slipped away.

46

Mackenzie came to on the cold metal floor of the cargo van, her unsupported neck bent at an unnatural angle. Every bounce and sway of the vehicle intensified her agony. Struggling to inhale, Mackenzie discovered that she couldn't open her mouth and that her nasal passages were partially obstructed. A wave of panic ran though her, the sudden jolt of adrenalin helping her break through the effects of the physical assault, pain, and nausea.

As she tried to pull herself into a more comfortable position, she realized her hands were bound behind her. As she strained she felt zip ties cut into her skin. She realized that her ankles were bound also.

Pushing her tongue against the surface of the tape that covered her lips, she focused on not vomiting, breathing slowly, trying to relax her muscles and control her panic.

Mackenzie tried to remember the events leading up to this nightmare. There was the shower of glass, the burning sting and high-voltage jolt, the biting chemical scent. *Ether*, she thought. She could still smell it. The nausea came back. She focused on her breathing again, trying to keep from retching, frightened she might drown on her own vomit.

Breathing deeply, she concentrated on opening her eyes. The right one cooperated, giving her an oscillating view of the floor of the van and storage bins attached to the wall. Her left eye was a source of pain. Groggily, she tried to comprehend what that meant. Was it damaged, swelled shut, missing? She pulled her eyes tight and slipped toward unconsciousness. Pushing against oblivion, she roused herself.

Inventory, do an inventory, she thought. Starting at her toes, she concentrated on sensations, what she could move, how was she bound. Feet still in boots, protected. Zip ties, painfully tight above the boots. She moved, her eyes closed, trying to visualize the condition of her legs, knees and thighs. *Intact,* she thought.

She felt a nagging pain in the hip she was resting on, but her chest and back seemed unharmed. One finger at a time, she probed the condition of each hand, then pulled again at the ligatures that held her wrists. *Nothing broken, both securely bound.* Her tongue ran along her teeth, left to right, top to bottom. *Intact.*

The truck bounced hard several times, came to a stop, and started again. Mackenzie struggled against the nausea once more, pushing it back to the edge of her consciousness. She focused on her breathing, slowing everything down, filling her lungs as deeply as possible.

She opened her eyes again. Once more, vision from the right eye only. Lifting her head, she could see some of the front windshield and a partial silhouette of the driver. *How did this happen?* She closed her eyes.

When she was awake again, there was no motion. She shivered against the cold metal interior. Then there was the sound of voices and the opening of doors. She was pulled by her feet into the night air, her body falling hard to the ground.

"Careful," came a voice. "We might still have some fun with her."

Mackenzie was aware of a bright light, the interior of her closed eyes glowing red.

"God, she's a mess. I don't want her blood all over my carpet."

"Can't take my van. We'd be stuck before we got 10 feet."

"Got a tarp in that truck?"

"Yeah."

"Get it, and do a good job spreading it around. I don't want a trace of her left when we're done."

Mackenzie felt her body being moved again. She continued to feign unconsciousness. This time she was being carried. Then she felt the plastic of the tarp against her face, heard the sound of the hatch slamming and the doors closing, and then the rumble of a big engine coming to life. She was going with sensations, avoiding thinking about her situation. She could smell a leather interior and imagined the soft glow of the instrument panel.

"Did you check her for weapons?"

It was Sabotny's voice.

"Just like you told me. You coulda been there to help."

"No need to increase our exposure. No one remembers a white work van. Was she packing?"

"Yeah, a sweet little Glock right under her left tit. Big tits, just like her old lady."

"Fucking pervert, copping a feel off an unconscious…."

"Like it matters."

"No other weapons? You patted her down good?"

"Just the Glock. She had some kind of electronic device around her neck, though."

"What did you do with that?"

"I smashed it."

The men went silent.

Mackenzie listened to the mechanical sounds of the vehicle as it bumped along the uneven surface. Then things went silent. Doors opened. She was lifted out, carried a short distance, and dropped on sand—cold and damp against her Lycra shirt and tights.

"What's the deal with the fire?" came the other voice. Mackenzie shivered, partially opening her good eye to the twilight surroundings. She could feel the breeze coming off Lake Michigan.

"I like fires. You know that. I always make a fire on the beach at night. We made a fire that night with Terry. Remember?"

Mackenzie could see the glow of the fire increase. The two men were drinking, passing a bottle back and forth. One of them, the heavier one, moved behind the fire. A scar ran between his eyebrows. *Brewler.*

"Why did you make the hole so fucking big? You could bury an elephant in here," he asked Sabotny.

"I was trying to get the hang of how to use the backhoe on that old Kubota. Once I figured it out, it was too much fun. I was like a kid playing in sand. If we'd buried Terry like this, we wouldn't be messing with this shit now. Just another runaway; that's what they would have said."

"If Terry had let us have his sister, he wouldn't have gotten hurt at all. We'd a had our fun, maybe even started something regular."

"Drag her over here, and put her back on the tarp. I don't want her ass in sand. What a mess, she's got blood all over. I told you to be careful."

"Yeah, but you weren't willing to put your ass out there. I had to do the whole thing myself. No time to be dainty."

Suddenly Sabotny was standing above her, looking directly into her half open eye. "Good morning, darling," he sneered. "You're probably wondering how we figured this out." He bent over and snapped his fingers an inch from her good eye. "Easy, once we found that GPS. Had to be someone local. And new people don't go unnoticed, darling. And as luck would have it, Chris, here, serviced the back-up generator at your house, something you asked your realtor to take care of. That's when we heard about the rich woman from California. And then there was the Subaru, seemed to be around too often. Besides, I always knew you'd be out there sometime looking for revenge. I've been waiting for you."

"Why don't you pull the tape off? Let her talk," said Brewler.

"Don't mess with a good thing. I don't care what she has to say."

Brewler knelt at her side. She saw the flash of steel, the fire reflecting off a knife. He ran his hand under her shirt, then pulled the stretchy material against the jagged serrations of the blade. Then he slit through the bra, severing the band between the cups. He looked up at Sabotny, "I told you she had big tits, nice and hard with big nipples."

"Too bad you fucked up her face."

"Get a flag or roll her over. It's all good. Should we tell her about Terry before we fuck her?"

"I think we should have a drink, then flip for who gets sloppy seconds," said Sabotny. He tossed an empty bottle on the fire. Mackenzie watched as he walked to the Range Rover, returning with a fresh whiskey bottle. He stood near the fire, using a knife to cut through the foil, pulling the cork, then passing the bottle to Brewler.

"Too bad Jim ain't here for the party," said Brewler after taking a long hit.

"Yeah, too bad the stupid drunk cooked himself. He was just fucking drinking himself to death."

"This shit is good," Brewler said, passing the bottle back.

"Should be. Seventy bucks a bottle," Sabotny said. "Drag her over near the hole. Make it easier to toss her in when we're done."

Mackenzie felt the tarp under her sliding over rocks and clumps of dune grass. She clawed against the ties, trying to free her hands.

"I think I should have first crack," said Sabotny.

"Why's that?"

"Well, for one thing, I'm holding a gun. And I want her from the front. I'm not like you. Cut loose her ankles and wrists, then hold her down. And give me the knife so I can cut off her pants."

Mackenzie was pushed onto her stomach, and she felt Brewler's knee in her back. A knife ripped through the nylon ties, releasing her wrists and ankles. Then he rolled her on her back, violently pinning her shoulders to the ground with his knees, his hands pressing down hard, painfully holding her wrists near her shoulders.

She tensed her body, getting reading to make a move, focusing all her energy on breaking free.

Then, she saw the flash, followed by the roar of a pistol. Brewler's grip weakened, he fell backwards. Sabotny kicked, then pushed him toward the deep trench until his lifeless body tumbled to the bottom.

Then Sabotny came back for her, moving slowly, staggering. Mackenzie reached for the Rohrbaugh, fumbling with a numb hand, surprised to find the pistol still in its holster on the inside of her boot. She swung it toward him.

"What the...." he threw himself at her.

She squeezed the trigger. He kept coming. She continued pulling on the trigger until the explosions stopped and the only sound was a mechanical click.

Crumpling to his knees, Sabotny fired back, one shot, and fell face first into the sand.

Mackenzie felt a burning sensation in her chest. She clawed at the duct tape covering her mouth, pulling some of it free, filling her lungs with the cold air coming off the lake, and falling, falling.

47

It was after 6 p.m. when Ray slowly rolled to a stop at the top of his drive. Hannah Jeffers, leaning against the side of her car, was waiting. Ray could see that once again his kayak was strapped to the top of her Subaru.

"Get in the car. Let's not waste any sunlight."

"I've got to get my gear," he protested.

"Everything is packed. Your dry suit, fleece, and gear bag are in the back.

"Where will I change?"

"In the car or next to it. It's not likely that anyone will be around. It's not like I haven't seen you *au naturel.* Besides, I'm a doctor. You can trust me."

"What about dinner?" asked Ray, continuing to protest.

"Quiche. I ate mine while I was waiting for you. There's a bottle of mineral water, too. You can eat while I drive. Get in. We're wasting time."

Ray pulled off his sport coat, threw it on the back seat, and slid into the passenger seat. "I've still got a gun and a badge."

"Stash them under the seat."

"That's not secure enough," he said.

"Okay, we'll stuff them in a dry bag and put it in a hatch." Hannah was already rolling down the drive. "Put your belt on. I don't want to get pulled over."

"So what's going on?" asked Ray, noting Hannah's agitation.

"Lot's of stuff. I need to get on the water and drain some of this energy. Eat your quiche before it's completely cold."

Ray attacked the food, trying to remember if he had eaten lunch.

"There's some dark chocolate in the bag, too. Ninety-three percent, just what you like. I only ate half the bar, total self control on my part. Plus I like you."

Between bites, Ray counseled, "Slow down. The lake's going to be there." After a long pause, he asked, "Are you okay?"

"When I'm on the water, I'm okay. I need big, empty places."

"Me, too," said Ray.

"I've learned a lot by watching you."

Ray looked across at her. She briefly turned in his direction.

"How's that?" he asked.

"You know how to control the static. You own a TV, but it's never on. Classical music is usually playing, the local NPR station. You read more than almost anyone I've ever met, and faithfully reflect on your day every evening in a journal. You always have your mind chewing on something. In between, you're focused on food, making sure the next meal is worth eating. And at the edge is always the lake, the water, paddling or walking the shore. You seem to be able to keep the bad stuff in perspective." She paused briefly. "I'm not sure how women fit into that scheme, but thank you for letting me into your life, at least a little bit."

Ray pondered Hannah's statements. He had never thought about his life in those terms before. She had seemed to nail it. He was still savoring the last bit of chocolate when she pulled into a circular parking area at a road end.

"I'll undo the boats while you change," she said, climbing from the car.

After carrying the boats to the water's edge, they sat quietly for a while, watching the surf, each lost in their own thoughts.

Hannah slid behind Ray, putting her arms around his neck. She pulled him tight and playfully nibbled at an ear, then stood up. "How much light do we have?"

Ray looked at his watch, then at the horizon. "Two hours, with the gloaming, then some moonlight. The lake should be flat by then, and we can paddle in the dark. North or south?"

"South. Get your GPS going. Do five or six miles, then turn back."

They launched through the surf, Hannah first. Ray pushed her into the waves, then followed. They settled into an easy rhythm, more relaxed than usual. The sun moved toward the western horizon and slowly sank into the gently curving lake.

The light was almost gone when Ray and Hannah neared the take-out point. Ray's phone, in a protective case under his front deck lines, started to ring."

"Don't ruin the moment," said Hannah. "Don't give in to the static."

"It's Sue, it's important" he replied. "Raft up with my boat."

Ray answered and listened as they floated on the still water. He pulled his GPS from the deck and illuminated the screen.

"We're about two miles south. I see the fire. It'll take us about 20 minutes. Get all the resources in place. When I'm in position, I'll text you. Come down the beach fast, lights and sirens, on. That should create enough of a diversion for me to make a move."

"What's going on?"

"Something bizarre. There was an apparent kidnapping, a possible hostage situation. We're going toward that bonfire. Get my gun." He leaned over Hannah's boat, holding onto her deck lines, steadying the two kayaks, so she could pull open his back hatch cover. She passed him the dry bag and re-covered the hatch. Ray pulled the pistol from the bag and stuffed it in the top of his PFD. "We need to paddle fast. We'll land where a stream dumps into the lake. We've been there before. Sue's going to create a diversion, and I'll see if I can get to the hostage. Stay with the kayaks until I yell."

Ray and Hannah paddled furiously along the shoreline, 30 or 40 yards from the edge of the beach. As they neared the area of the bonfire, shots rang out. Ray paused, grabbed the phone, and hit Sue's number. "Now Sue. Shots fired. Now."

He paddled toward shore, releasing the spray skirt, grabbing his pistol as he tumbled from the boat and scrambled up the embankment, cautious at first, then fully standing up to survey the carnage. "Hannah," he shouted. He held a flashlight for her as she quickly did a triage on the three gunshot victims.

"The guy in the trench is dead. That one," she motioned, "may be salvageable. This one," she said, soon after she began checking the woman on the ground, "has a sucking chest wound, and was severely beaten. I need your hand here." Hannah pointed to the torn flesh with a flashlight. "Enough pressure to keep air from escaping. I'll be back."

Ray stayed in position, his hand covering the warm, slick flesh until Hannah and an EMT returned, took over and dressed the gaping wound. They loaded the woman onto a basket stretcher and trotted toward one of a collection of four-wheel drive vehicles waiting on the beach. The other shooting victim, clinging to life, was also quickly carried from the scene. Ray stood on a bluff above the dwindling bonfire, watching the receding lights.

Sue came to his side.

"What just happened?" asked Ray.

"It's going to take some time to sort all this out. I don't even know where to start. Probably there," she said, shining the beam of her flashlight on the body in the trench. She half circled the body from above. Two eyes, unaffected by the glare, stared up at her.

It was almost light again when Ray caught up with Hannah Jeffers in green scrubs and a dark blue surgical skullcap.

"You were amazing," he said, putting his arms around her. He felt her puddle against his body. They clung to each other for several moments, and then she pulled away.

"How's my boat?" she asked.

"On your car. In my garage. How are…?"

"The woman, gunshot wound to the chest, broken rib from the bullet, tissue damage to the breast. But lucky as hell. The bullet was on a non-lethal trajectory. I can't say about her eye yet. We'll know a lot more when we wake her up. What do you know about her?"

"Very little at this point. How about the man?"

"Four wounds, two in the left shoulder, one to the gut, one to the groin."

"Will he live?"

"Probably. The gut shot is the most problematic. He's been in surgery for hours." She hugged him again. "We're both in desperate need of a shower."

48

The noon rush was long over and the room was near empty when Ray and Sue sat down at a table far in a corner of the hospital cafeteria with Ken Lee Park.

"Thank you for believing me," he said, half standing to shake their hands. "That was my first fear."

"As soon as our dispatcher put you through to me, you sounded credible. And then when I checked the address you provided, the car with the broken window, blood all over the interior...."

"Did you have to force your way into the house?" asked Ken Lee.

"No, the garage door was standing open. Her assailant was in too much of a hurry or just careless."

"How did you know she was in trouble?" asked Ray.

"She was wearing a satellite communicator on a lavaliere. It allowed me to keep track of her. It also had an emergency communicator on it. The device suddenly went dead. First I called, then I viewed her security cameras."

"How did you know about the Hollingsford estate?" asked Sue.

"The people she had been watching; it's a complicated story."

"So start at the beginning," said Ray. "Tell us about your friend. Why was she here?"

Over the next 50 minutes Ken Lee Park talked. He provided a carefully crafted tale of why Mackenzie Mason, née Caitlyn Hallen, had returned to

Cedar County. He left out actions on his part or Mackenzie's that probably violated state or federal law.

"So what did she intend to do to these men?" asked Ray, after Ken Lee had finished.

"That was probably the weakness in the plan. She didn't know what to do. She wanted justice rather than revenge. She wanted them to go to jail, but didn't think there was anyway they would ever be prosecuted. By yesterday she was ready to give up on the whole idea and fly back to California."

"The cell phone, the one she left at Jim Moarse's place…."

"The original intent of that device was to make sure that she could get the attention of local law enforcement if she was in trouble. As it turns out, it worked perfectly when she wanted you to find that crime scene."

"How do you know about this stuff?" asked Ray.

"Corporate security and intelligence. This is what I do."

"And Ms. Mason?" asked Sue.

"She works as a project manager for tech companies."

"What's the nature of your relationship with her?" Sue pursued.

"Good friends. She often employed my company in recent years. But our involvement was more than casual."

"Why now?" asked Sue. "It's been decades."

Ken Lee ran his hands over the stubble on his face and head. "The death of her brother…I don't how to explain it…the festering wound… which sounds too clichéd. But it was always there. She told me about his death soon after I got to know her. Every so often she would search for Sabotny. Finally finding him was the key to…well, the key to something. One day his name popped up. There he is back in Cedar County, living very openly. She needed to come back here. Try to figure out how to get some kind of retribution. I tried to talk her out of it. But that was what she needed to do, so I did my best to support her." He looked from Ray to Sue and back to Ray. "What happens now?" he asked.

Ray shook his head. "I don't know what the prosecutor will do with all of this," he said. "In the end, circumstances suggest that Mason was acting in self-defense. As for Sabotny, if he lives, he'll be charged with two murders, kidnapping, and a host of other things."

"How about the death of Terry Hallen?"

Ray looked at Sue and back at Ken Lee.

"I guess I know that's impossible," he said, shrugging. "Sabotny managed to take out all the guys involved. The truth will probably never be known." He paused briefly. "Having him in jail; I think that will be enough. She will be able to get some kind of closure."

"Sabotny—did you do any background work on him?"

"You hear things along the way. On the plane last night I was thinking about that, thinking someone might be interested in him. I put a few things together. It's just the surface, public info, gathered legally. But I think some of it might be of interest to all sorts of folks." He reached into his shirt pocket and held out a thumb drive. "Is there anything else, Sheriff?"

"I'm sure there will be."

"I'm not going anywhere. It's pretty up here. I hope to get to know the place while Mackenzie is recovering. Now if you will excuse me, I'll go up and see if she's awake yet."

They watched him walk away.

"Interesting man," observed Sue. "A rather exotic couple. They would turn heads up here."

"Doesn't take much," said Ray, passing her the thumb drive.

"What do you think?" she asked.

"Need to know. He told us just what we needed to know, and nothing more. There will nothing on that drive that came through illegal channels or would compromise any of their sources, but I bet they know a lot about Richard Sabotny and his associates.

"You know the dance at this point. We need to get everything on paper and really tight. Sabotny will have sufficient funds to put together a good defense. Let's make sure we don't give his lawyers any openings."

49

Simone arrived in Ray's lap before Sue had cleared the door.

"We do better at co-parenting than most," she said, setting a bright purple milk crate on the conference table.

"She's very special, and neither of us is poisoning the water. She picked mature parents. How are you today?" asked Ray.

"It's amazing what a couple good nights of sleep will do. That and the weather, the wonderful sunshine and warm temperatures. How quickly we forget about the months of gray skies and barren landscapes. And the ever enthusiastic Simone seems even more so. I took her for a run on the beach last evening, and she was beside herself playing in the surf and chasing gulls."

Sue paused for a long moment and looked at Ray. "Getting some closure on the Fox murder, that was a special gift. I was absolutely frustrated by all the wheel spinning. You are more patient than me," she observed.

"Does anything tie Richard Sabotny to the Vincent Fox murder?"

"No. That said, I need to work the Moarse home again, same with the Jeep. At this point nothing suggests Sabotny was part of that crime. My guess is that Moarse was solo on the Fox abduction, a desperate man going after some low hanging fruit."

"When time allows," said Ray, "I'd like to connect the dots in that investigation, as if we were preparing to take the case to the prosecutor. I want to make sure Moarse had no accomplices, including Sabotny. I don't want anyone to walk from that crime."

"Like they were almost able to do in the Terry Hallen murder," said Sue. "Justice delayed is justice denied. And our finding the truth in this case was a matter of luck. Think if his death had been thoroughly investigated at the time."

"It's justice of sorts, and sometimes you have to be thankful for what you get. The bad guys all paid a price. If Sabotny survives, he'll never see the outside again. And Mackenzie, bruised and battered, will heal. She got justice for her brother. Now she will have closure, and that's a good outcome."

"If everything hadn't fallen into place…."

"But it did. And we, especially you, did everything right to get a good outcome."

"The Doc, too, Ray. She's a good woman."

"The planet's were in proper alignment." Ray pointed to the crate, "Money in there?"

"Yes, everything is signed for, complete custody trail. I thought your plan was to hold on to it until we were sure that…."

"You've got all the serial numbers and photographs. Now that we have several federal agencies involved, it might be months or years before this is all resolved. Ma French called yesterday wondering about the money, saying she had a bit of an emergency. She found it. Let's return it to her. We're doing everything according to law and policy. In this matter it won't be justice delayed."

The words were hardly out of his mouth when Jan was standing at the door, Ma French, at her side.

"Please come in," said Ray, "Why don't you sit here." he pulled a chair for her at the conference table. "Sue has the cash you found. We need you to count it and sign off that we have returned it to you."

"Oh, Ray, do I really have to count it. I trust you."

"Yes, you really do. We will sit here quietly so you can concentrate."

They watched as Ma French made stacks of bills, counting out loud to ten as she constructed each pile. "It's all here," she said after she finished. "Okay if I keep this envelope?"

"Absolutely," answered Ray. "You mentioned on the phone about needing money. What's going on, Ma?"

"Well, I need to get some roofing done. It was bad to begin with, and a big branch came down on it a couple of weeks ago when we had that last ice storm. But the big thing is Roxy. I mean she found the money and all."

"What's going on with Roxy?" asked Ray.

"Well, the vet says it's hip dysplasia. Both hips. She's a young dog with lots of years left. And Ray, that dog means everything to Bobby, especially since Pa's gone. Roxy, that's his friend, his constant companion. And when I'm over at the school working, I'm comforted to know Roxy is there with him."

"So what's the cost?" asked Sue

"I think it will be about $5,000. The vet says after the surgery I've gotta be sure that Roxy doesn't get fat. It will be hard to teach Bobby not to keep giving her treats. But Roxy should have a long happy life."

"So is $10,000 enough?" asked Ray.

"Well, it will take care of Roxy and do the roof over the back of the house. Maybe the rest of the roof will last as long as we need it. The money is a godsend, just a godsend."

"Before you go will you sign on this document that we've returned the money to you, and that you've counted it," said Sue, sliding a form in Ma's direction and handing her a pen.

"Thank you so much, both of you," said Ma, using the table to help push herself to her feet.

"Thank you," said Ray, reaching for her hand. "I hope things go well with Roxy."

"They will Ray. They've got to."

After Ma left Sue said, "We need something like this every day to keep things in perspective."

"We do. Let's order some sandwiches to go, take Simone to the beach for a run, and celebrate spring before the weather changes. The mountain of paperwork these events have created can wait till later this afternoon."

Author's Note:

I am greatly indebted to Heather Shaw for the cover photo, design, and interior layout. I am in awe of her artistic skills and literary sensibilities.

Special thanks to Sergeant Roy Raska and members of the Grand Traverse Sheriff's Office for sharing their knowledge and expertise in answering my questions about police procedures.

And, finally, Mary K, who provides support, friendship, and wise counsel as the book moves from a few random notes to a final draft.

A Final Note:

Readers of this series are aware of the importance of sea kayaking in the stories. For more than a decade I have benefited from the friendship and instruction of many skilled kayakers. There is a special bond between members of this small community who share the exhilaration and danger of paddling on the Great Lakes. It is with sadness that I remember Dave Dickerson. He was one of the best waterman in the sport. I am so sorry, Dave, we missed that last paddle beyond the shelf ice.

Books in the Ray Elkins Series:

Summer People
Color Tour
Deer Season
Shelf Ice
Medieval Murders